Ancient Of Genes

Dan Gallagher

Published by *StoriesAmazing*

For information, please contact:

StoriesAmazing
800 Third Avenue #1079
New York NY 10022
E-mail **Pubs@StoriesAmazing.com**

Rights inquiries (TV-series pilot, spin-off short stories (also cinematic items for $ecret$): Contact **The William Pettit Agency.**

Publisher's Cataloging-in-Publication
Gallagher, Dan, 1959-
Ancient of Genes / Dan Gallagher
p. cm.   First Edition
Preassigned LCCN (paperback): 2021915102
Hardcover ISBN: 978-1-7376494-2-7
Paperback ISBN: 978-1-7376494-1-0
eBook ISBN: 978-1-7376494-0-3
Audio Theater: 978-1-7376494-3-4

Categories
Primary: Science Fiction / Action Adventure
Secondary: Visionary / Metaphysical Thriller
Tertiary: War / Spy / Military Thriller

Dedication

To Laura, wife for life
and mother to our four.

Also…

to all who yearn to experience what or
who was out there… and remains within.

Invitation

If high adventure and thought-provoking mysteries of the
prehistoric, archaeological, and spiritual kind intrigue you, please
reward yourself & others: Enjoy this novel & Dan's other works,
become an appreciated "Reader-friend" and please kindly enable
your friends & acquaintances to experience his work.

Note from the Author

Thank you for considering *Ancient of Genes (AOG)*. This provocative spiritual and scientific thriller is vastly improved in pace and prose over its 1998 predecessor, *The Pleistocene Redemption (TPR)*. Accolades reprinted herein for *TPR* are applicable to *AOG*. *TPR* sold 4,080 copies in fifteen months, earning twenty-seven rave professional reviews and two slams. But *AOG* was tightened from 148,000 words to 75,000 and meticulously revised using reader & professional feedback.

Now at least as stimulating and controversial as *TPR* was, *AOG* can enliven any book discussion group. Sign up for AuthorDan visual, audio and reading treats *plus* the privilege to influence new works! Please enable others to enjoy *AOG*, its spin-off short stories and my award-winning nonfiction by creating links on your website and sharing on social media. I try hard and listen well so that my work, including useful nonfiction, makes great gifts that show you care.

Enjoy reviews, excerpts, video trailers & more at AuthorDan.com. Please note this descriptive and age-appropriateness information:

AOG is grounded in real genetics and the only prophecy in common (in one form or another) among all religions & myth traditions.

No evolutionism & creationism themes; no dinosaurs. Reviewers praised its plot as no rehash of any prehistoric-related fiction.

AOG is a two-decades-spanning adventure for fascination-driven readers; a spiritual thriller to intrigue thoughtful readers.

Ancient of Genes is a "clean" read, but it is only appropriate for teens & adults mature enough to grapple with life's creation & meaning.

Thank you in advance for being my appreciated Reader-friend!

--*DG*

Accolades for *The Pleistocene Redemption* – <u>still applicable</u> to *Ancient of Genes*

by category: Literary, Scientific, Spiritual

<u>Literary:</u>

"... Solidly believable, sweeping me along its strong currents and evoking such emotion that I had tears in my eyes. It's not just good, it's damn good."
– Lyn McConchie, International Who's Who of Authors

"Intense... harrowing... will grip the reader from the first page to the last.... Another of those science fiction masterpieces... so hard to put down."
– Midwest Book Reviews (Cox)

"Gallagher goes into intense detail of every aspect of this world.... So much so that not only does the reader feel like a nightmare that won't stop has been created... so vivid that reading becomes a scary, yet thrilling adventure in exploring our own roots.... Profound... a wonderful job of connecting philosophy and the humanities with science... surprising... intense... sobering...."
– Bookwatch (Glodowski)

"A fast-paced new thriller and a great read."
– Prehistoric Times (Fredericks)

"A fabulous, wild, fast-paced story that combines an extraordinary amount of research with a real narrative gift. The ending will leave you overwhelmed with its profound philosophical and spiritual implications. I highly recommend it."
– Doug Preston, best-selling co-author: *The Relic* & *Mount Dragon*

"Fascinating... the Preserve... the Neanderthals... the perils. More authentic than *Jurassic Park*."
– James Gunn, author of *The Joy Machine* (Star Trek #80) and *The Road to Science Fiction*

"The whole family is fighting over it -- great stuff!"
– Anne Marie Duquette, author, *In the Arms of the Law*

"An important addition to science fiction.... Others have tried.... Now Gallagher... keeps the reader off balance with action: hungry Pleistocene megafauna, political tension and realistic military conflicts... a novel that is hard to put down."
– Thomas J. Bassler, M.D. (T.J. Bass), author of *Half Past Human*

"I truly enjoyed it. ... a mind-opener, challenging.... It may make you angry, but it will definitely make you think. A compelling read."
– Richard La Plante, author of *Tegné* and *Steroid Blues*

"Extraordinary vision... well researched... intriguing...."
– William Sarabande, author of "The First Americans" sagas

"An engrossing confluence of cutting-edge science, thought-provoking ethics, and storytelling that moves at the pace of a Gatling gun."
– Lincoln Child, best-selling co-author: *The Relic* & *Mount Dragon*

Scientific:

"Hard to put down.... Hauntingly close to real possibilities... terrifying. I truly enjoyed the action, excitement, politics, human drama, all mixed with enough science to make me think that perhaps this could really happen."
– Scott R. Woodward, Ph.D., geneticist and microbiologist, Brigham Young University

"A giant leap beyond *Jurassic Park!* Its foundation in real technology & biology enables the reader to hurtle into this very enjoyable and intriguing fiction."
– William W. Hauswirth, Ph.D. & Erin L. Hauswirth, Editorial Board, "Ancient Biomolecules"

"This is not a story to put down, but you may wish it to last forever. Thrilling, with a fine blend of adventure, politics, religion, and science. More scientifically plausible and better written than any other book I have read on regenerating extinct species."
– Neil Clark, Ph.D., Curator, Hunterian Museum (Scotland) & author of books on dinosaurs

"This thrilling, wild adventure uses just-beyond-current science to plausibly, forcefully and vividly place readers among astounding animals. As your muscles tense and your heart pounds, wipe the sweat off your brow and try to tell yourself that it's only a story!"
– Larry G. Marshall, Ph.D., paleontologist, The Institute for Human Origins

"A gripping and highly entertaining yarn, matching *Jurassic Park* in accuracy & plausibility."
– John M. Harris, Ph.D., Chief Curator of the G. C. Page Museum of La Brea Discoveries

"A high spirited, adventurous book worthy of the time and considerable thought readers will happily invest. Readers will definitely have things to think about as they turn the last pages."
– Kelly Milner-Halls, author of *Dino-Trekking*

"A fast-paced and imaginative story, based on wide-ranging background research, that prompts one to wonder what it really means to be human."
– Ian Tattersall, Ph.D., paleontologist, author: *The Last Neanderthal*

"Thoughtfully addressing critical issues confronting humanity, this science fiction/geopolitical thriller leaves *Jurassic Park* way behind. It's an intellectual adventure in… molecular biology, species regeneration, biomedical ethics, and spirituality. An assured classic and a 'must' read."
– J. Richard Greenwell, Secretary of The International Society of Cryptozoology

"A crackerjack adventure chock full of derring-do, with a grand bonus for the paleontologist.... Vast... innovative... far more ambitious [than] the *Jurassic Park* novels... global in complexity... - and what a cast! … a work of great philosophic complexity... quite readable... first class science fiction... ingenious... compelling...."
– *Paleontologia Electronica* (Anderson)

Spiritual:

"With skill, wit, and humor, Gallagher deftly propels readers. This pleasurable tale is hauntingly profound. Accelerating powerfully within natural and supernatural realms, it enthralls, consoles, and terrifies. This important thriller melds espionage, biotechnology, spiritual challenge, prehistoric adventure and more. A compelling and meaningful experience joining the ranks of Shelley's *Frankenstein*, Huxley's *Brave New World*, and Miller's *A Canticle for Leibowitz*."
– Russell E. Smith, STD, KHS, Past President, The Pope John Center for Bioethics

"Few science fiction writers also possess sufficient expertise in the religious and ethical fields to provide the balance necessary for a thoroughly compelling narrative. Dan Gallagher is an exception.... [*The*] climax, containing one of the finest action sequences in recent fiction, approaches apocalyptic dimensions.... While Michael Crichton's *Jurassic* stories were interesting..., Gallagher ups the ante dramatically and intellectually. His spiritual and ethical probing of characters and situations is also relentless as the escalating peril... reaches catastrophic dimensions....An extraordinary work...."
– Richard J. Woods, O.P., author of *Mysticism Prophecy, The Devil*, and fiction works

"Intellectual... timely..., and a most entertaining story.... A gripping science fiction.... Research, plot & character development, and intrigue are extraordinary.... In refreshing opposition to the chaos-deterministic theme of *Jurassic Park* and the neopaganism of *The Celestine Prophecy*.... I had a difficult time setting this fine work down and heartily commend it to the thoughtful reader."
– J. F. Bierlein, author of *Parallel Myths*

"Dan Gallagher has given us... this visionary... spine-chilling and

compelling work [and has] also given it the ingredient that separates the good books from the great books. It gets you to think! If you've been looking for a book that is provocative and controversial, look no further."
– Richard Fuller, Ph.D., Senior Editor, "Metaphysical Reviews"

"Science fiction with a soul.... Intriguing and insightful.... Controversial? Perhaps. Riveting? Definitely!"
– Book Reviews by Clancy Cross

"Science fiction, anthropology, religion & thriller for fans of *Jurassic Park* & the human spirit."
– Lynne Bundesen, author of *So the Woman Went Her Way*

"Thrilling new insight.... Not only is the style of writing riveting, but the scientific and ethical infrastructure of this remarkable work is faultless. A brave new voice!"
– Bernard N. Nathanson, M.D., author of *The Hand of God*

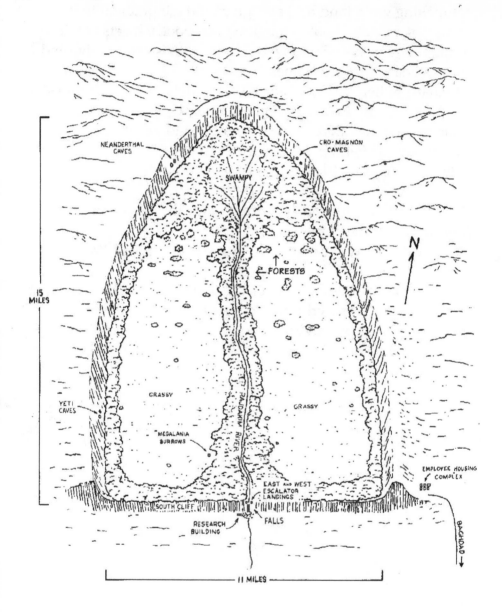

Al-Rajda, Iraq

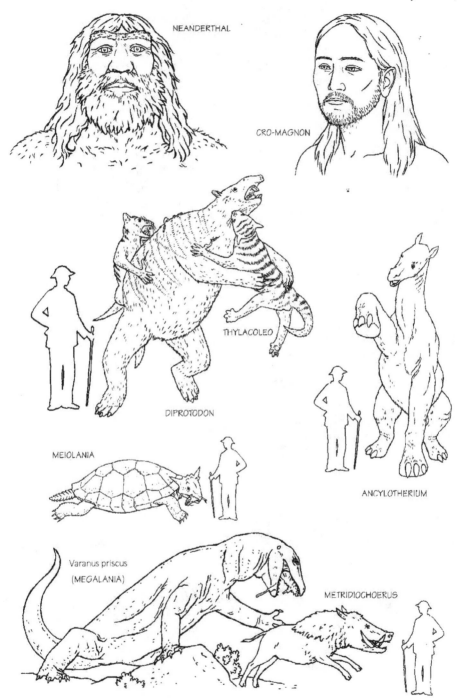

NEANDERTHAL

CRO-MAGNON

THYLACOLEO

DIPROTODON

ANCYLOTHERIUM

MEIOLANIA

Varanus priscus
(MEGALANIA)

METRIDIOCHOERUS

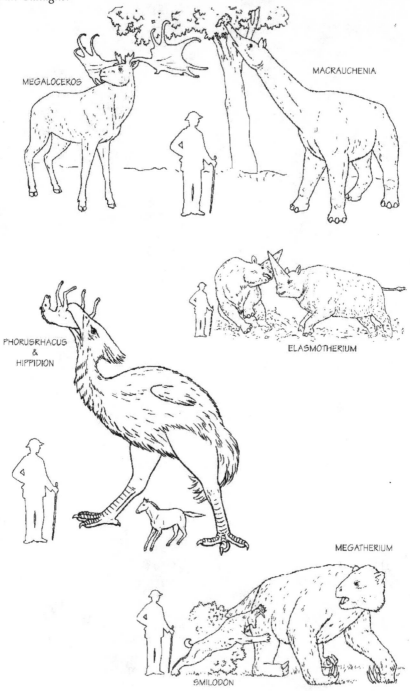

MEGALOCEROS

MACRAUCHENIA

PHORUSRHACUS
&
HIPPIDION

ELASMOTHERIUM

MEGATHERIUM

SMILODON

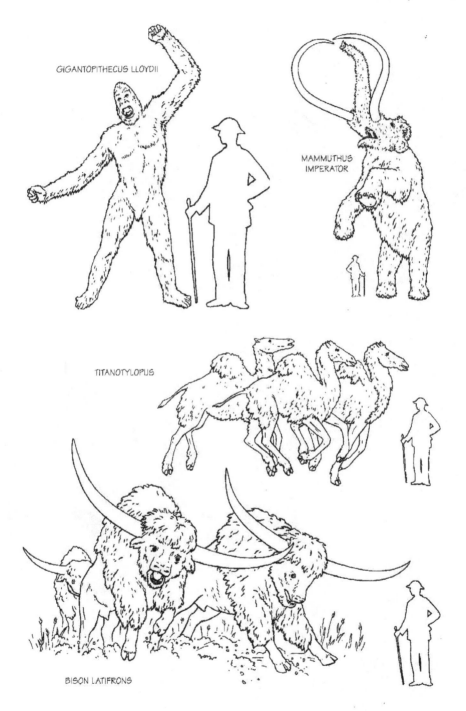

GIGANTOPITHECUS LLOYDII

MAMMUTHUS IMPERATOR

TITANOTYLOPUS

BISON LATIFRONS

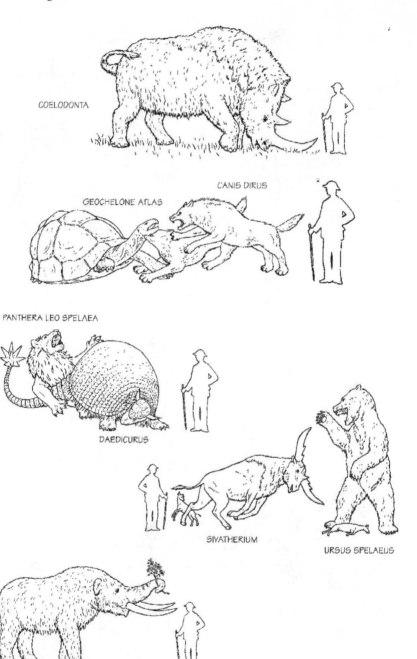

COELODONTA

CANIS DIRUS

GEOCHELONE ATLAS

PANTHERA LEO SPELAEA

DAEDICURUS

SIVATHERIUM

URSUS SPELAEUS

MAMMUT (MASTODON)

Wars & rumors of war, seen & unseen

Ancient Whispers:

God can raise up children to Abraham from these stones.
– Matthew 3:9

Children a year old shall speak with their voices, and pregnant women shall give birth to premature children at three and four months, and these shall live and leap about.
– 2 Esdras 6:21

Arrogant Answers:

The Bible and the Testament are impositions, forgeries.
– Thomas Paine, *The Age of Reason*

God is dead.... He whom they call Redeemer put them in fetters of false values and delusive words. Would that someone would redeem them from their Redeemer!
– F. Nietzsche, *Thus Spake Zarathustra* Second Part

Final Calls:

Roam the earth; see how God has brought the Creation into being. Then God will initiate the Latter Creation.
– Qur'an 29.20

When they have finished their testimony, the beast that comes up from the abyss will wage war against them...conquer...kill them.
– Revelation 11:7

Prologue

Humankind struggled for millennia to survive and understand this world. We hunted fantastic animals, even cousin-races. We sought insight into life's inception and meaning through superstition, religion and science. Has science shown that only we control our destiny?

Some say that there is a voice that calls our names before birth and as we mature, then pines to call us home at our deaths. Is this an archaic superstition, destructive of individual freedoms? Others believe that they have plenty of time before they will have to deal with the serious issues of life and death. Pontius Pilate, a man denigrated by history but esteemed by peers until refusal to worship Caesar cost his life, asked an enduring question: "What is truth?"

Why is "regeneration of Eden after destruction" the *only* prophecy that, in some form, is held in common among nearly all religions and myth traditions? Are socially erosive behaviors based in genetics and, hence, neither moral nor immoral? Were the Hebrews a people chosen by God or did they simply misinterpret natural phenomena? Who can discern meaning from the coincidences, personality changes and dreams that develop in the passing years of our lives?

Kevin Gamaliel Harrigan, driven by struggles deep within, pursued these questions. He sought the truth—or perhaps it sought him—about the human animal, destiny, and himself. A brilliant leader with vision, he was well equipped to capture the answers. Many accompanied him on his journey; among these, Manfred Freund who sought insight from both the seen and unseen. In a quest spanning two decades, the two men ultimately *did* find the answers.

Who could possibly have foreseen that such work would lead to the most ominous implications ever to confront humanity?

Science Journal
19 September 1991

Researchers at the South Tyrol Museum of Archaeology, Bolzano, South Tyrol, Italy, have announced the finding of a naturally mummified man. The Iceman, or Otzi, as he has been nicknamed, is dated as having lived between 3400 and 3100 BCE. The body was found in the Alps, between Austria and Italy.

His body and belongings are on display at the South Tyrol Museum in Bolzano, South Tryol, Italy, with one oddity: his genitals are missing.

Chapter One

Kevin Harrigan picked the yellowing newspaper clipping up off the floor, along with a dozen others on non-mineralized human bodies found ranging in age from a few millennia to tens of thousands. He filed all of it in the bottom drawer of Dr. Wentz's desk. Retrieving the pen he'd come for, he returned to the lab, pondering what it meant. *Did someone purposely pull that file? Did they understand the magnitude of what it meant? Missing genitals.* He often wondered how his professor got those missing genitals and other fossil meiotic material, but never asked. He needed pay as an assistant to recoup the Army its scholarship, be released to civilian status, and study genetics. Dr. Wentz had been initially skeptical of a short, redheaded Army medical student. But as studies progressed, he had recruited Harrigan into his secret work. After thirty years for Wentz — the last two assisted by Harrigan — they were finally close to seeing the results they sought.

Did Dr. Wentz leave the file out? He's pretty absentminded. No matter. The lab assistant, nobody would see that clipping and suspect that Dr. Wentz had actually found – stolen? – the genitals. Just old articles stuffed in an old file.

He refocused his attention on the specimen under his scanning electron microscope, and then the color print-out of an RNA molecule, the mysterious translator of genetic instructions. He thought, with great pride, that everyone except he and Wentz believed RNA functioned only to maintain DNA after an organism is formed and to translate DNA's instructions to the organism's cells. *Focus! No mysteries or cures uncovered without a doctorate.*

Dr. Wentz's clandestine genetics project consumed them both and demanded immense effort, in spite of Wentz's advancing age.

Harrigan shivered. *What if the unauthorized work were discovered, and the modern samples that donors hadn't authorized for…?* He focused again on the specimen. *Nothing to worry about.* This was Wentz' life's work, well hidden.

Three years before, in a thick Austrian accent, Wentz had pulled Harrigan in. "Shtudying dis specimen has to me given a renewed sense of purpose und deferred my retirement from…an unremarkable career. I haf confided in you because I cannot do all of this verk alone. Neider can I let it be lost if I should *sterb*-- uh, English -- die while the files und materials are intentionally mismarked. You are my brightest shtudent. Work with me." Wenz paused, then continued excitedly.

"By comparing modern genes with the archaic ones, we can track disease resistance, longevity, changes in the human species, redeem atrophied traits daht are useful und hunt down genetic defects. What do you say, Kevin? Discovery is why you left the Army, yah? Explore human genetic evolution with me. Mankind will owe you a debt of gratitude."

Harrigan had leapt at the chance to make his mark. *We'll pioneer a new field,* he had mused. *I'd do anything to study genetic changes over time, even speciation within genus Homo. Most importantly, we can eradicate genetic diseases — help Pete — improve humankind in myriad ways, transform medicine itself!*

Eventually, they used PCR to replicate some of the undestroyed segments of genetic material from the Ice Man sperm. PCR, the polymerase chain reaction, produced viable copies of fragile DNA segments. He had then inserted these copies into modern human eggs whose genetic strands were removed, manipulating a second set of male-contributed genes so as to produce a purely archaic clone of the Ice Man. The eggs were genetically coded so that they could not mature past nine or ten weeks. The resulting zygotic masses, embryos, helped Harrigan and Wentz isolate the effects of the archaic genes, and compare their nucleic composition and functions with modern genes. The embryos yielded clues to the production and chemistry of various kinds of RNA molecules. Harrigan found that the first of these to form existed only during the formation of new eggs in the female zygotes. It marked thousands of DNA sequences for dormancy. He called the molecule "primary" meiotic RNA. He suspected that this M1-RNA preserved as-yet unidentified traits, possibly inhibiting speciation.

Despite the danger to his career, Harrigan had become as addicted as Wentz, though for different reasons. For more than three years, he was consumed by the desire to unlock the secrets of what made humans human, and how the revealed secrets could cure genetic diseases.

Harrigan finally finished up the segment he was studying and headed home where he rapidly devoured two peanut butter and jelly sandwiches, then sat down to study for the tests he had to face the next day.

Two hours later, sleep began to seem more valuable than reading over material he already knew. Still nervous over the interrogatories, he finally fell asleep an hour later.

At midnight, the sudden ringing of his phone jerked him awake. He glared at the clock and then saw Dr. Wentz's name on the phone. "Hello?"

The Austrian's voice came fast, shaky, and thick with accent. "Kevin, it is I, Dr. Wentz. Someone has accessed the computer files. *The* files. *Und alle* the specimen flasks — They are gone. I'm almost out of *meine* mind, for *Gott's* sake. Come down, can you?"

After a moment, Dr. Wentz's words sank in. "I'll be right there."

———————

The following night, Harrigan sat nervous and angry in the white marble anteroom to the chancellor's conference hall.

Too late and too rude of the chancellor, Harrigan thought, flexing his jaw in suppressed fury, *but I'll hold my tongue for now. They had damn well better treat Dr. Wentz with respect.*

Harrigan's mind shifted into confrontation-ready mode — even violent fantasy — though his personal discipline held. Vivid memories of Ranger School flooded him.

———————

Dog-tired and too close together for proper tactical intervals, the Ranger students hesitated in crossing an icy stream. Harrigan's ruck held blasting caps, used to detonate the otherwise inert plastic C-4 explosives carried by another Ranger candidate. His close friend Manfred "Mannie" Freund, a German exchange officer, waited just ahead in the formation.

Bunching up again! Harrigan mused. *We're gonna give Jenkins another excuse to explode.*

To infamous instructor Sergeant Jenkins, this bunching up was an intolerable lack of tactical discipline. Jenkins brought up the rear of the formation and carried no weapon or ruck. With massive hands and a stern brow, he reminded Harrigan of a caveman. He wore three black chevrons on his sweaty camouflaged lapel and the coveted Ranger tab on his left shoulder.

"Maintain your damn interval," came Buck Sergeant Jenkins' angered shout. "You scum-sucking officers..." He flung the last man in the formation, a second lieutenant being tested in the role of platoon sergeant, backward several feet. "...think you can just have a preppy damn frat party..." The next soldier became a blur hurtling to the ground. "...in my friggin' swamp and expect me to give you the tab." The volume and pitch of his abusive tirade continued to grow. "I'm sick of you privileged, pansy dirtbags!"

Harrigan was about to turn with a retort to stop the abuse of his fellows when he felt a slap on his ruck. He landed hard on his butt and was abruptly energized by fear of the blasting caps as they bounced out of his rucksack. When they did not explode, his fear became outrage.

Harrigan yanked a quick-release to shed his ruck and sprang to his feet. He lunged at Jenkins and, with his right hand, grabbed the instructor around the waist from behind. He jammed his left forearm up into Jenkins' crotch and, on pure adrenaline, lifted the buck sergeant off his feet and slammed him head-first into a jagged stump.

"Who the hell do you think you are?" Harrigan screamed. "You think you can shove us around 'cause the rank is off our shirts?" With those words, the realization hit Harrigan: *This guy is going to cream me!*

Without a sound, the caveman-looking NCO ran his hand over his wound and slurped up a mitt-full of blood. He rose and spit it into Harrigan's eyes. Momentarily advantaged, Jenkins snatched the rifle dangling from the 'dummy cord' that linked it to Harrigan and thrust it, muzzle first, at Harrigan's teeth.

By trained reflex, Harrigan deflected the weapon just as it met his lips. He grabbed Jenkins' shirt and slammed his forehead into the bridge of Jenkins' nose. Harrigan dropped backwards to the ground, crunching his right boot in Jenkins' solar plexus and the other in his crotch. He launched the windless instructor into the air behind him.

The fight was broken up by the Senior Ranger Instructor, Master Sergeant Gaines. "What you need to learn, Ranger Harrigan," Gaines had said with almost evangelical fervor, "is that we are here to prepare for war. Better learn to distinguish friends from enemies."

The admonition triggered a vision in Harrigan of himself diving into a cold river full of giant reptilian jaws. *Distinguish friends from enemies,* came the echo. He blinked hard, dismissed it, and continued this last patrol telling himself it was a stress-induced hallucination. But when Harrigan later pulled a coral snake from Freund's arm, sucking away venom and spitting it into Jenkins' face, Gaines had Harrigan and Jenkins disciplined by the Camp Commander...and Jenkins swore revenge.

The commander ordered Harrigan to assume the front-leaning rest, a stationary push-up. After the tongue-lashing with grudging praise for saving Freund and standing up for his platoon, the Captain admitted that Harrigan would receive the Ranger tab. Then he spat tobacco juice in a cup and scowled. He handed Harrigan newly faxed orders and growled, "You must be special, just like you think you are. Hey, don't medical programs start in the fall? You're in for a major ass-kicking, starting in the middle like that. You may speak, you sawed-off little whelp."

Harrigan smiled broadly and strained to turn his head and shout his triumphantly sarcastic answer, "Yes, Camp Commander. Just like West Point, two academic majors, Officer Basic, Ranger School, and Jenkins *all* kicked my ass."

"Dismissed, Harrigan. One of these days somebody's gonna *kill* you."

Refocusing on his crisis at Harvard, Harrigan assured himself that courage and moxie would aid in facing it. He'd recover from the penalty.

He watched Wentz exit the conference room and sit, tearful and silent, next to him. Harrigan felt like hitting someone for this humbling of Dr. Wentz but told himself to cool. The massive oak door opened and the chancellor's assistant's face jutted out. It struck Harrigan as a pin-head and a pencil-neck.

"You may come in now, Dr. Harrigan."

The assistant ducked from Harrigan's glare and yielded the passage.

Harrigan stood rigid before the Board. *Ethical-immaculates*, he silently branded them.

The chancellor, visibly tired, addressed the accused. "It's been a long thirty-some days, Dr. Harrigan, and it's late, so I'll come right to the point. The Board has determined that your unauthorized and unethical research was independent of that conducted to fulfill your doctoral requirements. As such, it has declined the Disciplinary Committee's recommendation that your degree be rescinded. I concur. So, you will retain your degree.

"But it is a fact that you participated in the creation and destruction of fetuses, using University resources and donor eggs not authorized by the donors for such a purpose. The University will, tomorrow, release a press statement to that effect, announcing that all findings, data, and specimens involved have been destroyed. Those items will be destroyed after this meeting.

"You and Dr. Wentz might be relieved to know that we will not disclose the origin of the specimen, since it could not be verified. But you are permanently barred from this institution and a summary of the case will be released. I doubt you'll be able to make anything of yourself in genetics."

"Your opinion, Chancellor, of my career prospects is as wrong as your ethics. You're just trying to avoid lawsuits from me, the donors, and the Italian government. Dr. Wentz gave you years of loyal service and important discoveries, but now you kick him when he's down. You've got a lot of nerve. This institution teaches abortion techniques, and its medical plan pays for RU-586. I suppose that's appropriate. But you are hypocrites if you think my research on fetal material is any different. Hypocrites!"

Harrigan fought the impulse to violence and left the room. In the anteroom, he grasped Dr. Wentz's hand firmly.

"Should have taken my advice *und* gotten a lawyer. Vill you keep your Ph.D., Kevin?"

"Yes. They decided to avoid a suit, but they'd better be careful how they publicize this. What will you do with your retirement, Dr. Wentz?"

"*Weis nicht*—I just don't know. But I want to stay away from the public for a very long time. Did you read the *Science Journal* article? They are saying we made hybrid fetuses *und* killed them. Lies. How can they view it that way? We discovered gene repair during the formation of eggs."

Wentz held Harrigan's shoulder and resumed. "You discovered how to redeem archaic genetic material. This could be of monumental importance. *Und* they are destroying all the research. Imbeciles! Man was meant to study man." Wentz's voice clogged in his throat. "Now it's all lost. Your brilliant research career *ist vorbei* before it's begun." His voice turned melancholy and quiet. Wentz looked at the floor. "*Und* mine is ended in disgrace. I can never face friends *und* colleagues again. We're beaten, finished."

"You've long needed a rest. Take a cruise. Maybe put your notes back together to defy these sanctimonious jerks. And don't be so sure they've beaten *me*. As for the gene redemption process and 'primary' meiotic RNA discovery, they can't take those out of my brain."

"Vat vill you do now, Kevin?"

"I haven't decided. My folks have been great through the controversy. I'll visit them for a few days. Then maybe go on vacation to plan my next moves, career-wise; duck the press. If those bastards think they can wave a pen and stop me, they're wrong."

"Goot luck, Kevin. I hope you can build a life after this."

"Thank you, Dr. Wentz, for everything. Don't get despondent. It's like Mannie Freund, my old college buddy used to say: 'It's how you view life.' You do have at least one friend; I respect you and appreciate you. So, chin up, okay?"

"*Ja*. 'Chin up.' That *ist* the way."

Harrigan smiled warmly, shook Wentz's hand, and left.

———————

That evening Harrigan drove, stone-faced and steaming over the chancellor's prediction, past the Cathedral of the Holy Cross toward his apartment on Union Park Street. He parked, eyeing the cathedral's huge circular window above the arched entrance. He knew the red-stained glass depicted the figure of an English king, but it looked distinctly like a blooming rose to him now. He concluded that he was hallucinating due to stress and that it might also have been prompted by the scent of roses surrounding the Madonna statue on the cathedral lawn.

That's odd, he mused, *my windows are rolled up; no AC*. Harrigan saw only dark mist. Infants weeping reverberated from a one-story, flat-roofed building below a cliff. His breath became shallow, halting. Then a glistening woman in a white gown and blue shawl appeared against a pitch-black sky. Ashes flew from a gash in the earth as dividing bubbles streamed from a jagged hole in the building's roof. These soared behind her as a red-sashed rider on a white horse appeared in the distance. A dozen stars shone around her head, only to burst into countless suns, filling the firmament with light.

"Much is at stake, son of Ephraim," she whispered in a comforting yet challenging voice, "for you eternally, for all humanity. You who must choose between your prideful will and the source of redemption. Choose humbly."

He blinked, now gazing at the cross atop the cathedral. His eyes filled with tears as he considered going to confession and Mass. He let out an awkward, pitiful moan that surprised him, embarrassed momentarily for having yielded to what he thought of as superstition. He put the car in gear and proceeded to his apartment. He wrote a few to-do notes and slept. The next morning, he left for a four-day visit to his parents' home in Connecticut.

On his last morning at his parent's Hartford home, just before light, Harrigan sat sipping coffee in the small but cozy kitchen. His father was not yet up. This morning he felt guilty that he had anticipated an "I told you so" attitude but encountered only moving support from both parents despite all the media criticism and debate of the last four weeks.

His mother stared at him from across the kitchen. "The newspapers say all the work you were doing has been destroyed. Why?"

"The university said they destroyed everything because findings may only be added to the genetics body of knowledge if obtained ethically—by their self-serving definition of ethics. They didn't want anyone to have any possible incentive for doing unauthorized research—any possibility that their work would be kept. The real reason is that they didn't want an investigation that could enable the anonymous egg donors to sue them."

"The *Time* article said you were able to rejuvenate destroyed sperm. A Fossil Gene Redemption process, they called it. How could that be done?"

"It can't, exactly. I wanted to study how sperm and eggs are produced; how the genes are assembled when they're first created. That production process is called meiosis. For boys, meiosis occurs when they're several years old and practically impossible to study. The sperm would have to be observed forming in *living* testicular filaments. But for girls, meiosis occurs while they're still in the womb. We can study fetuses in a genetically modified pig uterus. So, fetuses are vastly easier to obtain and work with.

"For years, Wentz couldn't get permission for an unrestricted study of meiosis. Finally, he and I just went ahead and did it, and we discovered an RNA molecule that occurs only *during* meiosis. We thought it may inhibit certain types of human mutation. It might also..."

"Also what, dear?"

"Don't talk about this, okay? I suspect it makes some traits dormant for generations. This could explain how saber teeth appear in one species of cat, skip another species that arose from the first, and then reappear in another that evolved directly from the second. Re-emergence is called atavism. It could be a key to reviving prehistoric traits of extinct animals, even human ancestors. We could only find traces of it in animals, but lots in the Ice Man. We suspect it's even more prevalent in modern humans."

"*Gawd* between us and harm, Kevin!"

"The Ice Man specimen offered us the chance to go further. When I discovered this new RNA, I wanted to find out whether it occurred only in humans and how far back in the development of sapiens this trait arose. I couldn't implant any of the genes from the specimen into a modern egg, but I found a way to stretch out the convoluted genetic material without destroying it and enhance the way computer-controlled scanners could follow and read its segments. That enabled that PCR machine I showed you last year to reconstruct most of the genetic coding in the archaic sperm. It's like this, Mom:"

Harrigan grabbed a thin booklet that his father had left lying on the table. It was the instruction manual for assembling a cabinet.

"Imagine you have instructions, say four pages typed, for making a cabinet. These printed pages represent the genetic blueprint of a possible baby the Ice Man might have fathered, less the egg's half of course. Now imagine I tore each page into five or six pieces."

He ripped the booklet as his mother gasped but held her tongue.

"That tearing represents the damage done to the sperm's genetic instructions over ten thousand years. Got it so far?"

"I think so. You could put them back together if you could read the language. You could tell which words and sentences would make sense as you put the puzzle together. Right?"

"Exactly. And we have a mental model of what these pages ought to look like. The words and sentences are like gene segments. The computer can read and make sense of them. That's because it has a database, like the language that the cabinet instructions are written in, from the recently completed human genome project. Remember I told you about that project to decipher and map human genes?"

"Yes, but there must be many different children any given man could father. How can the genes be put back together with all of that complication?"

"First, siblings aren't as different as you might think. I've begun to suspect that far more extensive 'personality sequences' exist in genes than were discovered in the last decade — that these produce the really significant differences. Even if so, personality genes are a tiny portion of all sequences. Second, I discovered that all the instructions for marginally distinct potential children can be estimated by the computer. The genetic coding in each sperm is only slightly different. For any given man — and the 'Ice Man' was no exception — *most* segments in the genes of each sperm are identical.

"All of the segments were damaged, *but* that damage was never in exactly the same place for every fossil sperm. The computer read the instructions — the genetic sequences — in hundreds of sperm. It could infer what the destroyed segments were by reading the *corresponding intact segment* from a different sperm in the same sample.

"I had the computer build a model of what the most common configuration of genetic sequences were, then compared its readings of each sperm scanned to the model. That way it kept updating and perfecting the model of the most common configuration. It eventually built a model of the coding of the typical sperm in the sample. It's like reassembling these printed pages — by being able to read and know which words and sentence fragments would make sense if you put them together.

"Then, we just waited a few days while the enhanced-speed PCR machine manufactured an actual set of gene sequences from that perfected model — the reassembled instructions. I added instructions that mass-produce a sort of editing tool — my own version of the CRISPR molecule that gene therapy clinics have used for years to splice and insert genes. CRISPR's a long acronym I won't bother you with, and mine's different anyway. It multiplies and moves along gene strands to accelerate the whole process. Then we put the new genes into a donor egg — a kind of artificial mating.

"The reconstruction was very good but imperfect, so to avoid creating a freak, I inserted genes that coded all the embryos to be female and to terminate just after meiosis would occur. The RNA molecule *only* appears during meiosis. It falls apart once the female embryo's own eggs form. I think it's the same for sperm production. Evidence from doing this with donor eggs of several races suggests that it's present in every modern population. The Ice Man showed us that 'primary' meiotic RNA was less prevalent long ago. The significance, Mom, is that a biological process might be occurring that keeps humans from evolving further! This isn't published and I'm not *about* to give the press any interviews. These Harvard fools won't even study it. This research could lead to genetic cures! Did I explain this clearly?"

Harrigan saw horror, possibly a deeper understanding, in her eyes.

"Kevin, you created human beings using living women's eggs and a dead man's sperm — and prearranged for the little-girl fetuses to be unable to grow to experience a mother's love — while you studied what went on in the doomed fetuses' ovaries."

"I started it all for Peter! I wanted to be able to fix genes for individuals — even humanity's genome — so no one has to suffer from Down Syndrome... or other genetic flaws."

"Your brother doesn't suffer. He's just different, and he's the way God intended him to be. We don't love him less because he's not a brilliant scientist like you."

"He's not normal. Someday anyone will be able to be made normal by correcting genes."

"Who are you to determine what is normal?"

Kevin stared at her, not comprehending how she could be so dense.

"Don't you tell your father," she continued. "It would kill him. And God help you, son of mine. I'm not your judge. But I *am* a mother, and I know what a human being is. Caring about human suffering hasn't kept you from wrong judgment."

Harrigan's face turned ashen. He realized his parents must not have completely read or understood the many articles that taunted him when they offered their warmth. Then his face reddened and hardened in an indignant frown. "Then you *are* judging me. Stop it, Mom. It's not against the law. Look: It's man's destiny and purpose to study every aspect of himself and his world. So, don't lecture *me*. I'm doing this for the good of mankind."

"All right, Kevin." Her voice sounded sad and quiet, almost defeated. "I won't lecture you. I'll just pray for you."

Harrigan noticed his father standing in the kitchen. The man's eyes brimmed with tears. "I understand now, Kevin." And he walked, head low, silently from the room.

Harrigan stared after him, equally vindicated and ashamed. *I can't teach them anything.*

After gathering his belongings, he drove back to Boston to pack for a Florida vacation.

Just after noon, a man arrived with an ornate envelope. Inside was a note from a diplomat from Iraq's newly reformed government. It hinted at joint scientific projects with the Israelis to promote peace, and it involved the newly famous African-British explorer Dr. Bart Lloyd, captor of a yeti — abominable snowman of the Himalayas — alive.

The envelope also had tickets for a London flight that very evening.

Why not? Harrigan thought, grinning for the first time in weeks. *What could go wrong?*

Chapter Two

Harrigan's gray pinstripe suit, traditional black Florsheims, starched white shirt, and red silk tie gave him a sense of authority even as he strode into the meeting suite just behind and to the left of his overly polite Iraqi escort. The escort stood stone-faced by the breakfast cart. A gleaming crystal chandelier hung above a gold-leafed coffee table, centered in the spacious suite.

Dr. Bart Lloyd stood munching on a grape jam-covered bun, which amusingly matched his purple dress shirt. His black tie hung loosely while his white cotton suit seemed to beg for a splotch of jam to slip from the bun.

Harrigan took to him immediately and extended a hand in greeting. "You English wake up at an ungodly hour. But it's an honor to meet you, Dr. Lloyd. I've read the accounts of your discovery with absolute fascination."

Lloyd wiped his mouth and moustache with a linen napkin and shook Harrigan's hand. "Thank you. But you must be exhausted, what with being five hours behind England and arriving only yesterday. I've read of the controversy—such a ghastly affair—that seems to have befallen you. I must say, Dr. Harrigan, I think Harvard was *most* unfair to one who has made the brilliant breakthroughs you have."

"Thank you."

"By the by, call me Bart, would you?"

"Sure. I'm Kevin. Bart, where is our host?"

"Hassan there said that Minister Mon would be unavoidably late; not too. Let's have a sit, shall we?"

Hassan offered breakfast as one not used to serving. Harrigan politely declined and sat in one of the three embroidered armchairs by the coffee table. *Clearly*, Harrigan thought, *this place was selected to impress.*

"Hassan," Harrigan asked, "would you mind if Dr. Lloyd and I speak alone while waiting?"

"How da—Not at all, sir." Hassan grimaced as he shut both doors behind him.

For about ten minutes, Harrigan and Lloyd exchanged descriptions of their work and theories, though Harrigan was careful not to be too specific. Their discussion became friendlier and livelier as they progressed.

"Your tomographic sensor sounds amazing," Harrigan said. "I understand it enabled you to find the yeti's lair."

"Oh, yes, my dear Dr. Harrigan! And it can find fossils from the Pleistocene epoch just as well. You see, it detects low-density spaces, like caves and non-mineralized fossil tissue. That's my specialty, by the bye: Pleistocene Fauna. These creatures existed during our own evolution. Can you just imagine the goings-on! But enough about my work. What I'd like to know is how that mysterious Fossil Gene Redemption process of yours works."

"Bart?"

"Yes?"

"I've read about your yeti find, but I've never seen the video from the shoulder mount. You wouldn't have it on that tablet of yours, would you?" Harrigan asked as Lloyd sheepishly activated a video on his device and handed it over.

A massive red-and-black-furred figure gaped up and let out a birdlike, growling scream. There was a bloody gash in long fur atop its wide, cone-shaped head. It clutched something shiny, jet-black, and squirming in one of its claw-like hands, an ice shard in the other. The enraged yeti hurled the shard at Lloyd and missed. Then a blurred black object slammed into Lloyd's chest, flopping its furry hand onto the camera. The baby yeti's feet appeared as Lloyd fumbled to stuff it beneath his thermal-regulator undershirt. Rock, ice, and Lloyd's breathless screams followed — the adult ape's growls growing louder in the background.

Suddenly, a rope appeared as Sherpas shouted and Lloyd struggled, glove over glove, to escape the cavern. Snow-covered, rocky ground bounced as Sherpas ran headlong off a cliff. Lloyd's camera flashed into the mile-deep valley below, then turned skyward. The yeti came briefly into view, standing atop the cliff and shaking its fists wildly. Next came Lloyd's command to his friends. "Now – *lose* – *the* – *pack!*" Backpacks sailed off the men. "*Wait!* Fall away from each other. Away! Now!" Lloyd screamed as the view jumped with the tug. Now a multicolored, squarish parachute appeared against the sky as Lloyd checked his canopy.

But, as Harrigan gaped wide-eyed at the screen despite having read the account, he instinctively clamped his knees together in his chair. The ground lay carpeted with closely spaced, man-sized, razor-sharp ice formations. The razors loomed larger, faster and faster. The ice razors seemed to be but twenty-five feet away. The view righted horizontally as two Sherpas hit a vertical rock outcropping, avoiding the crystal blades. The view turned as Lloyd skimmed backward, about five feet above alternating flat surfaces and areas studded with ice daggers.

"Uuuh!" came Lloyd's and a Sherpa's grunt as they collided four feet up, abruptly ceasing lateral motion. Sky, then rock, then ice, the sky again appeared as Lloyd toppled, sprawling, and moaning upon a boulder.

A Sherpa came into view as Lloyd twisted, struggling to sit up. The Sherpa stripped off Lloyd's wire-laced equipment harness and set it on a boulder, facing two more holding Lloyd upright. Lloyd suddenly ripped open his parka, then thermal undershirt. The ravenous primate had a bite-suck on Lloyd's left nipple and a tight grip on the other. Hopping and hooting, Lloyd quickly fumbled through an interior jacket pocket, extracted a milk pouch, and pleadingly coaxed the baby off his chest.

"Bart, that's the world's most famous purple nurple, but we Airborne can take it."

"Indeed. My doctor and support group helped tremendously. But, still, when it's cold..." Lloyd rubbed his chest with the heel of his hand as Harrigan smirked. "I know that look, Kevin," Lloyd quavered, "It's become quite common, I must admit."

Harrigan turned away, muffling a laugh, then returned the tablet closed. He turned slowly, inspecting the room. "Why do you suppose the two of us have been invited here?"

"I had supposed it was so Minister Mon could buy the yeti and put him on display. He's developing all those joint projects for tourism and industry in Israel, you know. But the infant belongs to Oxford now, my alma mater. The ingrates wouldn't even return my book rights when, not two days after I signed the papers, I told them I hadn't intended to include book rights in my donation! Bloody *bamboozled*, I was."

"Sounds like a very tough break. I'm sorry."

"Indeed. Thank you. And on top of that, fire destroyed my electronics firm's only facility while I was in Nepal. It wasn't insured. Fortunately, I have the tomographic detector prototype, so things will be just grand financially someday, I should think."

Suddenly Harrigan sensed that they were being overheard.

"Hmm. Bart, let's just sit quietly until he gets here, okay?"

"Well...fine. That's fine with me, if you like."

Minister Ismail Mon strode in moments later alone, smiling, and apologetic. The researchers stood as he entered and greeted them both.

Mon's accent was Iraqi Arabic: long "r" sounds but few errors. "Doctors Lloyd and Harrigan! Thank you for coming. Please accept my apologies for my unavoidable tardiness. Please sit. Be comforrrt-able. This will take but minutes. I am impressed by the work you two have done. I take great issue with your obviously jealous and self-righteous detractors."

Mon towered over Harrigan, sophisticated in his impeccable navy-blue suit. "Gentlemen, I will honor you with brevity in relating what I beg of you and what I can do for you: We in the Middle East are approaching a new era of peace. But it is incomplete and still demanding of many Herculean tasks in order to change hostility into economic interdependence. You may be aware that the commission I serve is engaged in building up nondefense industry in several nations in my region.

"If we can enable the hungry to feed themselves, we can eliminate a major cause of strife. If we can better develop economies of the region to become both strong and interdependent, we can establish more safeguards against the senseless fighting of the past. Finally, if every family can own and work land without crowding out neighbors, we can quell the hatred spawned by the coveting of land."

Harrigan and Lloyd exchanged nods, impressed by this articulate and apparently compassionate official.

"You may recall the risks which many in my Justice Party in Iraq took to forge a day-mo-cracy; to establish safeguards against the aggression of past regimes. Our nations *can* cooperate to assure peace. We in Iraq are proving honorable intentions with action. You two can contribute to an historic effort and be handsomely compensated."

Harrigan replied first. "I commend you for what I understand is a re-emerging democracy in Iraq. But I'm not very political."

Lloyd added a small measure of joviality: "Nor am I, I'm afraid. But God save the Queen, nonetheless, eh?"

Mon's eyes flashed as he turned to look Lloyd directly in the eyes. "Of course. God save her." He paused, grinning. "Forgive me, gentlemen. My exuberance has kept me from speaking plainly as I promised. One of our projects may be of interest to you. It is an endangered species preserve at Megiddo, Israel to be primarily funded by Iraq as a gesture of peace toward the Jews, ah, toward Israel. We plan many de-ve-lop-ments: a monument to peace, a new college, and a natural history theme park. Megiddo was the site of so many battles of old. It was therefore decided that no more appropriate location existed for such powerful symbols of progress and peace, of man's defeat of aggression and his ascension to master his world."

Mon paused, leaned forward, and resumed excitedly. "I offer you an opportunity to greatly expand the concept of the animal preserve recently approved—something never attempted successfully. If you agree, we will expand the species preserve to include regeneration of extinct fauna. Yes, extinct animals for the enjoyment and fa-scin-ation of the world. It will be a multi-faceted project for peaceful development and zo-ological research."

Mon looked squarely at Lloyd and continued.

"I have been reliably informed that you, Dr. Lloyd, have developed a device that can identify subterranean formations if they are sufficiently different in density from the surrounding earth. This, of course, means you can quickly and reliably locate non-mineralized fossil soft tissue, like sperm and egg of recently extinct animals. Your own published research shows that it is the lack of mineralization, even if remains are crushed, which is key to redeeming any genetic instructions from a fossil spe-ci-men."

Mon turned to Harrigan. "It has been likewise reported, Dr. Harrigan, that you have successfully redeemed non-mineralized fossil genetic material despite damage to the DNA strands. You have been successful in activating such replicated strands to produce life."

Mon opened his arms to the pair. "Gentlemen, I realize that you have other demands on your time. But we will fund this change to the species preserve project if you are willing to combine your talents and make the preserve one which regenerates extinct species."

Lloyd's jaw dropped. "My dear Minister Mon, even if we could do something so fantastic, we could never provide an adequately cool and watered environment in the Mideast. Why, I've heard of the Israeli's plans for a high-tech desalinization plant on the Dead Sea and the attendant dreams of reforestation and the like. But all of this seems impossible; sensational journalism, pie in the sky, that sort of thing."

"It will be my pleasure to show how all these projects will bring prosperity and peace to the region, Dr. Lloyd. I have a fascinating surprise for you both regarding the water and environment for such a research preserve. Regarding the other issues, you are far too modest, Dr. Lloyd. I, for one, believe in your work and for years have been fascinated by it. You see, zoology and related sciences were for me hobbies when I was so long exiled from my country.

"So, Dr. Lloyd, while some may not appreciate you or your work, I do. You are able to find such specimens in media which permit some soft tissue to survive hundreds of thousands of years. Collapsed burrows, anaerobic sinkholes, petroleum seams, frozen tundra, or desiccated sources, right? If you allow it, your talent can enrich the lives of children and adults alike by changing our faulty understanding of the past; your theories can be proved."

Mon paused a moment and turned to Harrigan.

"Dr. Harrigan, I am one who has endured rejection in his own profession. Like you, I resolved to go on to accomplish my dreams. Let me help you actualize your dreams of discovery and accomplishment. I would be honored if you would recruit and lead a team. Staff I am prepared to place at your disposal. While Dr. Lloyd would be in charge of specimen location and recovery, you would head the finest laboratory facilities available. I understand such work can only be done with meiotic material, sperm or egg, rather than other tissue — at least once an animal is dead. This makes things difficult but far from impossible. Your expertise, Dr. Harrigan, and ability to lead are in-dis-pensable. You have the opportunity to show a hypocritical scientific and academic community not only what *they* are made of...you will be able to dramatically show them what *you* are made of."

Harrigan checked him. "You didn't mention medical research on birth defects and..."

There was silence. Harrigan stared at Mon for half a minute, wondering how this man's words could be so well targeted—so persuasive, almost hypnotic. Lloyd was already fidgeting and focusing an expectant grin at Harrigan. Though excited, Harrigan felt uncomfortable with how much detailed knowledge Mon had about their work and their inner feelings.

"Minister," Harrigan inquired with rare timidity, "Harvard destroyed my work. Non-mineralized fossil genetic material has been found, but only from the mid-to-late Pleistocene—within the last half million years—extremely rare and in near-useless condition. Then, too, is the problem of genetic compatibility. The extinct species would have to have close extant relatives. And how—if we ever could regenerate them—could ice age animals thrive in a warm region?"

Mon's reassuring tone pierced Harrigan's nervousness. "Achievers of our caliber don't let humility hamper choice. If I had a solution, would you join me in this historic endeavor?"

Lloyd blurted his answer even before the question was complete: "Yes! Yes, absolutely."

Harrigan hesitated a moment, sensing that something was wrong. Still, if he could maintain control of his secrets.... He spoke slowly, deliberately. "If I can run the show, yes. One more requirement: for personal reasons, I'll need a salary of a hundred seventy thousand, U.S."

"I want to build a solid, trusting relationship. The salary is two hundred fifty thousand. I hope you, Dr. Lloyd, will not mind reporting to Dr. Harrigan."

Lloyd dropped his jaw a bit further. "Of...uh. Of course!"

Harrigan spoke up. "So, what's this 'solution' to accommodate such animals in Megiddo? Climate-controlled warehouses?"

"Captain Hassan!" Mon called. The escort appeared, opening a suitcase. Mon turned back to his guests. "Now, computer simu-lations. Preparations in Megiddo should take the rest of this year. Then you'll be VIP guests Janu'ry two in Morocco to witness my climate miracle."

Harrigan and Lloyd stared at each other, incredulous, silent.

Then the two exclaimed in unison, "Morocco?"

The presentation was quick and hard-hitting. At its conclusion, the amazed pair stared at each other and at Mon.

Harrigan sounded almost winded. " I didn't even know Israel was developing such a weapon, let alone intending to use it for this purpose!"

"The announcement of the Atlas Mountain Range project is tomorrow," Mon declared. "This massive effort, gentlemen, forges spears into plowshares. Israel and we are partners."

"If I'm to lead a staff, I'll need security that reports to me," Harrigan interjected.

"Yes, safety and security are paramount. I will make certain our security personnel respect your position and, as you Americans say, 'you have my ear.' I heard you have many leaderr-sheep trraits." Mon nodded approvingly as his voice lifted. "Your people will appreciate your concern," he added with a wink. "They will trust you. There are mo-dest offices waiting for you both now in Megiddo."

Lloyd smiled warmly at Harrigan. "My old bosses and professors never cared!"

Harrigan returned the smile and gripped Lloyd's hand, pulling it up once then down before releasing it. "I do," he replied in a firm voice, and turned again toward Mon.

"In six months," Mon continued, "you will likely have your teams together with you at the demonstration. Its effect in the eastern Mediterranean will be less than we'd like, so we're installing a unique misting and cooling system at the preserve. You can depart for Israel whenever you like. Temporary accommodations are available. But now, I regret that I must leave you. Hassan will see to your needs."

Harrigan had not felt such giddy anticipation since he was a boy visiting Dinamation's lifelike prehistoric animal robots. He and Lloyd enjoyed breakfast together, brainstorming plans and smiling at the checks and airline tickets Hassan left with them.

The next day was all smiles as they boarded a flight for Israel.

In Megiddo, they began to recruit the personnel they would need, and a half-year passed quickly. Harrigan was amazed to see the once-undeveloped valley studded with new construction. Pipes and fiber optics were being buried everywhere.

Several miles east of the archaeological dig of Har-Megiddo was a massive north-south tear in the earth and a sign in three languages: "The Highway of Peace: A Triumph of Arab-Israeli Cooperation."

Harrigan was pleased that Lloyd reported securing access to several sites he suspected would yield fossil genetic material and had several of his tomographic detector manufactured in Israel. The report included several viable soft-tissue fossil finds: A *Smilodon*, the saber-toothed cat, and an Imperial Mammoth were discovered beneath four yards of stone in a shaft in Lepkin Cavern, California. Oxygen in the shaft was almost non-existent; the animals were mummified.

Also recovered was a mummified carcass of a grotesque moose-like animal from India. This twelve-thousand-year-old *Sivatherium* proved its species survived thousands of years longer than hitherto thought. It was found in a sinkhole that had high concentrations of tannic acid, a byproduct of rotting leaves. This is caused by a lack of rot-causing oxygen.

Harrigan approved Lloyd's request for an expedition to Nepal to recover another live yeti, a mating pair if possible. Specimens from existing collections were also purchased, but no genetic manipulation could take place yet. The lab would not be fully operational until mid-spring, 2021. Things were progressing well, despite the debris, mud, and dust that permeated the soon-to-be-bustling valley.

On Christmas day, Harrigan got up from his work-station in one of the few buildings actually completed at the Megiddo Species Preserve. He was alone in the building. He donned his heavy sweater, put a flash drive in his pocket, grabbed the two wide printouts from the oversized printer, and strode confidently to the jeep outside.

Mud, plumbing fixtures, fencing, and building materials were everywhere around him. The parking lot was mush. Harrigan knew it would get even muddier after the Atlas Project, Mon's historic endeavor designed to improve rainfall. The grassy plain around the Megiddo archaeological mound was transforming daily into a mix of red-domed, tan-sided buildings and western-style brick homes.

Minister Mon's office was a mile east toward the new highway, itself still unfinished. Harrigan parked right up on the new sidewalk, changed into clean boots, and entered the glass and granite building. The secretary gave Harrigan access with a silent smile. Mon's oak doors were wide open.

The Iraqi leader looked up from his laptop. "Come in, Kevin. I thought you'd be in the states celebrating Chriss-mas."

Harrigan placed the charts on the desk. He had some selling to do. "Just had to finish up these schedules and ask you a few things."

"Thank you. Is this a PERT chart or something?"

"It's similar. It's a new multidimensional scheduler. Most-likely-case is printed out for twelve-month and five-year projections and the program will run itself for you. Best and worst cases are on the flash drive. You can even put on the view-visor and visually walk through the preserve as it gets completed phase by phase. I've checked all the inputs for this with the contractors and it's accurate."

"Wonderful. I'll have a look."

"First, though, medical staffing. The Megiddo hospital has only one doctor and—"

"She's the finest. You hired her!"

"Yes, but she might leave one day and we need a backup."

"Kevin, the patient load isn't large yet and the Commission isn't made of money."

"He's an intern, but the best. He was RIFted – reduction in force -- from a German army hospital five months ago and he's available cheap. Ismail, he graduated top one percent at the University of Munich's medical school. He even took extra courses. He can work part-time here and you can pull some strings so he can finish his internship at Tel Aviv; do his residency here. By the time he's finished, the patient load here will be three times what it is now. See? There on the projections."

Mon studied the paper covering his desk. "I see, yes. How cheap is cheap?"

"Seventy thousand, U.S., and he'll need a bump in the usual relocation package. Ninety thousand to settle a loss on his house."

"Well, at least the salary is rea-son-able. You vouch for him?"

"He was my only friend at the U.S. Military Academy and Army Ranger School. An exchange program with the German Army. His name is Manfred Freund. He's the best. He'll be a major asset on the research end, after his residency. His forte is neurology."

"Neur-o-logy. Top one percent. Inexpensive backup. Interesting. Okay, Dr. Harrigan. You have asked and, this time, you shall receive. You know, Kevin, you and your research have enormous potential. You are going to have the scientific community, maybe all mankind, in the palm of your hand one day. I'm just glad to be a patron; no, a bit of a mentor for you. If men like you and I could have true freedom to create, the world would be a su-premely better place! But one step at a time, eh? As I said, the Commission is not made of money. Half from your budget and I'll get the rest from the theme park or something. All right?"

Harrigan felt, oddly, both exhilarated and uncomfortable. Only Mon gave him such high praise or exhibited faith in Harrigan's ability to attain glorious achievement.

"Thank you, Minister. Now about these projections: I think you'll be pleased with..."

Harrigan, most of his team and international dignitaries, stood transfixed. News camera operators jostled for positions. The thirteen-hundred-mile-long northwest African mountain range called the Atlas chain was going to be reduced in height by at least a third, a massive and historic effort, combining mostly Arab oil revenue with previously secret Israeli sound-beam weapons technology to change a major planetary feature. The plan had been carefully computer-modeled until the result was certain. The reduction would permit rain to pass eastward from Atlantic weather systems to quench the barren Sahara and even improve precipitation somewhat as far east as Iran.

According to the data in the report, Harrigan felt confident that the local forces had done a relatively humane and efficient job at clearing the small populations of villagers from the target areas. By the New Year, the thousands of protesters, scruffy Berber villagers along with radical environmental and human rights groups from around the world, had also been cleared.

A tense stillness filled the moment. Even the reporters had gone silent with expectation. There was only a slightly high-pitched sound. The air seemed to become refractive. The long mountain range blurred a bit, as if heat were rising through the air and distorting the view.

Suddenly the entire range exploded in a cloud of gravel-sized particles, sand, and dust. The rumble followed moments later. It grew loud in a few seconds. Already it appeared that the steeper faces of the range were pouring like liquid down their slopes. Portions of the peaks collapsed slowly, flatter, wider. Then the high-pitched sound ceased. A rumble continued briefly, quieting. The air calmed and dust began to settle, revealing that the once awesome peaks and ridges were flattened at the top and heaped at the sides as if ground with a router.

Ominous clouds invaded from the west. The humbled mountains grew dark within minutes and became striped along their slopes with what could be seen through binoculars as mud slides. Aerial viewing by the speechless crowd was canceled as the advancing rains soaked everyone and grounded the observation helicopters.

Harrigan activated his tablet and checked the progress of work on his house, labs, and animal facilities as he sat on the sofa in his Megiddo apartment. *Six years for everything, two to five for the total lab facilities!* He switched to the news app.

Newscasters hailed Minister Ismail Mon as being the hero of the century, and at the very least, the Man of the Year. Mon's Atlas project was touted to reap billions of dollars' worth of copper, zinc, and other previously hard-to-reach minerals from the remnants of the mountains. They sang his praises for land distribution as well as compassionate relocations of Berbers. Fertility was forecasted to return to the northern third of the Sahara, and mean summer temperatures as far east as Western Iran were expected to drop twelve degrees.

One newscaster was bold enough to predict that Ismail Mon would be elected Chairman of Iraq's Justice Party, a five-year term.

Harrigan turned off the app and leaned back on the sofa. *Mon promised priority of completion to the Megiddo Preserve over his 'Tower of Babel' monument. Victory number one. It'll all take years, but this research can advance genetics decades… new therapies, resurrecting prehistoric animals, even…*he grinned to himself…*Lloyd's just the guy to find non-mineralized genetic material…maybe even hominins!* He wondered about reactions to his research, but worried most about Mon's controversial monument, six years from completion.

Chapter Three

Each tour group passed security to approach the monument after the research zoo tour and a sumptuous supper buffet. As families strolled in through the towering monument's doors, camera crews dogged Mon for comments and scientists for video narration.

"These are so placid, Dr. Lloyd," a reporter asked, showing him a video and directing her cameraman at Lloyd, "and able to reach high browse. How did they go extinct?"

It showed two small groups of totally different herbivores lazily feeding together. Six tan, horse-like *Macrauchenia* easily reached feed cages twelve feet up using almost elephantine snouts. Beside them stood one male and six female *Megaloceros*, the enormous "Irish Elk". The male flaunted wide-dished, sharp-pronged antlers that spread six feet on each side of its stately head; the females all appeared pregnant.

"We don't have a bloody clue how *Macrauchenia* died out," Lloyd offered, "but p'raps, as glaciers receded, *Megaloceros'* antlers caught in trees, impeded mating, migration, and evasion of predators. Their routes were then more predictable to human hunters, too."

Without a "Thank you," the reporter next pulled Australian biologist-veterinarian Carl Smythe bumping against Lloyd and continued with a sequence showing a pair of angry-looking, ten-foot-tall mastodons, *Mammut americanum*. Their bulging neck and shoulder muscles and fluffy red coats made it seem that they had no necks at all. They had smaller ears than their mammoth cousins and sharp but subtly curved tusks.

"These, too are *so placid*. Dr. Smythe, Compare them to mammoths?"

"These mastodons possess low-crowned, conical mol-ahs for mashin' leaves, unlike their grass-eatin' mammoth cousins. Jungle 'n forest dwellers, they were, from the American Great Lakes down to Patagonia. Strictly leaf eaters but bloody mean brutes. Early on, we 'ad 'em with an *Elasmotherium* — that's our rhino from 'ell — and they savagely gored each otha'."

"Thanks. We're at the turnstile. So, let's, uh, enjoy the monument."

The tower rose two-hundred-twenty feet in smooth, helical form like a tightly rolled silver scroll whose center had been ceremoniously pushed up. A revolving brass door at its base permitted entrance; another at its top provided exit to the spiraled exterior walkway that led back down. A United Nations flag crowned the narrow pinnacle.

The windowless monument was a cone-shaped, aluminum spire with anthropological displays. Its floor formed a ramp spiraling up around its one-hundred-eighty-foot-tall central core. The core formed a cone, twelve feet wide at the top and forty at the base. Its hidden, central shaft was empty, save for steel supports, exposed bolts, and electrical wiring. Outside the core, in the long, curved display hall, most kiosks were animated with 3-D TV or robotic exhibits highlighted by blood-red carpeting and glare-free lighting.

In the service parking area, the Syrian parked his food vendor van and booted his laptop. He spoke coolly through it to his operatives. "Number Three, check door codes and report."

It took over a minute. Then, the screen flashed, CODES OPERABLE.

The man left the vehicle to deliver more food then returned to his van. As he drove away, he eyed the brass and steel revolving door at the base of the Monument to Peace and Man.

"Sacrilege and desolate abomination!" he muttered. "You who would be gods in God's land deserve no mercy. Wolves, masquerading as lambs!"

Harrigan's group followed Mon, discussing points broached by the displays. The VIPs leisurely ascended from the base toward the top, Freund's group next.

Near ground level, the displays focused on ancient human ancestors and included paintings, interactive screens, and mounted artifacts such as spear points. Exhibits portrayed ape-like pre-human simians evolving societal and other traits that compensated for physical vulnerability. Simulations dramatically showed the formation of clans, division of labor and invention of tools for hunting, gathering, and war. The abilities to think symbolically, imagine, cooperate, vocalize, and manipulate tools all were touted as key attributes of hominin survival and development.

Still, as the displays made clear, evidence of brutal individual and group fighting and killing had been unearthed. Wall placards and displays defined the issue repeatedly: Was the urge to kill and all other propensities in humans genetic, and thereby not subject to moral judgment? Harrigan knew that Freund recognized evolution theory as sound, and that many behavioral propensities were genetic. But he also suspected that Freund would erupt over the implications of the monument's displays. He nervously watched Freund glare at Mon.

"These displays," Freund growled, "obviously promote the assumption that acting on genetic proclivities is morally neutral."

Harrigan frowned as Freund gained momentum. *Great, we're gonna have an argument in front of everybody and Mon'll overreact.*

Freund's tone hardened further. "Humans make choices with an understanding of their impacts upon individuals, society, and the natural world. So, even if a behavior is genetically influenced, the fact does not render any human behavior morally neutral—however expedient it may be to mischaracterize genetic tendencies. I'm sorry, but the truth is *not* established by humanist or rationalist philosophy, opinion polls, or political correctness. Stand in the truth, sir!"

Mon's tone seemed unemotional. "Dr. Freund, what is truth? You must admit that this concept of 'morality' differs from society to society and is, therefore, an imperfect *human* construct. This monument, however, should please you: You will see as you walk onward that it celebrates man's conquering—by reason and societal evolution—his most dangerous inherited traits, from selfishness to the propensity to murder. We are at that threshold now Doctor, and neither religion nor morality has brought us here. Civil and secular mastery of ourselves has."

Quite a few in the spiraled hallway clapped and cheered the impromptu speech. Freund did not respond but did smile as Harrigan broke off and stepped back to speak with him.

"Okay, you're right," he whispered to Freund. "Just don't mar the tour by arguing. Mon could fire you! His Commission and some U.N. committees designed this. It's kinda like the International Public Radio news, promoting its agenda while only appearing to impartially inform. This next display of how religion developed I think is more on target. Look at it impartially."

"Impartial? The truth makes demands on us. Remember that."

The group wound its way past primitive simians toward depictions of near-humans, such as *Homo erectus* and *Homo ergaster*. One theory, based on recent finds, asserted that *Erectus* continued to survive, side-by-side, with Neanderthal and Cro-Magnon man, and that Cro-Magnons deduced that they and the Neanderthals both were the children of the more primitive species. It postulated that stories, like that of Cain and Abel, were passed down orally as Genesis-like myths. Other displays evidencing shamanism among both subspecies came next. There was a common thrust: man's history and scripture were not revealed to him; rather, he created them.

Freund grimaced as he read the only reference to creationist views. "I wish creationists wouldn't get so wrapped around the axle. They give rationalists ammo to denigrate religion. They attack anyone who believes that God used evolution as a tool. If God wanted to use evolution, the saints, or even Kevin Harrigan—God help us!—who are we to deny it?

"Even if creationists are right, it's unimportant because Christ made no reference to the issue. What'll happen to their kids' faith as evolution gets closer to being proved? Just look at that!"

Freund directed his wife Gertrude's attention toward the collage depicting numerous examples of shoddy science once used to refute the theory of evolution. These included a fossil shell coil, which Irish monks had carved at the blunt end to appear as Satan's snakes turned to stone by divine punishment.

Harrigan listened as Gertrude admonished her husband. "Manfred Freund! We may not share fundamentalists' views, but their hearts are righteous. You corrected Hans for talking mean to playmates yesterday. Besides, maybe the Creation Story is true, and evolution began afterward. How can you presume to know?"

"Number Three, test the door codes," commanded the Syrian in the white utility van.

He smiled as CODES OPERABLE appeared on his monitor.

He brought up a schematic of the monument, scanning his typed notes and mumbling as if humming a song. "Soft plastic panels on steel supports. Maximum kills once the infidels spread throughout the building. Blast goes up from the core at the base level. Perfect!"

He checked another's status. "Number Two, are you at the platform?"

The computer screen in his van flashed one word: IMMINENT.

Harrigan was engrossed by depictions of hominin evolution as he led his group slowly up the Monument's incline. One theory posited that *Homo heidelbergensis* gave rise to three races: Denisovans disappeared before Cro Magnons, modern humans who arose a hundred fifty millennia ago in the Mideast or northeast Africa. Neanderthals appeared three hundred millennia ago, but died out thirty millennia ago. Fossil and genetic evidence pointed to Cro-Magnons extinguishing Neanderthals. War, enslavement, and rape were alleged. Modern peoples' genes are one to five percent Neanderthal.

Computer simulated conflicts, even societal change, from megafauna-hunting to nomadic and agricultural lifestyles, fast-forwarded before everyone's wide eyes. City-states, wars, migrations, and trading routes waxed and waned before Harrigan's and others' wide eyes. Destruction and diasporas of peoples were traced globally and in time. Harrigan let out a "Wow" as he devoured evidence that the Hebrew tribe of Menashe ranged as far as north India and up the Amazon to the Andes around 700 B.C.

Progressing farther up the incline, groups saw representations of the medieval crusades. These vividly showed Christian fighters massacring whole Moslem towns and Moslem knights also using religion to justify disemboweling Balkan women and children. All religions were portrayed as deleterious, particularly Christianity. One display, void of evidence, alleged that the Catholic Church was silent during the Holocaust. Warfare between competing sects of Buddhism, Hinduism, and Islam followed. The gist was clear: Humanity progressed most when governments controlled, and when religions restricted themselves to serving people's philosophical musings.

Freund gave Mon an irritated scowl. "This monument's presentation is one-sided. You've ignored clandestine help to the Jews by the Church in World War II and trashed all religions."

Harrigan cringed as Mon pointed at depictions of war and terrorism. "What about abuse of the ignorant masses' loyalty to religion and national identity? Killing over resources and superstition proves the destructive influence of competing nations and religions. Only one confederated government regulating religions can halt strife among nations and faiths."

"Did you learn nothing from the Martyrs, Fatima, or Zeitun?" Freund growled, "Did you not sense God pining for us to love him, not prosperity?"

Mon grimaced, then smiled and responded in a condescendingly patient tone. "Einstein knew God, but he knew it was a unifying property of the universe. If only religion were a force for unity! You worship the bogus 'Ancient of Days', but we explore our 'ancient of genes' to advance humanity." Then Mon trained his gaze toward the crowd to continue triumphantly, "It is ignorance and poverty that enslaves, my friends; not what's branded as sin. One day, prosperity-generating reason will be the mortar that will bind nations like bricks in a wall."

Freund turned red. "Like bricks in a prison wall," he shot back.

Mon's voice rose inspiringly. "We will only be free when we reject the oppression of clerics and put human economic and personal freedoms first. No nation or religion gives happiness. Science, government, and freedom from religion do. The U.N. *will* build a global village, conquering the very stars to carry the torch of peace and the supremacy of *man*."

Applause and cheers rose from the crowd as Freund eyed Mon, then turned away, silent.

The remaining displays credited the Arab-Israeli Development Commission, the World Bank, and other institutions, for progress.

Mon stepped just ahead of the crowd to a ten-foot-wide landing atop the ramp. Between the revolving exit door and a maintenance door, an impressionist painting hung bathed in bright spotlights. It showed a nude, racially vague couple stepping out into bright stars from a dimming silver-gray volcano, shaped like the monument, in whose bowels boiled symbols of religions, nations, and wars.

As Mon turned to address the audience, a red light lit on a panel beside the exit door. Two metallic clangs rang out as steel bars popped into the exit's curved turnstile, locking it.

Machine gun fire burst from two guns behind Freund, who threw his family to the floor. Mon flew backward, blood bursting from the right side of his head. VIPs dropped, screaming. In a few seconds, the shooting ceased. Mon's bodyguard trained his pistol down the walkway past Freund. Before acquiring a target, he fell, his neck ripped open at the left jugular by automatic fire. Two Israeli soldiers sought targets without success. Their heads snapped back, blown open.

The gunmen turned and fired down the hall toward the crowd, most of the bullets striking the sloped ceiling. The thugs ordered silence, but moans continued.

Two men in jeans and cotton sport shirts—one dull red, the other navy blue, jumped over Freund and pulled a fat-looking man in gray slacks and a black parka-style shirt up through the crowd. As they bounded past bodies toward the maintenance access door, Harrigan hurled himself at the three and bowled them to the floor. He managed to hold down the two gunmen, but they quickly clubbed him unconscious with their gun butts.

The 'fat' man rose to his feet, his open shirt revealing foam padding with cavities in which his co-conspirators' weapons had been smuggled. Harrigan subdued, the smuggler pulled a small putty-like cube from his false belly, pressed it onto the bulky door handle, drew away, and pushed a small green plunger linked to the cube by wire. The explosion blew the door open.

The other assassins raised their guns to Harrigan's head and...

"Aaaahhh!"

Freund's yell distracted the two long enough for him to pounce. Shots ripped a quarter of an inch deep valley below Freund's left ribs. The noise revived Harrigan, who wrenched the weapon from one assailant's hand. The fat man turned, pointed his gun at Freund, who lay atop the gunmen, and fired.

But a rising attacker met his death instead, as the short burst split his back. The other prone gunman tried to push Freund off. Harrigan fired point-blank into the terrorist's head. The spray of bone shards and hair appeared to frighten the explosives man, who disappeared into the maintenance room.

Freund and Harrigan chased him through the mangled door. Foam padding falling off him, revealed rows of C-4 plastic explosive bricks studded with wired blasting caps. Harrigan's heart skipped a beat as the true threat flashed into his mind, *He's not fleeing – this is the real attack!*

Freund screamed. "He's wired! Caps *und* C-4 all over him!"

"Get him," Harrigan roared.

The man was already climbing over the maintenance platform's railing, which overlooked the monument's deep central cavity.

"He's jumping!" Freund screamed.

Harrigan lunged for the man's arm and missed.

Freund dove for the floor, almost sliding off the platform. He grabbed the man's right arm and waist, but his hold was insufficient. The terrorist continued to fall away from the railing – pulling Freund precariously over the edge. Harrigan kneeled to grab Freund and pull both men back through the railing. Freund was losing his grip on the struggling terrorist.

Bart Lloyd rushed into the room and leaped onto the platform. He reached his long arm over Freund to grip the bomber's other arm. Pulling against the terrorist's substantial strength, he managed a headlock and began to strangle the "filthy blighter," as he shouted.

Harrigan and Lloyd now hauled the man in, throwing him against a workbench, which tipped, spilling tools and thick extension cords. Harrigan, still on his knees, pushed Freund and Lloyd out of his way and grabbed a long torque wrench. He swung the heavy steel club into the man's temple. The bomber started to tip, as if dead, but Freund steadied him before the C-4 and blasting caps could strike the floor. Then Freund laid the body down gingerly, announcing that the man was still alive but out cold.

"Shouldn't we tie him up or some —" Lloyd was almost breathless.

Harrigan was dressing Freund's wound with clean work rags and his belt. "Yes, do it now. No. Wait. Get everyone to the lower levels – slowly. I don't want a stampede."

Lloyd pushed open the mangled door and found a stampede in progress. He chased the sound of the screaming crowd and was gone. Freund and Harrigan began to wrap the man tightly with the hundred-foot electrical cords from the workbench, tying hasty knots.

"Vee need to tie him bedder! He could wake up any min —"

The man's eyes opened and he sat forward, pulling a detonator from his right side. In a flash, he was through the railing. Harrigan went for the man and Freund reached for the detonator. Harrigan caught him at the edge of the platform. The detonator plunger was almost all the way down to its base, so Harrigan grabbed for the plunger as well.

"Ahhh. Aaah." Harrigan's finger felt as if it were being crushed, but it did effectively block the plunger from its base. Harrigan and Freund tried to wrest the detonator from the terrorist. As Harrigan and the man struggled,

Freund released his own grip on the device and grabbed a carpenter's hammer from the floor.

Freund struck the man with the blunt end, but the bomber kicked Harrigan away and was almost over the edge. Freund spun the hammer in his palm and crashed the claw end down, gouging the top of his skull. The man somehow continued to struggle; he was out over the edge again. Freund struck again, harder, well into the brain, and pried the hammer back viciously. It spattered a red and gray jam-like substance on his face.

The man began to convulse wildly. He floundered back under the railing and away from the pair; through the air and down—five feet, then ten, twenty feet, more. Harrigan and Freund blanched. Both knew that in seconds the blast could kill hundreds.

Freund saw it first. Then Harrigan. One of the cords they had tied him with had fallen over a banister post, providing a chance to halt the deadly fall. The two got in each other's way grabbing for it. Only four feet of cord remained and they still had no hold.

Harrigan managed to grasp the cord, pull it back, and form a single twist around the base of the post. He pulled it tight and wrapped it one more twist around the pole. All he had left to hold was the plug and ten inches of cord. Freund clutched it tightly. Together, the two held it fast.

"We've got it, Mannie!"

The binding was holding easily. Too easily. They looked downward in horror: The deadly, explosives-laden body was still falling, spinning furiously as it unwound.

Then the line tugged. The body bounced. They held their breath and Harrigan even prayed, "God *help* us!" out loud.

The prayer seemed unanswered: The body slipped the confused loops and began to fall again, to lurch, and flip. Precious little cord remained wrapped on the body, now tumbling eighty feet below.

Another tug. A snapping sound, like bone cracking.

The cord tangled about its neck. The body-bomb bounced and swung.

A moment passed as the two men took breaths in short, halting gasps. Tears as much as sweat dripped from their cheeks as they knelt, holding the cord and staring down in terror. The body still dangled. Another moment passed. It swayed. Then it hung almost motionless.

"Mannie," Harrigan whispered. "We've gotta go down and get it. His cord could let go any minute. You know what'll happen if it falls."

"*Ja*, I know. We don't have enough cord here to tie it. 'nd if we pull him up, the disturbance could unbind him."

Harrigan saw duct tape near his leg. He pulled it to himself with his foot and a free hand. With that hand and his teeth, he pulled some off. He taped the cord at the base of the pole, almost dropped it, and continued to expand his bind. Freund released his grip.

They looked for more extension cords and found a hundred-foot roll. Feverishly searching the lockers, they found three more rolls. They secured square knotted lengths to the railing, three feet on either side of the pole to which they had taped the dead man's line. Next, they gathered three empty tool belts with a few hinged D-shaped safety rings, four smaller extension cords, and pairs of heavy-duty gloves. Rapidly donning these, they wrapped the long cords once each around the D rings on their tool belts. They pulled the field-expedient ropes around their right sides and held them centered on the small of their backs. Set to rappel, they dropped from the railing.

They bounced downward more quickly than they knew was safe, but they could not assume the binding around the bomber's neck would stay. At the one-hundred-foot point, they breathed sighs of relief. The tangle around the man's neck looked secure, for the moment. Freund and Harrigan reached the corpse and began to tie the small extension cords between their own bodies and the dead man's arms. But they soon realized they would not be able to haul him back up.

"We're going to have to lower him to the floor," Harrigan sighed as he fumbled to wipe sweat from his eyes.

"We'll have to unhook ourselves to get our D rings below the knot to descend. Gimme a sec before we try *that* suicide maneuver!"

Freund closed his eyes and slowly wiped his drenched face. Then the men unhooked their D rings, hung on precariously with one hand each, then re-secured the rings below the start of the next cord. They heard moaning and crying through the walls below them, but heard no indication of rescue.

"Untangle his neck and lower him down?" Harrigan asked hesitantly.

"Let's do it!"

On the eighty-foot journey. Freund winced each time his wound got constricted by the tethers. They reached the base, without dropping the body.

They set it in a sitting posture, its head resting on its chest; the coagulated skull wound matted with blood clots and hair.

"Okay. We're safe from *this* guy. I think it'd be easier to break through that heavy plastic wall than to climb back up, don't you?"

"Absolutely." Freund's accent was dissipating as his confidence bolstered. He rose to look for something with which to attack the wall. There was nothing. They both wished they had thought to bring tools. Freund examined the wall bolts. They were not removable by hand. Harrigan did not assist but instead remained at the body, nervously looking the dead man over. Harrigan cocked his head and listened.

"You gonna keep gawking at that horror show or help—"

"Shh! Mannie, this thing's got a backup detonator. Listen."

"I don't hear anyth—"

Harrigan grabbed the corpse and carefully rolled it on its side.

"Zhzhzhzhzhzhzhzh," came the faint noise.

Harrigan tore the shirt open with his teeth, careful not to disturb the hundreds of blasting caps. If just one went off, it would detonate everything. Then he saw it between two bricks: a red box with two blinking green lights.

"I see it. Maybe… it's a battery pack," Freund said hesitantly.

"It's a friggin' timer, and we don't know how to turn it off. If we disconnect it, it could detonate right then."

Harrigan was fidgeting, frantic but not panicked. "It could blow any second. I need ideas, Mannie, *right now.*"

Freund took only a second to respond. "Look, pull the C-4 from the blasting caps *und* separate them. He and the caps blew up, but the C-4 isn't detonated. We'd need at least fifty feet distance, with so many caps on him."

Harrigan grimaced at Freund. "I was gonna suggest that."

Freund was already loosening blasting caps, just as they had been taught in Ranger School. "I know you were. Let's go!"

They feverishly ripped tape from the rows of C-4, avoided wires, and wiggled bricks off the corpse. They stuffed blocks into shirts, breaths now shorter and sweat dripping into eyes. Cries and moans continued from beyond the wall as Harrigan took the last brick, sweaty and smelly, off the man's lower buttocks. There was no more room in his shirt or pockets. No bricks could be left on the floor—even one would blast through the plasti-panels and kill many in the huddling crowds below. Harrigan had no time to think. Reaching, he wiped the brick and stuffed it in his mouth. The men climbed as fast as they could, but they were exhausted and cramping. The two progressed forty feet up and absolutely *had* to rest and catch their breath. They were not getting enough air with bricks in their mouths.

Freund looked almost as if he was having breathing convulsions.

Harrigan was concerned and spoke through the impediment of the smelly C-4 block in his mouth. Freund looked at him and winced.

"Mannie," Harrigan mouthed. "Breathing problems? Not far now till we get this stuff out of range. You can do it!"

"I'm okay," Freund mumbled. "Just winded. I was laughing."

"Laughing? We could die any second and you're laughing?"

"You know, Kevin, all you had to do to keep that butt-sweat-soaked C-4 out of your mouth was exchange it with one in your shirt!"

Harrigan's eyebrow popped up. He cursed and resumed the climb.

Freund called to him. "You were going to think of that any second."

They were forty-five feet up when Lloyd leaned out over the platform.

"Are you chaps all right? We're still stuck in here and I don't think anyone knows we're locked in. The crowd has some serious injuries, I'm afraid. We're waiting for the outside guards to notice that we're late in exiting. Hey, can you hear me?"

Harrigan and Freund had no more energy to respond. They strained to keep their position, to keep from falling back down. They were still within the range of what could easily be an ejected, live cap.

Harrigan saw Lloyd rappel down. All three met halfway, ninety feet.

Lloyd slipped. He swayed too much and tangled his feet in the wiring hanging along the plasti-panels, lost his grip, and hung upside down by one leg. He struggled to pull himself upright. Harrigan and Freund tried but could do nothing for him.

The blasting caps around the corpse detonated within milliseconds of each other, creating the effect of one big explosion. It melted and shattered the surrounding plasti-panels, injuring several people in the adjoining hall. The terrorist's chest imploded as the shattered head and some of the neck rocketed upward. The bloody comet lost speed just as it reached Lloyd. He gasped and struggled. It temporarily lodged on an exposed bolt, then fell to the floor.

The shock knocked Harrigan and Freund into the steel supports, spilling C-4 blocks. They recovered their senses and waited a full minute to be sure no late-fuse caps remained, then they tossed away the remaining C-4. They managed to help Lloyd right himself.

All three shook from muscle fatigue when they finally reached the top and clambered onto the platform. After lying and panting momentarily, they walked weak-kneed and bloodied to join the others below.

"Who were those bastards?" Harrigan asked Freund as they descended the curved hall, "and why this attack?"

"Who knows," Freund sighed, "and what does it matter, anyway? It's always been like this. If 'religious' warriors, the IRA, Jihad, and the rest, genuinely subscribed to their beliefs, they'd bury the hatchet and work for peace. God sends iterations of prophets, but we arrogantly ignore the prophecy, an incentive to rise above our nature. God hasn't given up — but there *is* to be a final call and I'd bet humanity is approaching that point."

Harrigan dismissed the thought. Cries and moans grew louder as they neared the crowd. Tykvah Strauss tried to stand but collapsed, moaning and ripping her skirt. A pen protruded from her bloody right hip. Harrigan held her hand away and wiped blood from her thigh, his mind reeling as he glanced from her face to her exposed thigh.

"Don't pull it!" he ordered, scooping her up and whisking her outside to medics. "You could bleed worse." He paused, waiting for the ambulance to arrive. He felt as if he were swimming in her glistening brown eyes.

She smiled demurely. "You can put me down, Dr. Harrigan.

"Th—that could...your thigh, pulling out, worse bleed," He fumbled.

He placed her gently into the ambulance as she raised her head toward his. Then he blushed and stumbled backward, exiting toward the wounded but holding eye contact until the ambulance doors shut.

Inside, Harrigan found Gertrude tending to an ugly bullet wound that had destroyed Mon's ear and entered his skull at the temple. She looked up as Freund rushed in to attend.

"His pulse weakened and now I can't feel it at all!"

"He's lost too much blood, Gertrude. He's gone unless—"

A blow torch's flame suddenly flared through the wall. In minutes, a three-foot-by-two-foot opening had been cut. Mon and the wounded were evacuated to the hospital.

Within twenty minutes, everyone was out, including nineteen bodies for the morgue. Three were religious terrorists. Eight had been murdered by the "devout" deceased. The remaining tourists were trampled or crushed against the unyielding entrance door.

Mon, initially declared dead, was "miraculously" revived at the hospital and regained consciousness late that evening to the sound of cheering crowds in the parking lot.

Harrigan assumed that Mon felt indebted for his life, making him a confidant. Days later, Harrigan received a note that reinforced this belief: Mon, having returned to Iraq, wrote, "Kevin, your work is too important to ever risk again. I can give you no details now, but be assured that you will soon continue the vital work that you were forced to abandon years ago."

Chapter Four

Al-Rajda Village, Northern Iraq
0934 hours, 11 September 2026

Major Hassan eyed Mon from his seat in the roomy ten-passenger jet. He coveted Mon's discipline, station, and the colorful medals covering his commander's crisp, forest green, lieutenant colonel's uniform. He admired the work done on Mon's ear and scalp. The segments had been regenerated in Harrigan's lab from Mon's own cartilage and flesh but attached by Mon's personal physician.

Hassan noticed Mon peering out a window and imagined his leader was surveying the somewhat enhanced greenery of his desert realm. Perhaps Mon was angered by this minimal environmental improvement, given the computer projections of lush forestation. Mon's ominous reticence made him nervous. Hassan wanted dearly to get inside the mind of his mentor.

The new research site preparation was three months behind schedule, still not cleared of Kurds. He watched as sparse desert turned to grassland, then became verdant as the plane approached the plateau and the rugged olive-gray mountains that surrounded it. As the jet passed a bend in the river, the tiny village came into view near the base of a high cliff. Up on the plateau, mountain ridges formed a northward-pointing arrow framing sparse grasslands. A small river cascaded off the southern cliffs.

It seemed to Hassan that the ridges were jaws closing on the settlement. He smiled. Below, military vehicles parked in a deep ditch beside the dirt road that ran northward into mud-brick homes ringed by a white stucco wall. A convoy of construction vehicles and trailers clogged the road.

The jet slowed a hundred feet above the grassy plain as two powerful engines rotated on its wings to support the aircraft's vertical landing. Some stragglers were being shoved into the crowd of two hundred or so Kurds. Most of them bore the weight of heavy sacks on their stooped backs and waited in uneven ranks for the order to load the buses. Two lines of guards, leaning lazily on their weapons, bracketed the Kurds. Armored vehicles formed the ends of the troop lines.

Mon descended the jet's staircase and curtly returned Lieutenant Colonel Vaj's shaky salute. Vaj began to offer excuses for the lateness.

Mon ignored his babbling commander and marched past an old BMP armored troop carrier crowned by a small gun turret. He stopped to face the executive officer, Major Najik, who stood at the edge of the ditch that hid the bottom half of the BMP. Najik snapped to attention. Vaj rushed beside.

Mon finally addressed Vaj, his voice flat and quiet. "Have you been standing here looking at each other for three months?"

"No, sir. Only today have we had support to force these stubborn—"

"Shoot them."

Mon's soft-spoken command was loud enough to be heard by the crowd of Kurds fifty feet away. They gasped and shifted about.

"Sir, we will have them out in mere moments. The buses are—"

"Give me your sidearm and you will observe how to control."

The commander hesitated, nervously shifting his gaze from Mon to the crowd of Kurds. Vaj handed his pistol to Mon.

"Minister, please. If I may have my pistol, I will kill one of the Kurds. That will motivate them to board the buses. If you will allow me a mo—"

Mon turned to Major Najik and placed the pistol in his hand. "You are now the commander of this battalion. Shoot Lieutenant Colonel Vaj and execute the order I gave him."

Vaj blanched, his eyes darting between Mon and Najik.

The crowd began to murmur and retreat. An old man near the front shook his fist and swore. A teenager, barely showing pregnancy in her white smock and blue shawl, quivered as she called out, "Let us live!"

In a split second, Najik raised the pistol to the center of Vaj's forehead and fired. Vaj's body collapsed face-up, forming a halo of blood in the grass. Najik pointed the pistol at the left side of the Kurd ranks, traced an arc across them, and called to the BMP's gun turret operator.

"Abrih, open fire."

A priming handle clanked back and released. The Kurds abandoned ranks and cringed into a tight crowd, but the girl—no longer trembling—stepped forward holding her stomach. Then, slowly, she turned her work-worn palms up and outward.

Armor-piercing rounds ripped the girl's belly, splashing red, white, and gray shreds of the tiny person within like balloons and confetti at a political convention. She fell back, sitting upon baggage with her head drooping to her right as if nuzzling a child.

Hassan watched in giddy awe as the rounds exploded seven other Kurds, whizzed through sixty feet of air, and scarred the village wall. Despite the carnage, not every Kurd was killed. One gripped his wounded side, repeating "Allah, forgive them," until bullets opened his chest and knocked him onto the girl's lap. Najik ordered soldiers to use their rifles to quiet the rest of the screaming, moaning survivors.

Taking initiative for Mon, Najik ordered that power shovels dig a mass grave, dozers push the Kurds into it, and his men to burn the contents.

Soon, gasoline fumes, burning flesh, and ash permeated the air.

Searing reflections of the flames glinted off each officer's eyes. Only Mon, Hassan, Najik, and half of the soldiers appeared tolerant of this change in this area that would soon be a laboratory lawn.

Mon spoke again to Najik. "You will watch your 'weaker' men carefully after this. You will assure complete security."

"Of course, sir."

"Your unit, all these men, will remain here throughout the building phase and will become the permanent security garrison."

"Yes, sir."

Mon's voice skewered both of his officers' attention. "This project is of paramount importance to me. Therefore, it is of paramount importance to you. I will remember you two as I rise to my rightful place as premier, and ultimately, even greater leadership."

Najik and Hassan thanked their teacher. Mon led Hassan back to the jet, tasting the ash on the rail with his finger as they climbed the steps. Hassan, astounded by Mon's carriage and confidence, coveted his mentor's mysterious mettle. But he was sure no one could fully penetrate Mon's mind. *Perhaps*, he thought, *if any were to gain this insight, they would be unable to conceive or endure the awing immensity of its powerfully seething and insidiously effective malice. I would give my very soul to have a mind such as his.*

Inside the plane, Hassan listened to his mentor. "Your people are still ignorant, so I must personally convince the fool Harrigan, to head the project. Are your scientists ready to learn from him and achieve my assignments?"

"Y-yes, sir. But we look forward to ultimately…replacing Harrigan and his staff!"

———

At the Megiddo lab, Harrigan and Tykvah paid scant attention to work, less to coworkers. Tykvah sat at her computer screen nuzzling her head under Harrigan's chin. His arms embraced her shoulders as he leaned forward from behind, resting his hands upon hers.

Harrigan smelled her long brown hair. The aroma flooded him, a comforting scent that meant she was with him. He swiveled her chair around and gazed into her gleeful eyes. They were a temptation to him, but more. To Harrigan, Tykvah's probing eyes promised companionship, acceptance, and patience. He sensed, beneath his ego, that Tykvah knew his faults yet would not ridicule him as he painfully and sporadically tried to grow beyond himself. Now he drifted in the glassy sea of her gentle brown eyes.

He tried to kiss her quickly and refocus on work, but her soft, warm lips held him longer until he had to force himself to the computer screen.

They stared at the computer analysis of differences between the DNA of two *Panthera leo spelaea*. One had been created using both modern and archaic genes while the other was completely archaic. The analysis was another attempt to determine whether the building criticism of Harrigan's FGR was justified. A plethora of adverse articles blasted his and his team's work as creating only hybrids — new species — rather than regenerating extinct ones.

Harrigan frowned. "I admit, they're right about the *Smilodon* and *Elasmotherium* recreations. Those hybrids are way off," he sighed.

Tykvah's end-of-sentence, almost-a-question inflection pegged her New York Jewish roots. "So, you should expect perfection? The cave lion you made using both egg and sperm, Lloyd's team recovered it essentially the same as the one you made using archaic egg and *modern* sperm. Not bad for kibitzing!"

"The modern lion is closer to the cave lion than these other extinct species are to their modern relatives. What we've got to do is refine FGR, and see if there really are dormant genes in moderns. That we can use them to compensate for not having both egg and sperm of the extinct species. Otherwise, it'll just be more 'humiliate Harrigan' articles and I'll never show those arrogant —"

"You will, Kevin. Such an impatient mensch!"

"Expressing dormant prehistoric traits in modern genes is still just my theory. I'm not even sure if there are ancient traits preserved that way. When I try to complete an ovum's gene set by doubling and modifying the single-sex contribution, genetic errors are too numerous for it to get past the zygote stage. Maybe we should focus resources on helping Bart find useable male and female specimens," Harrigan said, almost resigned to the obstacle. He mumbled in dejection, "Maybe I should stop work on the toads and —"

"What toads?"

Harrigan studied Tykvah, unsure whether he should let her see the second avenue of FGR research. He took her hand, silently led her into his office, shut the door, and moved a huge bookcase with ease. There, in an aquarium, was a toad — breathing underwater with gills. Tykvah's jaw dropped, then she gasped at the cat purring in a cage. The orange tabby's saber fangs extended three inches from its mouth.

"I do this alone. I'm trying to find ancient haplotypes, and gene sequences at the chromosome's centers. They code for traits archived when species split from their ancestral species. But it only *appears* that I'm getting somewhere, because the special RNA that *I think* preserved those traits are rare in animals.

"If it was rare long ago, the traits are just not preserved well enough to express fully in modern animals. That chicken over there—"

Tykvah followed his gesture. Her eyes popped at a chicken with yellow scales among, sparse red feathers and thick reptilian talons.

"—is merely an improvement on a 2005 atavism experiment by Harris and Fallon. Very few traits survive, and in a very incomplete state. Or I can't find them. I found the genes that produce these traits by looking for similarities between these animals' genes and those of species that share their ancestry. It takes trial and error to release the genes from dormancy, and I have to cheat by splicing some genes in. I just can't get beyond this flawed method because I don't know how to find, target, and express the haplotypes. I worry that it could be a dead end."

"This is astounding, Kevin. How can you even think of abandoning what you're onto here? I'm not a geneticist, but finding and expressing dormant genes may be the key to a lot of mysteries. Both FGR methods are viable options and don't you dare abandon either one! Why do you do this part of your research alone?"

"It could be stolen. Or, worse, it could be used to—"

"To what?"

"Make a weapo—a waste of assets on a technique that only seems promising."

Harrigan led her out, re-secured the laboratory, and returned to her workstation. "You and I are the only ones to have seen this, Tykvah. I…trust you. Maybe I just needed a little encouragement. It's hard having to work alone, in secret, with my self-doubt."

"If anybody can make one or both methods work, Kevin Gamaliel Harrigan can."

"Thank you. But, Tykvah, I told you I can't stand my middle name! Geeze! I share private things with you, bare my soul to you and—"

"I'm sorry, Kevin, you're right. You make me feel special."

Harrigan put his lips to Tykvah's ear and whispered, "You *are* special. Let's take the day off and…"

"I'm game," she giggled.

Music to Harrigan's ears.

His phone rang and the video filled with Freund's smiling face.

"Hey, Kev. Hello, Tykvah. It's a boy! Now when are you and Tykvah gonna tie the knot and have one?"

Harrigan stewed, more so when he saw Tykvah blush and peek at him with an expectant grin. He spoke his mind with joviality. "Yeah. Like I need to get married… tied down." He now spoke of Gertrude and Mannie's new arrival. "Congrats!" He tried to read Tykvah's face, but she turned away.

Tykvah broke in, inflecting and elongating the names. "And how's *Gertruuude* and…I guess it would be little *Ottooo?*"

"They're both doing fine. Can't put 'em on screen just yet. It was a rough labor. I've got cramps in my arms from massaging Gertrude's back!"

Harrigan took his turn. "Better not let Gertrude hear that stuff!"

Gertrude called from across the room: "Your arms are not the only appendages daht vill be hurting you, if I get my hands on you!"

Freund laughed sheepishly.

"Guess *you've* been told," Tykvah reinforced.

"When can we visit?" asked Harrigan.

"Supper time, I would think—" Freund glanced at Gertrude and received a nod. "Yes. Five or six, if you like."

Harrigan sealed the agreement. "Great. We'll see you then." Freund smiled and the image went black.

Tykvah reached up and grabbed Harrigan by the ears, pulling him to her for a protracted, deep kiss. "Isn't that exciting? A little baby. They've got a houseful!"

"I don't know how they all fit in that little house now that you mention it. I think he must give all his pay away or something. Well, let's take off. Want to swim at my place?"

"Why don't we just go for a walk here? Have you even seen your own petting zoo?"

Harrigan looked disappointed. "Zoo? That's not the kind of petting I had in mind." Tykvah pouted at him, and it worked. "All right. Okay. We'll go to the petting zoo."

Harrigan sighed. *Why are gorgeous women such outrageous teases?* Yet he knew he was addicted to this one; to her long brown hair, mesmerizing eyes, challenging intellect, and caring passion for him. She could always make him laugh and forget himself. Her conversation was so natural, so soothing and familiar to him now. *All right!* Harrigan admitted to himself.

"I love you, Tykvah. Do you know that?"

"I knew. But it took you long enough to say it."

They shed their lab jackets and silently crossed the tourist-packed quadrangle, walking hand in hand toward the sun-drenched petting zoo. Tykvah smiled and kissed him as they reached the pens filled with baby animals and laughing, scampering kids. He knew exactly why she was leading him there. For now, he would let her lead.

"Kevin, look at those silly kids!"

A group of girl scouts was screaming and chasing a soft, furry pygmy mammoth. It had tiny, blunt tusks and was about two feet tall. The animal squealed and jumped with them like a frisky dog used to playing gently with children. The girls could not resist flopping its ears. The sign on the pen clearly read "Do Not Pull Animal's Fur, Tail, Trunk, or Ears." The attendant pointed at it and yelled at the mischievous girls, who flopped its soft ears again when he was not looking. Tykvah laughed and motioned for Harrigan to watch.

Nearby, a little boy in a red striped shirt and too-big, rolled-up jeans sat in another pen hugging and feeding a bottle to the baby *Smilodon*. Its downy fur was shedding on the boy's clothes. It already had the famous canines showing but, like the rest, had been engineered to grow only slightly larger and not become aggressive.

They drifted to the marsupial section. A baby koala clung to a motherly three-year-old girl. The girl was trying unsuccessfully to get it to drink from her doll's pretend bottle of milk. The attendant eyed this carefully for possible inadvertent abuse as her enraptured parents took pictures from every angle. A five-year-old boy was trying to ride the baby ground sloth, whose claws had been clipped. Suddenly caught by the stern attendant, the boy adopted a puzzled, sheepish expression, which almost made him appear innocent.

Harrigan could not help but become caught up in the charm of it all and even directed Tykvah's attention to a young couple kissing on a bench near the exit. Her response was predictable: they embraced and gazed into each other's eyes. Slowly they stepped apart, still holding hands, and strolled toward the preserve's main gate. They walked left out of the exit and continued several blocks past the greenery planted along the preserve's property limits.

"I came here when I was twenty-seven," he said. "This place was just archaeological digs and farms then. Now, in just five years, it's become a beautiful city of fifteen thousand."

"And you, Kevin? Have you changed? Will you change more in the years to come?"

"Me? I don't change. Still work out, wear the same thirty-two-inch military belt from college, hair still short. Gettin' gray, though."

"*Not* what I meant!"

The relative cool of the late summer morning tempted them to brave the theme park's exhausting safari adventures and thrill rides. Talking and laughing intermittently, they entered the park, showed their passes and proceeded directly to the Time-Safari area.

The giant structure reverberated with recorded bird calls and scary growls. The ceiling was painted and illuminated to look like the sky but was composed of computer-controlled tracks. These could move riders in special harnesses across the make-believe earth of a hundred thousand years ago.

The floors sensed impact, absorbed it and sprang back at twice the force so that one could jump very high to avoid the realistic robotic animals and pre-humans of the Pleistocene. One could counter the bouncing by buckling the knees, thus reducing the thrust-off reaction of the sensitive, computer-manipulated flooring.

Harrigan helped Tykvah don her padded harness. Its hand-held controls enabled rising, hovering and gliding in the make-believe world. This environment was composed of forests, swamps, jungles, glaciers, and other creature-filled 'dangerous' terrains. He laughed and made airplane and condor noises like some kid. But he knew it was Tykvah, not the ride *per se*, who could bring out the giddy kid in him.

The pair continued on to other diversions in the park. The lines were short since the school year had resumed and families were not vacationing. They rode roller coasters through fake but intimidating volcanoes. Tykvah marveled in the shops at the realistic toy animals, some of which even interacted.

He was nervous that Tykvah might press a marriage proposal. Eventually, they noticed that they had missed lunch and it was nearly four o'clock. They entered the Holocene History Restaurant, whose theme was the natural and man-made history of the last ten thousand years. Dinner was Australian emu steak stuffed with cheese and crab.

Tykvah ate lightly, because they were obliged to eat at her father's home around seven-thirty. As she searched Harrigan's eyes, she considered whether she should break that engagement.

As Harrigan grasped her hand across the table, she listened expectantly.

"You know, Tykvah, going to a military college, not relating with many females, I kinda got the wrong idea about girls — women."

Tykvah winked and sipped her white wine. "You're trying to say that men are pigs and you're a man," she quipped.

"Yes, something like that."

"But I'd wallow with you…"

"I dated airheads I wouldn't think of spending time with now. Not like you. You're a mind, a person, to me."

Tykvah composed a warm and kidding response, softly intonated. "I love you, Kevin. You're just a growing boy, that's all. Won't get any taller, though, I don't suppose."

"I'm trying to say that I've just always been mostly a lone wolf." Harrigan's tone lowered. "I still am."

She studied his face, lowered her eyes, and excused herself to go to the lady's room where she wiped her eyes and re-applied eyeliner. When she returned, she directed lighter talk for the rest of the meal.

Harrigan paid the bill and they left to visit the Freunds. Tykvah picked out flowers and a card for Gertrude on the way. They parked at the hospital and went up to Gertrude's room.

The Freund's other children, Eva, Hans, and Marian, along with a neighbor, were there. The visit was brief since the small room was getting too congested from adults talking and children running around. Tykvah blushed, enraptured by the baby. She wondered whether Harrigan noticed Freund and Gertrude's wink.

Freund, as he often did, philosophized to Harrigan despite the latter's rolling eyes. "It's a big parlor party thing to pronounce shallow insights into the meaning of life. But, you know," Freund directed his hand toward his wife and children, "*this* is the meaning of life."

Tykvah smiled at Freund, noticing Harrigan's grimace. *Does he realize Mannie's right?*

"Time to leave you to your evening," Harrigan told Gertrude as he shook Freund's hand. "Congratulations, Mannie, Gertrude. You two have really got it made."

Tykvah gave Gertrude and baby Otto a careful hug and led Harrigan to the elevator.

Outside, she pulled Harrigan to a bench. "Hold up a minute. I have to call my father."

"Is something wrong?"

"No. It's fine." She stood and stepped away but made sure to remain within Harrigan's earshot. "Shalom, Father. Daddy, something important's come up and—I'm sorry—I can't come tonight. I don't have a lot of time to speak. I'll have to miss Shabbat tonight."

"Tykvah, Shabbat is—"

"You'll have to accept that I've grown up," she growled, then softened her tone. "Daddy, you don't understand. I just can't."

No one spoke for a moment. Then she added nervously. "Later, Daddy. Love you."

Harrigan took her hand. "I don't want to cause a problem with your father."

She looked into his eyes, then off to the distance. "He'll get over it."

They drove through the security gate at Harrigan's gray brick house and parked below it. Taking the oak-paneled elevator up to the foyer, they silently crossed the green marble floor into the adjoining cherry-paneled study. Tykvah nervously joined Harrigan, sinking into the burgundy sofa, its cold leather sending a shiver up her spine.

"Fireplace on three," Harrigan called.

The marble fireplace's gas logs glowed softly. She tried to relax.

Harrigan rose to select a spicy Australian Shiraz from the cabinet and returned to the couch with two overfull glasses.

"Tykvah."

"Yes?"

"This is…Well, I feel as if… I mean, you and I, are from totally different backgrounds."

She bit her lip as Harrigan continued. "I have this sense that you need to be…you ought to be…cherished by…someone. I love you and I feel I've…like I've needed you all my life. But mine has always been a life alone, despite appearances."

Tykvah lowered her head, eyes brimming. She watched him rise and immediately sit.

"Tykvah," he blurted quickly, "will you marry me?"

Bleary-eyed, she gasped, then whispered hoarsely, "Yes."

"Yes," she repeated, slightly louder. Recovering her composure, she inflected her told-you-so: "I suppose that hurt to finally ask?"

Harrigan's smile and kiss released tears for them both, then laughter. He breathed deeply, wiped her eyes gently with his thumbs, and held her tightly as they stood.

Tykvah gazed through the foyer at the stairs and back. "Catch," she commanded, jumping near-horizontally into his arms.

He carried her up the stairs as she stroked the back of his neck.

Harrigan spent a good part of Monday morning grinning at objects on his desk at the Preserve, alternately fearful and excited by his question and Tykvah's answer.

He noticed Tykvah attempting to focus on work but repeatedly giggling and smiling at everyone, and misplacing lines of computer code. Every few minutes, the two winked and whispered, unsure when to tell the staff.

Just before lunch, Mon appeared at Harrigan's office door.

Harrigan looked up. "This is a surprise, Minister. We don't see much of you these days. What can I do for you?"

"May I close this door, Kevin?" Mon motioned for his guards to wait outside the room.

"Sounds big. I'll get it for you. Please, sit. Coffee?"

"Yes, thank you. Kevin, our intelligence feels there will be another attempt on my life…and on yours as well."

Harrigan shrugged his shoulders. "There's always going to be something. Security's revamped here. I think we're okay and you have even tighter security than we do."

"There is more."

"Sorry. Please go on."

"Your work is too important to risk, Kevin. You're still refining the FGR process. You need a lab where jealous academics cannot pry or ridicule. To the extent that your people have been largely unable to find both egg and sperm of a given species, there is valid criticism. But both can be found with supplemental support for Lloyd. You need a bigger, more capable staff. You need a larger preserve where the animals can interact. And, above all, Kevin, it is pre-human DNA that you need to continue the work Harvard quashed. Only *then,* will you be able to refine your FGR and show those self-righteous bah-stards what you really can achieve. Like genetic improvement of mankind itself."

Mon waited for Harrigan's blush, then resumed. "My people found two Neanderthal females and a male. They were thirty-five thousand years old and among the last of their kind. You have a chance to study genetic evolution in the natural environment of one of the warmer interglacial periods. We have professionals waiting for the privilege to make history as surrogate parents of pre-humans under your direction. My facility is secure in the north of Baghdad. It will be ready in eight months. Our people want to do it themselves without you, but I insisted on giving you a chance. All of this, Kevin, I give you. What do you say?"

Harrigan did not know. His heart started to race. *Fantastic,* he mused, *a dream come true.* Yet something bothered him. He generally trusted Mon. But he was also keenly aware that, not so long ago, America and its allies had had to track Iraq's biological, chemical, and nuclear materials. *Mon's right about terrorist threats, and the need for better facilities,* he reasoned. *But I could be in over my head. Got to talk to the Feds on this.*

"Minister, I'm really caught at a bad time for thinking right now. I just got engaged. May I consider it for a few days?"

"One day remains, Kevin. I have been assigned to staff the project with Iraqis. National pride and all that. But as Party Chairman, I have demanded permission to put you in charge. I was given until tomorrow morning at nine, your time, to obtain at least *your* commitment."

"I understand. I can decide by then."

Mon stood abruptly, shook Harrigan's hand and left. Harrigan's heart raced even more as he considered how to report this, whether it even required reporting. He called the American Embassy from a landline at the concession's office.

Harrigan's voice was deep but worry shook it slightly. "This is Doctor

Kevin Harrigan. I'm an American. Who would I speak with on a matter, potentially, of national security?"

"I'll connect you, sir."

"I asked to know who I'd be talk—"

"We're glad to hear from you, Dr. Harrigan."

Harrigan hesitated at the odd greeting. "I'm the Research Director for th—"

A beep sounded and Harrigan heard muffled speech in the background. Then he heard a rushing sound like a hand coming off the phone's microphone. "Yes, we confirm. We're well aware of who you are, Dr. Harrigan. Do you have a problem to report?"

Have these guys been watching me or something? "I'm not really sure, I just want to discuss a potential problem with some research in Iraq I think would be all right but—"

"Your line is unsecure. Hang up and wait. We'll come to you."

Five minutes later, two men in gray suits called from behind.

How did these guys…These sneaky bastards were already nearby!

"Were you two already watching me?" he asked accusingly.

"No. You have something to tell us. Take a seat," one said flatly.

The three sat and discussed his work in more detail than Harrigan wanted but he felt it was necessary. One agent, an Israeli, said practically nothing the entire time. The other, an American, evaded all questions but probed Harrigan like an inquisitor.

"You did the right thing, Dr. Harrigan," said the American. "We've been instructed to ask you to accept the offer and continue the project as you've described it."

"You've been instructed? But how did you—"

"We have no reason to suspect that your work could or would be misused for military purposes. But we have no way to monitor Iraq since the new government took power. So, you're our eyes and ears."

"Uh, no I don't think so! Anyway, how would I—"

He took Harrigan's phone from his belt, inserted a SIM card, then returned it. "Now your phone encrypts video, voice, or text and sends to us, provided there is no metal or concrete between it and the sky. To report in, blink a few times *then* hold a warm thumb or fingertip within a half-inch of the camera aperture. Don't get observed. If there's nothing to report, the code is 'zip.' Report as briefly as possible, but at least monthly, with any news of spying or suspicious behavior by the Iraqis. Plan 'B' is to call or email any American Embassy or consulate. Ask for the Science Publications Ombudsman.

"If we conclude there's no threat—or need to get to you—the

ombudsman contacts you. Maximize *your* people staffing the Iraq facility. The fewer Iraqis the better. Any questions?"

"Did you even hear me? No!"

"Before you ducked out of the army to play God, Dr. Harrigan, you swore an oath to defend your country. Does that matter anymore?"

"Yes, but—"

"Just keep your new toy. You may need us."

The men got up and left. Harrigan walked away, stewing. *Sneaky, presumptuous bastards! Well, regardless, I have to sell the staff on this. Mannie and Tykvah will go through the roof if I ask them to participate in pre-human reproduction. But I've got to try. And if Tykvah refuses?*

Harrigan quickly returned to the lab, looking for Tykvah and considering how he would recruit Freund, on whom he hoped to depend on exploring pre-human development. He felt he needed his Ranger-trained buddy for more important reasons. Harrigan now felt the struggle within himself rage more intensely: *This frontier must be explored. And yet I will be leading my people and their families…into a potentially enemy nation.*

Chapter Five

Harrigan glanced around the slightly dimmed conference room, not an empty seat anywhere. "For those of you afraid that the hominins we will create might be maltreated, let me summarize. Despite Neanderthal depictions in movies, this cousin species was not entirely human. We will treat them with greater care than the other species to be released into the Al-Rajda Preserve.

"Gene coding will cause maturation to be three times normal during gestation, slowing to a halt at adulthood. They will not lose adult years. Just think back to when you were a kid, impatient to grow up. Archaic hominins died young...diseases, unpredictable food sources and worse winters than they will experience in northern Iraq. They'll live safe and satisfactory lives.

"There could be harassment of Iraq and us if the sapiens research got out. The contract forbids disclosing that aspect, even to family and children, in case any of you make rug rats."

Some staff members smirked.

"What about their health care, especially if there's trauma from animals?" Freund asked.

"There will be extra protection during the initial formation of clans. After that, Mannie, there will be physical danger, but they will have been taught how to deal with animals. Surrogates will train them in safe hunting and trapping. Evacuation to the clinic is possible because anesthetizing gas outlets will be installed in cave ceilings. Periodically, some will be drugged and removed for study and clandestinely returned. We'll have to learn the terrain, taxa behavior, etc.

"Surrogates are selected based on physique and scientific credentials in psychology and anthropology. Hormone and cosmetic treatments will enable Neanderthal appearance. They'll develop well in the semi-protected ridge areas. The young will be taught Nostratic, our best reconstruction of the root language of all Indo-European tongues. Once functioning as a clan, we'll relieve the surrogates and continue study posing as another trading tribe."

Harrigan projected an aerial photo of the plateau, touched-up to distinguish key features.

"Our next speaker will go over this slide in more detail. But for now, please note these wide strips of forest. They will be quite dense, discouraging large predators from reaching the sapiens in the northern ridge caves and yetis in these southwest ridge areas. A swamp and the Rajdakim River separate the two hominin groups. As you can see, the plateau is a triangular valley bordered by two rocky ridges that converge in the north and this cliff in the south. For five years, sound walls will keep animals from reaching the ridges, which end at the south cliff; then they'll be removed. The herds should stay near the river and sparsely forested plateau. Predators will follow them. Our lab building will be about centered east/west near the base of this waterfall.

"Caves will be provided for Neanderthals, yetis, and possibly other hominins. These clan homes will be rigged with surveillance gear. They will even have sanitized warm water springs."

Gene Recovery Technician Olivier expressed concern. "What of '*omo sapiens sapiens*, Dr. Harrigan, *s'il vous plaît?*"

"We have no Cro-Magnon specimens now. But Dr. Lloyd's team or an Iraqi team should have success soon. Let's keep in mind that, despite continued debate, earliest Cro-Magnon — some hundred-fifty millennia ago — only gradually became...*us*. So, regeneration and study of our immediate ancestors cannot be said to be some 'barbaric' act. We'll separate subspecies to avoid conflict. The yetis, by the way, are naturally reclusive so there's no danger from them."

Cabral, from Lloyd's paleontology team, raised his arm. "When moderns began contact into ancient Amazonian communities, there were culture shocks. The natives' behavior patterns and societies changed. How will we keep from — eh, avoid — ruin of their way of life or invalidating our study of their behavior?"

"Paulo, all field contact will be disguised or done while the subjects are sedàted. The gas formulations inhibit memory. Robotic heavy-lift suits resembling a cave bear and equipped with tranquilizer darts, will be available for our camouflaged use and animal defense."

"What about our lives and duties here?" Tykvah asked in a hostile tone.

Harrigan was irritated and sweating but still confident. "The Committee will hire replacements for us here. We will have to keep flying back to get them up to speed and obtain certain specimens, but eventually we will work only in Al-Rajda. I understand it's quite nice. As lush as Megiddo and cool enough, due to its location and elevation, to require no cooling plumes.

"There will, of course, be liberal furloughs. I'm certain none of you will have a problem with expenses, given the compensation packages. Travel back to this 'zoo' for research purposes or to work with your replacements will be at the expense of the Al-Rajda Research Preserve. You are all free to publish findings but only per the contract rules. By the way, the FGR process software and some of the equipment will move to Al-Rajda. This is because I own the rights, which revert to the Iraqi government ten years from now."

Geneticist Dr. James Fong looked nervous. "What if something of military value is discovered, Kevin?"

Harrigan hesitated. "An important question, Jim. This project, though closed to the public, will not be used in any way for military purposes. Iraq has many times proved itself trustworthy and stable. I would never permit that use."

Tykvah still glared. Harrigan returned it to no avail. He again flashed his laser pointer.

"I want to conclude my portion by re-emphasizing our primary objectives and what this new venture means. The objectives are: a) to create *authentic* regenerations — self-sustaining and interacting populations of Pleistocene fauna for study, b) to map the genetic evolution of subject species, especially sapiens, and to determine the instinctive versus cultural basis of behavior, c) to discover the basis of positive and negative genetic traits and behaviors through direct observation and evolutionary comparison.

"We now know from Dr. Lloyd's and many others' recent discoveries, that early humans and near humans ranged all over the world during the mid-to-late Pleistocene. So, we will attempt to recreate taxa from the six temperate continents. Most trees and plants, though, will have to be deciduous to withstand the winters."

He lowered his pointer, turned off the projector and looked directly into staff members' eyes, each in turn. "Friends, respected colleagues: You have a once-in-a-lifetime chance at a truly historic venture, an *ad*venture. You will be making profound discoveries, sheltered from interference. You will witness life interacting freely as it did at the very dawn of man's emergence. You may even find ways to advance the human genome and expunge genetic defects. You are the finest, most competent team ever assembled to engage in such discovery. Humankind may one day owe you a debt of gratitude."

Harrigan surveyed the room triumphantly. "Now, Major Hassan, our liaison with the sponsoring Iraqi government, will describe physical preparations and layout. Major."

Hassan thanked Harrigan. The aerial view map flashed again onscreen. He stepped to the podium. "Forgive, please, my English. I will be brief. The Preserve is fifteen miles long, north to south by eleven miles east to west. Its center is flat and grassy...small hills, stream...bottoms? No, stream beds — yes! It has subterrane — underground — irrigations and fast-grow forests in half-mile wide bands along the foothills, edges of the cliff and banks of River Rajdakim, a tributary of the Tigris. This conceals your access routes from sapiens.

"Notice now what this area will look like in a few months: The ridges are cut to a sheer face, forming an impreg-nable barrier to animal escape. The cliff cut near vertical, for impassable barrier. A minor five-foot-high cliff will be cut twenty feet deep into the entire length of plateau south edge as animal deterrent from the high cliff. The waterfall will be — how to say: with submerged catches, like a comb. It empties into a huge net, hard to see.

"As Dr. Harrigan noted, we will have cam-ou-flaged and computer-controlled sound guns to automatically repel animals which the system's surveillance finds breaching the pe-rim-eter. Troops patrol outside the plateau with…what is…real bullets? Yes: ballistic rounds. On the plateau, only tranquilizer rounds. These degrade to dust in days so the sapiens not to find.

"We camouflage this rectangular research building, at the cliff base just west of the river. It has two one-hundred-foot-long, thirty-foot-wide escalators for veterinary and research access. They open, one on each side of the river, upward into small clearings. Below plateau, the road and bridge will be replaced with a tunnel leading behind the east ridge; then out onto a paved road south to Baghdad. Your homes will be built to your spe-ci-fi-cations east of this ridge. It is ready before *sprring*.

"Eventually, my go-vern-ment recoups its investment by turning part of the preserve into a park and exporting some creatures to zoos. You have exclusive scientific use for ten years. You will be able to publish articles, with censor. This is because of commercial potential of this work, and avoiding con-troversy. Contract specifics are in your packages. There are any questions?"

The researchers had read the contracts earlier. No one objected, though Freund and Tykvah left the room.

Harrigan closed the meeting by telling everyone that he already agreed, but they had two days to decide. He knew he would still have a tough job with Freund and Tykvah. He took lunch and returned to work in his lab.

———————

Harrigan left the preserve near 5:30 p.m. to meet Tykvah at his house. The Brandenburg Concerto, Number Three, was playing. Tykvah sat on the couch in his study, flipping through a pile of unopened letters.

Harrigan felt his ire flare. "What are you doing with those?"

"You said before that I could roam free here; that you had no secrets or old girlfriend photos! Anyway, I haven't opened them. But why haven't you? They're from your parents."

Harrigan tried to force the anger from his voice, succeeding only in making it icy. "I just don't have the relationship with my parents that you have with your father. Look, Tykvah, those things are mine. Put them back, please."

"You don't communicate with your parents, but you keep their letters. You must still love them. Couldn't you patch things up and let me meet them?"

Harrigan's voice approached anger again. "Tykvah: Put those away. You pick and pick. Like when you kept pushing about my middle name. Some things inside me are private, okay?"

He felt his parry fail as she reposted. "You were going to tell me why your dad gave you 'Gamaliel' for a middle name. At least you *have* a middle name! Mannie hasn't got one and neither do I. But I told you on our first date that Tykvah means 'hope.' My parents had tried for years to have a child and I was their hope. Can't you share yourself with me even that much?"

"All right, look: My mother told me that Dad had gotten on this religious kick after my brother was born. He wanted a name that would remind me I was Catholic — which was stupid, 'cause it's a Hebrew name, anyway. It means 'The Lord is vengeance or recompense.' Mom said *my* choice is one or the other. They wanted me to be nagged about going to church and all that — even when they weren't around. Clearly, it worked, since you are nagging me now."

"There. That didn't hurt so bad, did it? Come here and kiss me."

He smiled and pulled her close. "We've got to leave to get to your father's on time."

"One more moment, hero." She stared into his eyes. "You know humans, subspecies or otherwise, are people. You can't just make them, put them in a dangerous environment, and define their lives as experiment subjects. Tell me what you know is right."

He had anticipated her demand. "You want sapiens research nixed?"

"Yes, at least—"

"Not happening."

"This is more important than discovery or fame or you or me..." her voice began to quaver. "Kevin, this is more important than our marriage."

He stared, sweating. "Tykvah, what about safety training for the surrogates plus highest tech protection if there are animal encounters? I can negotiate a safety regime clause that—"

"That, and let them out with counseling and the whole nine yards of psychological support after five years. Say it."

"Ten. I won't get that kind of control. Or when one generation matures. They'll have a normal lifespan, but mature in eight to ten years. That's the best I can get Mon and his—"

"Nothing less, or I cannot respect you, your caring for other human beings. You need that caring. I need to know you have it in you," she whispered, tearing, "or I'm gone. I mean that."

He knew she was right. "You're right. Absolute kid gloves with the sapiens, and I'll get an 'out' clause for them at ten years max. I love you too much, and I do care."

"Fine. You promised. Now I have a question. How do you feel about kids?"

Harrigan felt defeated by her, then further pressed into concessions. "We just agreed! Look, we have to study their parenting at least a few year—"

"You're going to be a father. I did the test."

His breath halted a moment. "You're going to torpedo moving to the new project anyway because you're afraid of dangers to us and our kid. That's all I can get from Mon!"

Her tone was surprisingly relaxed, even sexy. "Dangers? We eat danger for breakfast, you and I. So, yes, if your promise holds, *we* go where *you* go, Kevin,…if you want us."

Harrigan knew she was looking for verification of his commitment to her—now "them." "*We* go, then. I love you! I'm sure I'll love *the kid*. What are you going to tell your father?"

"The truth. He'll blow up, but what else could we tell him?"

———————

Later that evening at the Strauss residence near Tel Aviv, Harrigan observed that Tykvah was wrong. Her father did not get angry. His eyes filled with tears and he left the table, head low.

The aging Orthodox Jew returned, soft-spoken, from the kitchen to address his daughter. His gray beard and temple braids bracketed a kind face. It was obvious where Tykvah had gotten her habit of speech inflection. "Tykvah, *Tykvah*. A generation is lost. But, I pray, *not you with it!* You have shamed yourself, me *and your mother's memory*. And, yet, that slap at God and his Law has served to implement his will. You have made a child. A child, Tykvah. Are you ready for this baby? And you, Kevin, are you ready to care for it?"

Harrigan swallowed hard as tears skirted Tykvah's lips. "We *are* ready, Father."

"Speak for yourself, daughter. Kevin, have you saved Tykvah's life only to stigmatize it? Will you be a faithful husband to her and a dedicated father to this child — a *dedicated* father?"

"You can count on me, sir. I will."

"You have no regard for our faith; nor your own. If you would not become a Jew, you would still find your way...if you practice the faith of your birth. Will you reconsider this?"

"Sir, you demand what you cannot. You are wrong if you feel we are — I am — lost. But I will love Tykvah and our child. If she wants a Jewish wedding and to raise the child in your faith, I have no objection."

"Tykvah, you will abandon the faith of Abraham?"

Harrigan read her hesitation and almost answered for her. Then she whispered, "I will seek God."

"That was not a yes. But if you both listen for God's whisper, you have my blessing."

Harrigan had not asked for his blessing but raised his glass and smiled.

The old man hugged Tykvah and even Harrigan. His grin was contagious, then his laughter. "Mazel tov, children. *Mazel tov!*"

They finished the meal with a new sense of happiness. Harrigan did not even steam at having had to discuss religion.

They spent the night at her father's house — in separate rooms.

Harrigan awoke at four a.m. feeling tense and worried. He could not remember all of the dream that had plagued him. So he got up and went to the living room, adjusted the rheostat to dim so as not to wake Tykvah or her father. He sat in a plush easy chair, trying to remember; drifting asleep again. The dream embraced him once more, brushing him with cold exhilaration.

"I am...creator," he mumbled, "my will...supreme."

Suddenly, he jolted awake, oppressed by a panic akin to a child's first roller coaster ride yet different. It was as though he sensed that a parent could save him from the accelerating descent, yet as if he had just realized that no parent was with him on the ride. As he woke, Harrigan retained from the dream only accentuated fear and shocked loneliness.

He stood, nervously inventing a reason for these feelings. *My parents. That's what this is about. Maybe I need to reconsider the rift...or something. Yes, that's it.*

Dawn burned away some of the fog obscuring his view of the horizon as he stared out of the large picture window. A slightly improved view, far from clear, felt tentatively reassuring.

"Kevin, what are doing up so early? And what are you staring at out there?" Tykvah asked, still yawning and pulling her red robe closed against the cool air.

"Bad dreams. Guess this old thing with my parents is bothering me."

She laid her head on his shoulder and hugged him, almost pushing him over as she sleepily rested upon his muscular frame. "See? This family thing is good for you."

"You are good for me." He smiled and held her wild-haired head for a kiss.

"Ugh! A toothbrush would be good for you, too. Listen, forgiving your parents and letting them forgive you will do you a world of good. You know you want to do that."

"Hmm," he grumped, "I guess you're right. What would I do without you?

"You'd grump at people all the time."

"Maybe. Go back to bed and I'll see you tonight."

"Do you want something to eat or are you eating at Mannie and Gertrude's?"

"I'll eat there after I stop off at home to shower and change. Go back to bed, babe."

Tykvah yawned as she turned away, then squealed as Harrigan pinched her bottom. "You *might* have that later. Get driving!" She gave him a hug, squeezed his hand and headed to bed.

Harrigan grabbed his things and drove north toward his house, putting the remaining emotions from the dream behind him.

On the highway, he smiled, considering the irony of his Irish Catholic upbringing and his love for a Jewish woman. He felt relieved to have established a good relationship with his future father-in-law, for he had anticipated animosity. The more he considered his new life and family, the more he thought of his parents. He began longing to just be forgiven. He knew they would accept Tykvah, but he knew he had to avoid discussion of sapiens research.

Back home, he noticed the pile of letters that Tykvah was supposed to have put back on his desk. The handwriting on the latest one, which arrived a month before, was his brother's. He opened it. His eyes welled and he knelt on the floor. Sobs and one long, trembling moan tore from deep within. An auto accident had claimed them — and he had missed the funeral.

He composed himself after an hour, showered, and dressed. He headed out but stopped. In his mind Tykvah was holding him, giving him new courage. He picked up the phone, greeted his future father-in-law, and asked to speak with her.

"What's wrong, Kevin? You made my father look worried."

"I need you. I need you to teach me."

"Teach you what? Do you want me to come up now?"

"No. Not now. I'll see you tonight. I just want you to know that..." Harrigan paused, self-conscious at the confession he wanted to make. He side-stepped it and hit part of the mark. "I want you to know that I love who you are, our baby, and who your father is. That's all. I've got to get over to Mannie's house...I mean Mannie's and Gertrude's. Bye. I love you."

Harrigan replaced the phone and left. He felt humbled, thoroughly reprimanded, but he had a job to do, and made himself focus on that.

––––––––––––

Harrigan drove up the Freund's flower-edged driveway and parked behind their five-year-old minivan. He wondered why Mannie did not get himself a sedan — and a bigger house; he paid him more than enough! Freund came out to greet him and they strolled to his study at the rear of the house where the entrance was also strewn with toys and screaming kids.

"Want some breakfast, Kevin? It's still hot."

"No thank— Well, yes. Thanks."

Gertrude greeted him warmly. She placed two meals on a folding table between a pair of reading chairs and left.

Pictures of family members, friends, and scenes of mountainous southern Germany covered plain white walls. The desk alcove, enclosed floor and ceiling in polarized windows, and admitted sunlight. Atop the computer, a rosary of green stones hung from the Pietà, a statue of Jesus, derelict upon his disconsolate mother's lap.

Freund preempted his long-time buddy. "This is our home now, Kevin. We thought last year of moving back to Germany but decided to stay. The kids and Gertrude have friends. We're involved in the Lutheran-Catholic ecumenical program. Beyond that..." Freund's face tightened with concern. "I cannot participate in genetic manipulation or creating — then discarding — human embryos. God might very well bring good out of evil, but we can't do evil to create good."

"That 'manipulation' will take place whether you join us or not."

"That doesn't make it licit to do."

"But, Mannie, if you don't come, you'll never get to discover the genetic basis of behavior and instinct. You'll never be the one to discover what enables personality. And don't forget the pay bump." Harrigan could see no change in Freund's expression. "Mannie, look: I really need you with me on this. As a researcher and as a friend."

"I appreciate that. I know that zygotic and fetal research is inevitable. But I can't participate. It's against everything I believe; everything I know."

"Look, Mannie, all this Christian indoctrination clouds your scientific and ethical thinking. It's unethical to let religious rules hamper research on fetal stem cells and RNA that could cure disease and advance our understanding of the human animal."

"You want to talk ethics and reason, Kevin? Fine! Dismissing the faith-based argument for respect for human life is, itself, a fallacy. As a scientist, you must be open to the possibility that your tools cannot explore the mystical or moral. There's tons of evidence."

"Such as?"

"The Incorruptibles."

"Mannie, come on! Somebody in the middle ages made a secret flesh preservative."

"The fact that the Resurrection was recorded with female witnesses. In those days, women's testimony was dismissed, so if the story was merely invented, the witnesses would'da been men."

"Tenuous. Nothing else?"

"The phenomenal spread of the Church despite vicious oppression; records of the martyrs."

"People get fascinated with whatever's forbidden."

"Sure, Kevin, sure. What about testimonies and interviews of *tens* of thousands who saw Marian apparitions and miracles at Fatima in 1917, and *hundreds* of thousands — of all faiths — at Zeitun in the 1970s."

"Old news; mass hysteria."

"Thousands of exorcisms and miraculous cures, scientifically and medically substantiated."

"They just missed the real causes."

"There's Fanti's carbon dating of Shroud of Turin fibers to Jesus' day. Others dating it to the middle ages used sections tainted by repairs. Plus, it's scorched by unknown radiation."

"Even if it was his shroud, the dating and scorch marks are not proof of divinity. Maybe if he or his mom got in my face..."

"Talkin' evidence, Kevin, not proof! And you might be surprised! How do you explain away thousands of testimonies of spiritual experiences and conversions?"

"Psychological affects. Any serious evidence, Mannie?"

"Kevin, listen to yourself: You're rationalizing. You're making scientific proof the standard when the evidence is vast and science's tools are, themselves, limited. It's arrogant to assert that only science can find all truths."

"I'm — not — arrogant!" Harrigan protested.

"Oh, sorry. Since I lack the scientific tools to prove you are, that's proof that you're not."

"You are such a *dick!*" Harrigan chuckled.

"Look, Kevin, science can find the 'how' in physics or biology, but never the 'why.' Ask yourself why the universe was created and then evolution set in motion. Religion and philosophy are the tools for that. Faith and morality are God-given; ethics is a human construct. But if you want to look at this with reason — ethics — try a thought experiment."

"A thought experiment? Come on!"

"Focus, Kevin. Would killing a baby the day of normal birth be murder?"

"Uh. Obviously. Is there a point?"

"Walk with me here. What about the day before?"

"Sure. It would be. Just a day less developed."

"Another day prior?"

Harrigan's mind raced ahead — rather, backward — uncomfortably. "Human. And the day before, and so on back to conception. Mannie, you're going to say we can't find the day it's clearly not human, so we cannot find the day when its killing is licit. That where you're goin'?"

"Yes. Faith and morals shed more light than ethics. But ethical reasoning works here."

"Wrong! There *is* a point when it's not human. This is settled in courts and law around the world. When babies can survive on their own, that's when they become human."

"If survival on one's own is the test of humanity, it would be licit to kill invalid adults. Exercising power to make law is not the same as finding truth."

"What of a zygote, as we'd work with in our research? No consciousness, only potential."

"Kevin, you're right! So, it's okay to kill a mangled person in a coma who doesn't *look* human and who has only *potential* to recover, as long as you do it before he wakes. Of course! A zygote's fair game since it doesn't *look* human, and it hasn't *yet* attained the ability to think."

Harrigan, stumped, could only switch gears. "Mon says I can choose staff, but he'll fill vacancies with his own people. The remote possibility that FGR could have military potential worries me. I talked with the U.S. embassy. You can't know any of this, by the way. Their people want me to minimize the number of Iraqi researchers on the team. I need you, Mannie."

"I see." Freund stood and paced, then frowned and sat again.

Harrigan continued. "If there is a God, don't you think he wants humans to improve and understand themselves? Don't you think he would want us to advance our genes, alleviate suffering, prolong life — maybe even find evidence of a divine hand in our evolution?"

"Do you care about those questions, Kevin, or are they prepared for my recruitment? Do you seek the Ancient of Days — the truth — or only what Mon called the 'ancient of genes'?"

Harrigan felt inexplicably guilty. "I think about these things...sometimes. A scientist is open to evidence. Maybe there is evidence of God. This is your chance to show me."

"God needs us to just accept the faith he offers. Once in a while, though, he'll bonk someone like you in the head with a two-by-four, proof for one. Even if genetic engineering is a sin, it might actually serve his purpose. I don't know."

Harrigan looked absorbed in thought. "It's odd."

"What's odd?"

"That's what Tykvah's father said yesterday."

"You asked him to go to Iraq with you?"

"No, I mean...Oh, geeze, Mannie! I didn't tell you: Tykvah's pregnant. I'm glad, actually."

"But the wedding isn't until spring. Great wedding pictures!" Freund laughed until Harrigan's humiliated look stopped him. "Sorry. Are you moving the date up?"

"Yes."

"Well, what did he say, anyway?"

"He said the child is God's will, even though we shouldn't have been doing the deed."

"He's right. I met him once. He's a devout man who's found what you refuse to seek."

"I thought Christians think Jews are going to hell — like me, the Buddhists, Muslims, and so on, for not accepting Christ?"

"Kevin, God speaks unrestricted by time or prejudice to everyone in every language, in every age. Even prehistoric humans. God still reaches for us. Question is, will you reach back?"

"Well," Harrigan quavered, "I don't feel him reaching for me."

"People do, millions. Sometimes I do at Reconciliation and the Eucharist. Look, if you're so scientific, why are you unwilling to investigate miracles?"

Harrigan started a reply, only to be immediately flooded by the memories of his hallucination at Ranger School, then the one outside the Boston cathedral. But he would not be defeated in debate. "Mannie, science has looked at these things. Every day there's more evidence from chimpanzees that behaviors like theft, violence, even homosexuality are genetic and, hence, morally neutral. Not that I want to kiss you or rob a bank or something!"

Freund poured coffee on Harrigan's eggs and smirked.

Harrigan blotted his eggs with a napkin, taking it correctly in jest. "Thanks, jerk!"

"You're welcome. Look, Kevin, you can't validly assert that if something occurs in nature, it's morally neutral for humans. What if our genetic make-up is merely a way for God to challenge us to consciously choose to advance beyond a primal, selfish nature?"

"And what if pigs could fly? They've even found that sensations of a spiritual presence, like apparitions, can be induced by magnetic fields. That explains near-death experiences."

"Kevin, Marian apparitions have a common message of crisis approaching, so that's way beyond those experiments! Even if, one day, they can replicate physical reactions to spiritual experiences, that doesn't prove that real spiritual experiences don't happen."

"You're really into conjecture, now! Mannie, get a grip! You've got to admit that the New Testament contradicts itself. God's nature is supposed to be loving. If so, how can it be that he demanded the cruel, protracted suffering and death of his own son?"

"Hey, one's paradigm is the key here. You see a cruel death demanded by God as contradicting his nature. Has it never occurred to you that such a death was necessary to get our attention, to demonstrate love so strong he'd suffer for our wrongs?"

Harrigan sneered, dismissing Freund's assertions with a toss of his hands. "Mannie, if God loved us, his plan would be to help us here on earth and relieve our sufferings."

Freund's eyes widened. "God needs us to emulate his example of humility, self-sacrifice, mercy, and to use our gifts and talents to mitigate suffering."

"Mannie, if you really believed that man is supposed to use his 'gifts' to improve things, then you would come with me and explore any connection between the physical and the spiritual. You can study genetic transmission of behavior and personality. You could observe whether spirituality shows up where it won't be taught. This is your only chance to change *my* perspective or prove *me* wrong!"

Freund paused, frowning. "If I'm right, evidence of spirituality should be observable without it being taught." Then he smiled. "A fair challenge. I'll do it on three conditions."

"What?"

"I can fly back to my family and telecommute half the time."

"Fine."

"I won't create or doom any microscopic humans. Only study."

"But the tech is… Okay, I can work around that for your duties."

"And you have to be open to spiritual reality. You *can't* dismiss that there *is* evidence. Think about it when you witness death or birth... when you encounter what scientific tools can't explain."

"Plant a suggestion in my mind like that and I can't help but be reminded in the course of this work. But you promise not to lecture me. We'll both keep open, empirical minds. Gimme at least a year?"

They shook hands.

"Deal," Freund said. Then he glimpsed the statue on his computer and lowered his eyes.

Chapter Six

The Ministry of the Interior, Baghdad
1417 hours, 18 August 2027

Major Hassan's palms were damp with sweat as he entered Interior Minister Ismail Mon's lavish, new subterranean office. He closed the door and nervously took his seat facing Mon, a man becoming feared even by the elected Iraqi president. He felt Mon's eyes burning through him.

Mon queried his Special Activities Chief in a calm, almost friendly tone. "Are your people integrated with Harrigan's, and learning his FGR?"

"Yes, Minister. However, the techniques we have gained from his success with the animals in Megiddo and at Al-Rajda have so far failed at our lab here. It has been most frustrating. Harrigan is hiding something. He has been using FGR for the past eight weeks on the Neanderthal genetic material specimens. We have been monitoring him and the computer system more thoroughly than ever. We will have it soon, surely by the time he works on Cro Magnon DNA. And *then* we will replace dwindling oil revenues with myriad commercial applications. We will not need to wait the ten years of the contract. We can dispose of Harrigan and make it appear that we refined FGR independently!"

"Listen closely. I will confide something to you so that you will be more effective than you have been to date in directing your researchers' efforts. You will share this with no one."

Hassan looked puzzled.

"We are not after Harrigan's secrets to make money; even to compensate for diminished oil demand."

"But, sir! Funding for the project is based on —"

"Are you questioning me, Major?"

"No sir."

"The Arab nations have been kept at each other's throats for centuries by the West. They have made us dependent upon their increasingly meager oil purchases and forced us to accept those filthy Hebes dominating Palestine. They would have us cater like groveling servants to their fat, spoiled children in tourist parks. Eventually, they would not even need that. I will not allow this to happen to those who follow me. With greater mental capacity and longevity, our people will displace our enemies, whose progeny will serve us. Now, open your Alpha list. Follow along with what I tell you."

Hassan opened his tablet and touched the Alpha icon. A summary of research objectives for his main area of responsibility flashed on the screen.

"Would you like to live a thousand years?"

"Yes, sir!"

"Do you suppose we could gain the loyalty of leaders of the Arab League if we could control their longevity, reward them with better health — or punish them with the opposite?"

"We have discussed longevity, sir. My scientists place a high priority on tracing genes related to longevity."

"Hassan, it is not wise to tell me what you are aware that I know."

"Yes, sir. I didn't mean to—"

"Scroll to priority twelve: Meiotic Research. It is the highest priority."

"I do not understand, sir."

"That is because you are an idiot who will become more effective and insightful…if you wish to live. Those RNA molecules described there in the section marked 'confidential' are key. According to his notes, Harrigan believes they control ancient trait inheritance and expression. That must include racial and tribal markers, which we'll need on virus surfaces in order to target enemy peoples while protecting our allies. Why do you think Harrigan has attempted to keep that information in his ciphered files?"

"I supposed he felt sensitive about it. Studying those molecules requires destroying fetuses — and that's illegal here and in most countries now that RU-586 is distributed free."

"Don't be a fool, Hassan. RU-586 is but a convenient rationalization. The world can proclaim innocence for having outlawed abortions. Harrigan knows he is safe here even if he makes and aborts zygotes and fetuses. He never cared to save either the whales or the humans!

"What would happen, Hassan, if the West's women began giving birth to imbeciles like our primitive ancestors — while *our* women produced fearless, strong, fast-maturing children? What would happen if the non-Arab world's military personnel suddenly aged decades — in days? How difficult, then, would it be for Arabs — led by us — to inherit the earth?"

"How would we, I mean, what vector could distinguish genetic groups to carry such genetic instructions?"

"You will have your people develop the answer, then provide me with that capability. And I want those vectors in a form that is easily, effectively, and exclusively dispensed, at my command. In this vector, I want enhanced intelligence, rapid aging, greater longevity, disease resistance – everything else on your list, including the negative traits. I want mass production capability."

Mon took a page from a file, walked out from behind his desk, and placed it on Hassan's keyboard. "I will simplify things for you, Hassan. If you are successful — and I mean meeting the generously flexible schedule on this sheet—you will rise as I rise to lead the world. I can give you Iraq as your dominion. You will similarly motivate your underlings. But if this is beyond your ability, you will die. Are you more clearly focused now?"

Despite the intimidation, Hassan was awed by the reward. "You have honored me with your confidence, Minister. I will surpass your expectations! I will start by eliminating this spy."

Mon's eyes flashed at Hassan. "What spy? For whom?"

"This morning I received a report. I must give it to you myself."

Mon read the note from Hassan's Communications Bureau and handed it back.

"Idiot! Harrigan is trying to access *our* files, but he is reporting this word 'zip' to his handlers. That is American slang for 'nothing.' He is reporting that we have not accessed his most critical files. Don't kill him, you fool. Not now. Our dupe remains valuable. Just monitor him. Feed him the confidential portions of the Al-Rajda commercial plan. If he makes the Americans and Israelis think we're only out to monopolize prehistoric fascinations for profit, they'll leave us alone. If he appears to be communicating anything else, kill him."

Harrigan realized the previous two months of preparations had been exhausting for his staff. But spin-off discoveries, like the *in-utero* vaccine correcting Down Syndrome that partially helped Peter and millions like him, motivated everyone. These tools helped correct several genetic errors, some from inbreeding of his small populations of taxa. Each step in the FGR process had been progressively more exciting. His people were almost giddy. Implanting four Iraqi surrogates with thriving Neanderthal zygotes the day before had been a crowning achievement. And now, everyone treated the surrogates and their husbands like royalty.

Although more work loomed before them, Harrigan wanted to give his team a break. He arranged for a late afternoon cookout a hundred yards south of the complex so as to provide a better view of the awesome plateau cliff and waterfall at which he loved to gaze.

Harrigan had compartmentalized research between himself, Ruliev, his senior geneticist, and Freund because he did not want anyone to see the big picture. This precaution, he felt, was crucial now that Lloyd and an Iraqi team working in northern Iran has just found non-mineralized samples of hundred-fifty-thousand-year-old eggs and sperm of Cro Magnons—modern humans near emergence from *Homo heidelbergensis*. Soon this work would parallel that underway with Neanderthal samples. He feared its potential and did not want Tykvah to fully understand FGR, or the Iraqis to believe that she understood it.

His original FGR process was refined enough to work successfully with fossils of both egg and sperm of Neanderthal meiotic material. The past two months' intense development and experimentation, and construction and forestation, were sources of great pride, but what excited him now were the amazing feats that had just achieved the redemption of Neanderthal genes.

The FGR process had been executed in assembly-line fashion with three in-line laboratories. These were the Paleontology, or Paleo Lab, the Genetics Lab, and the Biology/Cryogenics, or BC Lab.

The Paleo Lab recovered nucleotides, pieces of gene strands, from damaged fossil egg and sperm. In the first five weeks, Olivier's team had separated and prepared specimens from the four fossil Neanderthals. Over the following six weeks, technicians tediously extracted damaged but redeemable fossil cells. The residue from the chromosomal cells was embedded along a thin bar of clear gel. Faint electron beams straightened tangled strands of residue. The gel bars were then semi-hardened and passed into the Genetics Lab.

He glanced across the windowless Genetics Lab at one of the huge flat monitors hanging on the wall, which showed colorized scans of DNA and RNA molecules, and statistical analyses. He crossed the room to the genetic sample scanner module, which received the gel bars from the Paleo Lab. One of its components, the Terahertz, or T-ray, illuminator, looked like a three-foot-long silver bar with hundreds of diodes. It functioned like a camera flash, while not affecting the reconstituted fossil nucleotides. A foot above and below it, two black bars produced a null-magnetic field that held the gel bars in mid-air.

A clam-like blue ceramic globe around these devices was the computer's eyes, receiving the T-rays bounced off gene segments in the gel. The key to proper computer modeling of the sequences was that few samples were damaged in exactly the same place. During this day-long mapping, the computer compared strands for sequence patterns, identifying thousands, and used this information to infer sequences that were damaged. After this, it took two weeks for synthesizing and assembling of raw genetic material into replicated sets of chromosomes for implantation into an actual egg.

Harrigan inspected his "assembly line" with growing satisfaction. Water and nucleotide storage tanks, raw materials, cable bundles, and a temperature control unit were the next components in the line of machines bisecting the Genetics Lab. The first manufacturing device was a nucleotide base-pair synthesizer. The synthesizer drew four nucleotides from the tanks to make DNA strands. Adjacent to the synthesizer was a gene strand assembler. It manipulated these strands of base pairs into complete genes, and the genes into sets called chromosomes.

He recalled how, years earlier, a breakthrough at Stanford had discovered human "growth microsatellites," which control maturation rate. His team now used his improved CRISPR coding to speed gene assembly, insert enhanced gestation microsatellites, and to error-check. Except for the fast maturation genes, the synthesizer had assembled the genes into chromosomes.

These chromosomes were migrated to the BC lab's microscope-crowned implantation station. Each completed set of twenty-three chromosomes was then placed in an artificial cell nucleus.

The nuclei, voided of their own genes, were inserted into eggs that had been harvested from four human surrogates. This "mating" produced forty-seven female zygotes and forty-four males. Harrigan alternated from pride to guilt as he mentally reviewed the final processes.

Forty-five female zygotes would attain the developmental state of ten-week-old fetuses within two weeks and produce their own eggs: meiosis. The girls in the artificial wombs would be terminated during meiosis and their eggs harvested to discover the secrets of that miracle.

Forty-two males were frozen for later study. The remaining zygotes, two of each sex, were implanted into the surrogates' uteruses to be born after a gestation period of only three months. These zygotes were cousins, so recessive genes had to be identified and repaired. The four Neanderthals were intended for natural breeding years hence.

Harrigan and his team had been confident throughout the long process because of previous successes with extinct animals. What had really excited the researchers' mood was the fact that they had created embryos of genus *Homo:* the once-extinct *Homo sapiens neanderthalensis.*

Harrigan scowled as Iraqi staff watched him summon Freund to his office. "Come in and shut the door," Harrigan said with a growl. "Mannie, I was going to fire you for not doing the implants. But I need you to monitor neurological and other physical development."

Harrigan touched a console on his desk and a dull vibrating sound made it difficult to hear speech more than three feet away. He pulled up a chair next to Freund.

"Mannie, I don't trust these Iraqis. They got into my personal computer files. For all I know, the whole building's bugged. So, this irritating buzz is necessary. I need your insight on something."

Harrigan took a wide, folded computer printout from his pocket and showed it to Freund.

Freund studied it a moment, sadness giving way to intrigue. He stared at Harrigan. "Have you run this analysis a second time?"

"I've run it three times, each with the same results."

"Could be a statistical fluke. But, Kevin, the odds are... millions to one. What does it mean?"

"Well, obviously implant number two — what'd they name it?"

"Kora. A modern name close to the Nostratic word for lamb."

"We got half her genes from the Pyrenees male specimen and half from the fossil girl Lloyd found at Shanidar. He thinks the three found there were a family. But, Mannie, Kora is genetically identical to the fossil mother of that fossil girl."

"An identical twin to the presumed mother... from the daughter's genes? The fossil sperm used was five millennia older, from an unrelated specimen! Any matches among other fetal or fossil Neanderthals?"

"None."

"Hmm. Matthew Eleven says John the Baptist was Elijah. That's the only scripture with anything like reincarnation. No! There are others. Plus, most religions and myth traditions have similar prophecies. Done with genetics, it'd be a botch. *Worse* than a botch! It could be used to masquerade as the returning Christ, to resurrect humanity...only not transfigured into divinely illuminated bodies freed from vulnerabilities and earthly needs."

"Oh come off it, Mannie!"

"Don't get me wrong. Reincarnation is a misinterpretation of a promise God gave humanity. The spiritual interacts with the physical. God said we die *once*... but coming back *once* in this final age... Her mom is back for a reason. God does what he wills, even exceptions that only *appear* to be reincarnation. Maybe Kora has a mission or it is a sign. Have you given any thought to what we talked — ?"

"Yes, yes, I have. Look, Mannie, I can't see how it could be a 'sign' or how she could be bearing some divine admonition. A warning carried by a resurrected Neanderthal...*please!*"

"I didn't say anything about a warning. You did."

Harrigan glared silently, sensing guilt. "Why do you insist on making me uncomfortable? Who elected you to minister to me?"

"Seeking that which is comfortable has never been your style in anything but spirituality. But, okay, let's just look at this from a purely scientific standpoint for a moment, Kevin."

"Thanks. That's what I've been asking you to do."

"If you shoot X-rays or T-rays through a box and get a round image, what would you suspect was in the box?"

"A ball. Is there a point, Mannie?"

"Why do you assume it is a ball and not a disk?"

"Uh. Well, I think in three dimensions. Wait. Four, including time."

"So, your interpretive frame of reference is from experiences of this world during your life. If you were really determined to find out what was in the box but couldn't touch it, what would you do?"

"I'd employ probe after probe, using the resulting data to build a list of known possibilities and eliminate inconsistent possibilities."

"So, then, is reincarnation—or some divine process that works like that concept—at least a possibility? Even if it never happened before, do you have evidence to eliminate it from all possibilities?"

"Okay. Something like that is a possibility—and no more. But what could possibly be the mechanism for spiritual occurrences? It's just not a supported hypothesis. What I want is the list and the probing tools. Will you track her neurologically and psychologically? It really gave me shivers when I saw this."

"Certainly, I will. I don't believe that reincarnation has ever occurred before…except for the Elijah and John the Baptist connection. Well, look, you keep the resulting children well cared for and I'll have this phenomenon pegged one way or the other: Random or otherwise. Now, what about this Iraqi prying? Are they trying to steal FGR?"

"I think they're after FGR because they don't want to wait the ten years under the contract before I have to give it to them. Fortunately, there is no way they can get it."

"Why not? The interpretation and mapping program is at easy access for them to copy. They have access to the equipment now."

Harrigan leaned forward, his voice congenial, secretive. "I had computer science grad students help me write parts of the program back at Harvard. None saw the whole picture, so they don't have my program. But their help enabled me to integrate a security precaution. The error-checking subroutine only uses the correct algorithm when I personally include a password in my voice commands. Otherwise, or if it's copied, FGR fails. Same for my database of eight hundred racial lineages. Another password permits correct operation for anyone but keeps the copy protection enabled. That's why the Iraqis can use FGR in this lab without me and not suspect I use a code word. It's in the program design so there's no virus to detect."

"You're a sneaky dog, you know that?"

"Arf! One last thing. I need to know more about these M1-RNA molecules and their function in humans. If we're going to learn what made Kora the same as her 'fossil grandmother,' we'll have to study human and Neanderthal meiosis. You with me on these things?"

Freund sighed heavily at the reminder. "You're terminating fetuses anyway. I guess if I want to be a part of the discoveries here and get you to consider deeper meanings, I have to study what remains. At least I *admit* my rationalizing. What'd you have in mind?"

Harrigan grimaced but let the 'rationalizing' shot pass.

"I've asked Major Najik to obtain female zygotes from donors at illegal abortion clinics worldwide. But before you say 'no', I told him to use only women who are intent on that. We'll get enough specimens to answer questions like which traits are preserved by meiotic RNA, in which groups of people. I want to know what changes are evolving in these molecules since the time of ancient humans."

"That's a tall order, old buddy. I have to admit, though, I'd like to know the answers. And any implication for modern behavior and personality traits. All right. I said in Megiddo I'd do it and I won't renege. At the enhanced maturation rate, it'll be three years 'till I can study Kora and others approaching neurological maturity. Adult behaviors emerge then, maybe beliefs."

Harrigan got up smiling and turned off the buzzer. The two men walked together through the halls, out toward the cookout. Freund looked troubled, head low, but Harrigan did not probe.

He turned hesitantly toward Freund as they walked. "Mannie, I think I need a vacation or something. Too much stress. I keep having these dreams every few months or so."

"Dreams? Of what sort?"

"It's nothing, really. I can only barely remember anything that happens in them. They're always different but they leave me with the same exhilarating...even ominous and lonely feeling. I get a hold of myself, of course, but I sometimes wake to find my eyes full of tears."

"Dreams affecting *you*? Well, we're all tougher on the outside."

Harrigan fired off a dirty look.

"Sorry. Recall any details?"

"Well, last night, it was like I was on one of the escalators, halfway up, alone. There was a sense that if I chose the 'up' button, I'd lose everything: myself, my family, the research—just a sad sense of loss. The 'down' button was no better: I sensed everything would prosper, like I could accomplish great things and be with my family—but the feeling of accelerating dread just chilled me. And there were these sad, high-pitched, voices whispering something. 'How long must' is the only phrase I remember. You're the doctor. Too much stress?"

"Stress, all right. Maybe something more. Maybe you should..."

Harrigan's voice turned to uncertain cynicism. "You think it's spiritual, don't you? Everything is spiritual with you!"

"I was going to suggest pentothal-II to dig into your brain."

"Whoa! Forget it. I'm just too stressed. I'll take a vacation. That should help. Right?"

"It might. But I doubt a vacation will be enough."

Up-beat music, raucous laughter, and children's happy screams cheered them as they left the building to join the party and kick off years-long sapiens maturation and study.

Chapter Seven

Neurological Research Lab, Al-Rajda Research Preserve
0923 hours, 8 July 2030

Dr. Freund entered the neuro lab questioning his ethics of the last few years. Now he conducted his deepest-reaching study yet of Kora, the Neanderthal girl now the equivalent of an adolescent. She had been removed from her cave under anesthesia six hours earlier. The gas would soon be replaced in her system by sodium pentothal-II to access her subconscious mind.

Dr. Ina Singh, the preserve's new anthropologist from Bombay, barely glanced up from reports on Kora. "Dr. Freund, what d'you make of the surrogates' reports of her trance episodes?" "I have an opinion. What is your interpretation?"

"The scans showed no epilepsy. But you are the medical authority. A recent report has an account of the sun changing color during one of her trances. Poppycock and hallucination on the part of the surrogate, I'd say. What do you think?"

"Yes. I must agree. I'm sure that's it."

"Well, then. Shall we begin?"

Freund smiled warmly. He had a strong sense that his response to Singh's inquiry was incorrect. Stretching wrinkles from his surgical gloves and closing his white lab coat, Freund noticed that he was developing a very slight paunch. He momentarily recalled with mild chagrin how his children had enjoyed finding his few gray hairs and plucking them out before his trip back here five days earlier.

He refocused on his task and started the audio recording. "System: Begin Recording, Kora One. Output to screen."

The large screen on the wall silently flashed three words.
RECORDING: Kora One.

The computer automatically recorded numerous monitored data, such as drug flow rates, Kora's blood pressure and her brain waves. It also recorded all sounds in the room.

"Present with me to conduct this experiment are Dr. Singh and Nurse Haddad. Nurse, please turn Kora on her side a moment as I begin the pre-experiment physical examination."

Kora lay nude and motionless on the cushioned examining table. She had thick brows, a receding chin, and eyes slightly smaller than those of modern children of her size. Such features had proved a century of artists' impressions of Neanderthals substantially right. Her eyes were grayish blue with surprisingly short black lashes. Her cheekbones were prominent and her neck and legs were short and muscular with thick and stubby fingers. The hips were much wider than modern girls of any race and her skin was nearly devoid of pigment. Her wide feet were covered with thicker hair than her hands and arms but, overall, she presented a more human than primate.

The long hair on her Kora's head splashed upon the table, forming a reddish-blonde corona. She was covered with the same reddish-gold hair over most of her body, inch-long but sparse on her chest, buttocks, and groin.

"Four percent of modern European genes are Neanderthal," Freund murmured, though he knew Singh and Haddad were aware.

He could not decide which emotion he now felt most strongly: awe at the very presence of this human cousin, or sadness. He knew her surrogate parents were only barely accepting. Freund often begged them to hold her and her siblings more, to be more patient. He appealed through Harrigan to their employers to force a change of attitude but they both were bluntly told that parents did not read Doctor Spock's classic advice tens of thousands of years ago.

"Thank you, Nurse. Now please release five milligrams pentothal-II into the stream."

Freund waited for the pentothal-II dripping through the I.V. to take effect. He glanced alternately at Kora, Singh, Haddad, and the monitors. Kora twitched her eyes and frowned. A REM sleep indicator on the secondary signs display lit.

Like her siblings, Kora's articulation of the vowels a, I, and u was shallow, slurred yet recognizable. Neanderthal voices were low and scratchy. She began to moan.

Kora's tone became suddenly loud, fearful. "Sera! Sera! Mana! Gandi palu bisa. Gandi qohl! Telh-laki; karipunyi qohl! Khayni qohl!"

Her heart rate, blood pressure, and breathing shot to alarming levels as she began to scream and contort on the table. Freund held her arm and hand but knew she was not aware of his touch. His eyes darted back and forth from her tormented expression to the frightening blood pressure readings, now at 181 over 143. She moaned and screamed, no longer articulating anything like words.

Freund was alarmed, taken entirely by surprise. "Twenty milligrams of labetalol *NOW!*"

The nurse drew the required amount from a small bottle with a needle and began to insert it into the hanging I.V. dispenser. Freund snatched the syringe from her hand and plunged the needle directly into the port at Kora's wrist.

The screaming stopped but was followed by continued moans. Her blood pressure returned to a safe range. Freund breathed a loud sigh, wiped his beaded forehead, and addressed his assistants.

"What *de* hell was tha—"

Kora's low, scratchy voice seemed relaxed, quiet. "Gepeh...gilda! D'mato-em."

The researchers' eyes now stared at the monitor in amazement. The analysis of the translation appeared almost instantaneously as Kora spoke.

VOCALIZATION SET 1, PHONETIC: "Sera! Sera! Mana! Gandi palu bisa. Gandi qohl! Telh-laki; karipunyi qohl! Khayni qohl!"

(AS ONE) ANALYSIS:

PROBABILITY IT IS A STATEMENT...98.23%

PROBABILITY IT IS A QUESTION...01.41%

PROBABILITY IT IS RANDOM...00.36%

SYNTAX CONFORMITY TO ENGLISH...80.00%

MODERN LANGUAGE...none

BEST FIT...Nostratic (90.91% match to etymology)

PRONUNCIATION CONFORMITY TO...Nostratic Model...35.12%

ALL POSSIBLE MEANINGS OVER 10% PROBABILITY THRESHOLD...One at 92.77 percent:

"Wake(!) Wake(!) Men(!) [Big men] many crush. [Big men] kill(!) Long-legs; black-hairs kill(!) [Khayni UNKNOWN PLURAL] kill(!)"

VOCALIZATION SET 2 (Y / N) ?

Freund stared incredulously at the monitor. For a mad moment, he wondered if Harrigan might have programmed the computer to generate a bogus analysis as a joke. But neither man knew for sure Kora would say anything at all while unconscious.

"Yes."

The screen blanked, then displayed a second analysis.

VOCALIZATION SET 2, PHONETIC: "Gepeh gilda! D'mato-em."

(AS ONE) ANALYSIS:

PROBABILITY IT IS A STATEMENT...99.81%

PROBABILITY IT IS A QUESTION...00.00%

PROBABILITY IT IS RANDOM...00.19%

SYNTAX CONFORMITY TO ENGLISH...100.00%

MODERN LANGUAGE...none

BEST FIT...Nostratic (100.00% match to etymology)

PRONUNCIATION CONFORMITY TO...Nostratic Model...38.57%

ALL POSSIBLE MEANINGS OVER 10% PROBABILITY THRESHHOLD...One at 94.29 percent:

"Light [PAUSE] shine(!) Two witnesses to call out [FUTURE

TENSE](.)"

NO OTHER VOCALIZATIONS RECOGNIZABLE. SELECT MAIN FOR OPTIONS.

Freund shivered visibly and turned toward Singh. "Ina, would you get the hard copy Nostratic Lexicon, please."

Singh left the room and returned with a thin booklet. "Here, Dr. Freund. Is this some form of joke? An error or some such?"

"Perhaps. More likely someone taught her this. The surrogates have been teaching them our best model of Nostratic. But I don't think all of these words were in the lesson plans. If they've tampered with these children's minds and our ability to gain valid insight, I'll...I'll have their jobs!"

Freund silently thumbed through the lexicon, checking each translated word. "She pronounced these words differently from the lexicon, on which the computer language model is based—and a few of her words are not in the lexicon."

Singh cocked her head. "What does that mean?"

"It means that we need to check the records on how she's been using these words to determine whether she's been coached. She would pronounce these words the same in waking speech as when she's in this subconscious state—if she's been coached in some unauthorized way by the surrogates." Freund paused and addressed the computer.

"System: Compare Vocalization Sets 1 and 2 to the model and to Kora's recorded usage. Time frame: last twelve months. Summary only."

SUMMARY COMPARISON...Neither Set 1 nor Set 2 Pronunciations match the model: no matches to any previous recordings (time = last 12 calendar months).

SUMMARY NOTES...The following words have not been recorded used by Kora previous to recording of Kora One:

Set 1: bisa, qohl, khayni

Set 2: gilda

...The following words are not in the model:

Set 1: khayni

DETAIL OF COMPARISON (Y / N)?

"No." Freund, jaw hanging, glared at Singh and the nurse.

"Her pronunciation for each word is different in her waking state from her subconscious state," he began. "No one taught her these things, Ina. She knows words not taught her. Yet all but one match Nostratic."

The nurse scowled as Singh whispered a Hindu interpretation. "Dr. Freund, Kora spoke words from the last moments of her life—forty millennia ago. But the future tense of witness..."

Freund was surprised by Singh's unscientific interpretation.

"Computer glitch, Ina, and that's not the translation. System: End recording. Nurse, Dr. Singh: Neither of you will discuss this until Dr. Harrigan or I authorize it. Nurse, please get Dr. Harrigan in here. Stat!" The nurse scowled again and disappeared. "And Ina, you and I can discuss this later...but please don't elaborate on your interpretation with Dr. Harrigan or the Iraqi staff."

Harrigan rushed down the hall and into the neurology lab. "Sorry I couldn't get here faster. What the heck is it, Mannie? Is there something wrong with the Neand— , uh, Kora?"

Freund stepped behind him and closed the door. "Kevin, listen to this. System: Replay Kora One. Output to speaker and screen."

The computer played back its recordings of every sound, readout, and command from Kora's examination. Harrigan stood, silently studying the replay, and frowning at Freund.

"Not amused, Mannie. We do science here, not practical jokes." Harrigan's cross tone was followed by a knowing smile and a look of triumph on his face. "Got you now! System: Run my validation check, code seventy-two." He glared at Freund, expecting to prove the ruse.

The metallic voice responded. "All components of Kora One were created in real-time and have not been modified."

Harrigan blanched. He stared at Freund, then at Haddad and Singh, embarrassed. "I owe you an apology, Mannie. I should not have suspected you of playing a joke. But this 'previous life' thing is garbage! I suppose you agree with Dr. Singh's comment at the end?"

"Something like that... and maybe evidence of events at both ends of Scripture."

Harrigan's rage built but he lacked confidence. "This research facility, Mannie, is not a damn theology discussion group. We don't jump to conclusions that hocus-pocus is the cause of an observation just 'cuz we can't immediately identify a mechanism causing a result!"

"Find the mechanism, then. Or continue to rationalize."

Harrigan bristled at the terse challenge and began to turn red. "No, *Doctor* Freund, *you* will find the mechanism; you and Dr. Singh will prove *yourselves* wrong or..."

"You sound more like you're worried that *you* could be wrong about there being spiritual traits which define humankind. And these children *are* human, physically and spiritually. Would you have us manufacture evidence that supports your position—*und* shield you from that which weakens it—or would you like us to learn about all aspects of human evolution? Perspective,

Kevin. How one views life. View it *mit* open eyes."

Harrigan felt caught. He knew the ability to detect a cause of a phenomenon was not a prerequisite to its reality. He glared at Freund.

Dr. Singh broke the tension diplomatically. "Gentlemen, I apologize for sparking this argument by jumping ahead to conclusions. But, *really!* Come now. Let's focus on studying her and — when they're ready — her siblings, shall we? We need a replacement for Pentothal-II because repeated use tempts stroke. We have a lot of work to do to determine whether this is mystical, natural, or just a fluke; an anomaly. Please, gentlemen."

Harrigan avoided Freund's eyes but offered a small concession to the physician's ongoing concerns about treatment and safety of the sapiens. "You're right, Dr. Singh. Let's get the Biochem Lab in on re-analyzing what levels and combinations of drugs are safe. I suppose you're right in some respects too Dr. Freund: She is essentially human, and you can't say I don't value human life. Safety is the primary concern in the operation of my Preserve!"

Chapter Eight

Harrigan awoke sweating and in tears. He glanced at the clock. Just after midnight. He felt a tremendous need to wake Tykvah, to have her reassure him that he was all right. Instead, he turned back the covers and strode to the bathroom, closed the door, and rotated the rheostat to produce the most light his eyes could stand. He stood at the marble sink, looking into its gold fixtures to see if the small reflection would replicate the first half of his dream. To do so, he would have to look in the mirror. He hesitated, staring below it.

He silently scolded himself. *You are not a wimp. So why aren't you looking in the mirror?*

He jerked his head up and peered suspiciously at his dim reflection, then deeply into his own eyes. He now spoke audibly. "Nothing. You're just yourself. What the hell are you afraid of?"

He turned out the light and walked to Ben's room. He watched his beloved five-year-old sleep. Remembering how he had vanquished the boy's nightmare with a hug only last night now reminded Harrigan of the rest of his own dream. *My subconscious has simply let Freund's superstitions get to me,* he decided, returning to his own bed, where he accidentally woke Tykvah.

"Kevin? What's the matter?"

"Just a bad dream, babe. Let's go to sleep."

"You never have bad dreams. At least you've never said you did. Wanna talk about it?"

"No. But it was so realistic. As if..." And Harrigan began to weep again involuntarily, overcome again by the emotions of his fearful dream.

"Honey, are you...Kevin, you're crying! What's the matter?"

"I need to talk this out another time, okay? It's just stress-related and I'd be better off going back to sleep, or maybe later blowing off some steam — something fun."

"You've been working too hard. Look, it's already Friday. We'll just take off for a long weekend back at Megiddo — you, me, and Ben."

"Can't. The last of the meiotic specimens mature Sunday and can't be frozen at this stage. If we're going to get any observations, we have to use the thirty-hour egg formation window — which should begin late Sunday morning. Then Mannie, Gregor, and I have some gene-tracing work scheduled for Monday afternoon."

Harrigan paused a moment, then gave in to a longstanding desire. "But I could take just tomorrow off. Enjoy the fall colors. Maybe have some fun in the Preserve."

"*Inside* the Preserve? With predators roaming free? Isn't that against your own rules?"

"Mannie and I will have to go in with teams anyway when the surrogates near the end of their contract. We need to learn the terrain, *animalistic behavior…*" He gave her a soft "Grr," and a hug. "Besides, the predators stay near the herds. It's me, Bart, Mannie, and some guards."

"Why Bart? There are no fossils there!"

"Bart's one o' my buds, and a party animal." Harrigan japed. "Seriously, he's on a rare stint here at the moment."

"Kevin, this is an unnecessary risk, and you know — "

"Babe! The heavy-lift suits are impervious to attack. We'll just explore. Only for the day. We'll get, experience, useful observations and video to boot."

"Well, *I'm* not going! And I thought you might spend some time with Ben and me."

"I assumed you wouldn't go into the Preserve. You've always been scared to death of the place. But you're right about the stress. Woods, buds, and danger…that's just what guys do, Babe. You and Ben and I will do something together next weekend."

"Okay. Have your 'big boy' fun. And good luck getting past Ben in the morning. You okay now? With this nightmare thing, I mean."

"Yes. Thanks. Aside from feeling childish, I'm fine. Let's get some rest."

———————

The next morning, Harrigan watched the rising sun illuminate the bedroom as Tykvah stepped out to the patio and pulled blooms from the fence to her face. The new day was breaking with clear, crisp weather. He followed her out to where Ben, an early riser, was playing with plastic prehistoric animals and placing two modeling clay figures, one head-to-toe with short brown strings, atop a box.

"What's that, big boy?" he asked, reaching for the hairy figure. "A yeti?"

"No," Ben replied. "She had less hair in the dream. I was grown up and she and I were on top of giant blocks with TV cameras all around. A reporter called us witnesses to something important. I don't remember what, but a lot of people hated us."

Harrigan smiled nervously, then called to Tykvah. "Did you tell him about the sapiens?"

"No. He's said that before. From movies, I suppose. No worries."

"Can I cut notches in *Megaloceros's* neck, Dad?" Ben pleaded. "*Smilodon* likes to jump and bite his throat and wait until he's bled too weak to poke with his antlers. Then he eats him."

"No cutting up toys, you little deerslayer-guy," Harrigan bellowed, chuckling.

"You don't have any knives out there do you, dear?"

"No, Mom. Geeze!"

Harrigan arranged for clearance and two guards through Najik. Then he phoned Freund and Lloyd simultaneously. They both jumped at the idea of exploring the Preserve and agreed to meet in two hours.

Harrigan went outside and dug holes and tossed Ben around before breakfast. After showering and dressing, he picked up his son in the hallway and held him upside down by the ankles. "You look funny upside down, little man!"

"You're the one who's upside down, Daddy!"

Harrigan righted the boy and held him up at his chest. "Ben, can you take care of Mom today until I get back?"

"I thought I was going to school today."

"You are, but no daycare before or after. Mom's staying home today. You and Mom can have an adventure. I'll be back for supper."

"Okay, Daddy, but I want to go with you!"

Tykvah stood by the kitchen door in her tight-tied, pink silk robe and eyed Harrigan with her "I told you so" look. She changed it to a pout and tapped her finger to her open lips. "It's still not too late to spend the day with us, Kevin. If you're looking for danger, I gotcha covered."

Harrigan stopped and considered his options but narrowly decided in favor of his original diversion plans. "Mannie and Bart are probably already at the vehicle bays. I'll see *you* tonight, Tykvah. Bye, big boy! Be good for Mom and…"

Tykvah was pulling a chain of black rosary beads from her robe pocket.

"Are you serious? Did Mannie give you those?"

"He said it would irk you to no end, so I like it! I'm reading the book he gave me, too: *Mere Christianity*," she said, changing her accent to mock Sicilian, "You got a problem wit dat?"

"Fine, I suppose. Fine. Just never expected…"

Tykvah gave him a stern frown, then hugged and kissed him goodbye.

Harrigan drove through the access tunnel to the research complex motor pool. He greeted his friends as he exited his car in the motor pool. The stale, subterranean air smelled like grease and electrical charging. Freund and Lloyd, grinning from ear to ear, stepped off footstools into the cushioned interior of their tall, furry heavy-lift suits.

The chest doors of the suits were open, and his friends' faces reminded Harrigan that, at thirty-nine, he was fit but no longer the young man of his memory. At forty-one, Freund had a few wrinkles and gray hairs, though his paunch was modest. Lloyd remained in excellent shape for a forty-seven-year-old man, but his mustache and short hair had grayed noticeably.

Tight fit for lanky ol' Bart! Harrigan mused as they entered battery-powered robotic suits, resembling cave bears — twelve feet tall. *An effective disguise, real bearskin.* He felt more secure, contemplating the improved latches and high-tech armor, responsible for no casualties since...Now Harrigan recalled two young soldiers, devoured on flora maintenance duty when they could not close their sloth-tractor to a vicious pack of dire wolves.

He closed the latches and checked its radio and other systems. The instant he stepped, the suit around him walked. Unlike a bear, it had dexterous mechanical fingers.

The mechanism was waterproof, but the wire-mesh viewports at the suit's neck did not seal. *Glass sealing visors on order for freakin' ever!* He smoldered as he tested a telephoto video camera that tracked the user's glance. He could hardly wait to play in the wild with artificially enhanced strength and speed.

Peering out, Harrigan saw his friends and two Iraqi guards, were suited up. "Follow me," he commanded, leading all to the escalator. "We'll stay to the eastern half of the plateau," he radioed his group, "head north along the wood line bordering the river, then loop south around the eastern edge of the open areas and return. The Neanderthal and Cro-Magnon families are now well established in the northwestern and northeastern areas respectively, far from our route. The clans continually post guards on the bare rock around their caves to give early warning of animal approach. So, if you get separated and go too far north, you could compromise the validity of our studies.

"By the way, gentlemen, the Neanderthal clan now consists of thirty-eight members. These are comparable in physical maturity to modern humans ranging from newborns to sixteen-year-olds. There are thirty-five Cro-Magnons ranging in human-comparable ages from newborns to twelve-year-olds.

"The sound walls have been gone for almost a year now with no predator intrusion into the sapiens areas. But *we* could encounter some, so stay in the suits until I call 'dismount.'"

Emerging at the top, Harrigan activated his camera. "Look at that fiery red and orange! Smell the fallen leaves. Reminds me of Ranger School and Georgia—remember, Mannie?"

"Yeah. Camp Darby and then Merrill in Ranger School's Mountain phase. Beautiful," Freund agreed.

"Ablaze. Marvelous. Like the autumn English countryside," Lloyd said.

"You guys want video for posterity?" Harrigan asked. "Switch on. But we can't take any sapiens clips out of here till the contract's up—unless you want to risk Najik confiscating it and docking pay!"

Najik, who was monitoring their transmissions from the Preserve's control room, spoke up. "That is cor-rect, gentlemen! Have today your privileged fun but keep the rules. A contract is one's word and one's word is…as you people say…one's bond, yes, Dr. Harrigan?"

Harrigan scowled at the remark. He knew communications within the Preserve were monitored but expected to be told when an officer was monitoring him.

The group progressed, in stops and starts, for a mile along the tree line before Harrigan cut to the river early. As they approached it, they surprised a group of eight huge *Sivatherium*. The bull siva—a black-maned, dark brown and shaggy, moose-like mammal nearly the size of its relative, the giraffe—obviously did not appreciate having its harem chased away into the river. Its two four-foot ossicones looked more like sharp-edged blades than antlers. It sported a smaller, second set that looked like deadly triangular horns above its eyes. The siva's nearly two-foot-wide head formed a frightful battering ram.

Freund pointed as it crouched and stomped threateningly. "*Ach!* It's going to charge!"

Lloyd shot back, "No problem! He'll get quite a surprise if he does!"

Freund's voice rose in everyone's speakers. "If he doesn't knock you on your can, he'll break his ossicones. Then, we'll have to evacuate him to the clinic."

"Mannie's right," Harrigan interjected. "Just back off, slowly."

As the bear-suits backpedaled, the beast directed its fury at Harrigan, who backed into a tree. The painful bump he sustained inside his suit gave him but a meager foretaste of the siva's crushing impact. Harrigan's muscles tensed, and he could not interpret his fellows' yells on the radio. He closed his eyes shut and screwed up his face in anticipation of the jolt.

He heard a crunch but felt only a slight bump. The air in front of him looked like thick fog. It was dust, he realized, as he dropped the mesh visor and peered out into the cloud. In seconds, the dust cleared and Harrigan's cheek received a tremendous blow from the siva's nose. It hesitated as Harrigan, stunned, failed to close the portal. The beast stuck its snout inside again to bite. Greenish teeth just missed Harrigan's nose. Then it raked his face with its foamy tongue and abruptly withdrew.

Lloyd prodded the siva's ribs with his partially retracted claws until it jumped and bucked away in another cloud of dust to join its harem in the river. Lloyd smirked on Harrigan's monitor, then switched the image to a zoom of Harrigan's own contorted face.

A tremendous itch suddenly flooded his sinuses. He withdrew his arms from the suit's sleeves to cup his nose. "Ff-phh-m-n! Ugh!" Harrigan's hands suddenly filled with green, foul-smelling, and bubbly saliva. He fumbled for a wet wipe as his right eyelid dripped a long strand and his whole face looked Christmassy: red and shining with particles of masticated shrubbery.

"You're lucky you've got a nose to blow, old boy! Those sivas can give quite a nip—and they like to taste their opponent's blood. Wonder if they would have become carnivorous if they hadn't died out twelve thousand years ago. Several species were moving in that direction."

Harrigan was not yet ready to laugh at himself. "Isn't *that* a pleasant thought? How about you guys covering me while I wash this *spit* off my face? Dismount!"

The three scientists got out of the cramped suits and fell down laughing at Harrigan's ridiculous luck. The guards posted themselves, and the trio walked over to the water's edge.

They remounted shortly and continued north along the river. After a mile, Harrigan pointed to a group of six *Coelodonta* crashing through the forest to reach the river. The male woolly rhino was nearly seven feet tall and fourteen long. Huge double horns and wind-blown black manes contrasted with dark brown body fur and made for fascinating video. The small herd plowed up a muddy cove as they milled at the water's edge. The men gave them a very wide berth and walked another mile before Harrigan halted.

"Care for a rest, gentlemen?" Harrigan ordered.

"Absolutely!" came Freund's response.

Lloyd was already opening the access panel to exit the suit.

Harrigan established security for the group, commanding the guards in halting Arabic. "Guards: You, one of you, watch all around. Only one of you can rest at a time and go no farther than five feet from your suit."

As he dismounted onto a large flat boulder overlooking the river, he told Freund and Lloyd, "We need to take out the tranquilizer pistols and put them on our belts."

"We should have brought some brew!" Freund declared.

Lloyd smiled and opened the right thigh panel of his suit and pulled out a gallon beer dispenser. "Have I got to think of everything?"

The scientists' faces lit as they poured the sparkling golden liquid, forbidden on the plateau, and began a late and long-desired lunch. They joked and pushed each other like kids. After scanning for giant spiked terror turtles, *Meiolania*, Freund and Lloyd grabbed Harrigan and threw him off the bank into the river. By the end of their meal, Harrigan had returned the favor twice over for each. They sat drying off and scanning the brilliant foliage, browsing herbivores, and rugged landscape.

They remounted and trudged through thick woods, which extended right to the river's edge, soon reaching a newly reforested area of saplings. A tiny, black, pony-like *Hippidion* bolted in front of them. Three feet tall, it was nearly an adult.

Then, out from behind a small ridge, came its pursuer, a fourteen-foot-tall *Phorusrhacus*. Bright yellow body feathers and a red and blue streamlined head plume marked it as a male. The terror bird moved at an incredible speed for such a huge predator. Never did its three-foot hooked beak waver from its prey, nor did the robotic vehicles faze the dinosaur-descendant.

Just as it seemed to lose its prey at a steep-banked creek, the terror-bird leaped forward and clasped the mammal in a crushing bite. It raised its brilliantly plumed head and threw the squealing horse to the ground. The *Hippidion* brayed once like a mule, then began to flop feebly where it landed. The bird of prey grabbed it again, this time slamming the pony on its head. The *Hippidion* lay still.

Lloyd whispered, "I'm sure there was no mercy intended, but I'm glad it died quickly."

The bird turned from its prize, lowered its head, and hissed at the men. Then it snapped up its meal, gulped it, and rushed off eastward toward a herd of woolly *Titanotylopus*. These eleven-foot-tall, one-humped camels had appeared complacent and aloof crossing the grassy hills beyond the saplings until the gargantuan bird scattered them southward. The *Phorusrhacus* gave chase but did not have quite the speed to catch any.

"Did humans know those two, Bart?"

"They did. The American Southwest for *Titanotylopus* and, for Phorusrhacoids, South America and the American South. But, only the first wave of humans—some fifty thousand years ago—knew Terror Birds. By then, they were going extinct and no more than four feet tall. The only direct descendant today is the South American Seriama, three feet at the shoulder — still a vicious blighter, mark my words!"

Relieved, Harrigan had all continue northward several miles until they approached the river's shallow headwaters. There they noticed a motionless ground sloth some sixty yards distant, west across the river.

The twenty-foot-tall brown and yellow *Megatherium* sat on its haunches on the riverbank, reaching into a leafy tree. It appeared to have a baby on its back.

"That can't be a baby," Lloyd exclaimed, broadcasting a telephoto image. "Whatever is on its back is white and tan. Let's have a look here."

Harrigan gasped as his lens clearly revealed the pelt-clad figure sitting upon the sloth's massive shoulders. "It's...It's Kora!" he shouted. "The surrogates were supposed to...*Dammit!*"

"Kora has been allowed to leave the cave?" Freund exclaimed.

Harrigan was livid. "I'll strangle th— You monitoring this, Control?"

"We have it, Doctor. Better moof back. I'll have surrogates to get her."

"No, the surrogates will be subject to predation this far out. We'll dart her and take her back ourselves. I want her surrogate to answer for this. Signal the surrogate to post herself as cave guard. We'll deliver Kora to her. Harrigan out."

Harrigan raised the right arm of his suit and moved his hand within it to disengage the dart gun's safety. He adjusted the dose to low. The first shot hit its mark and Kora grabbed her thigh. The sloth seemed not to notice the shot but did lower itself to all fours as Kora began to sluggishly climb down. In moments, she staggered and collapsed against the beast's furry hip. It gently licked her shoulder but only managed to knock her over with its thick tongue, then resumed its feeding.

"Follow me and stay close!" Harrigan began to ford the shallow river, hoping he would not step in a washout.

"Whoa, Kevin!" Lloyd called, "We need a cable link before fording this!"

"You're right. Everyone dismount with pistols. Link up."

The five accomplished the task quickly to remount their suits.

"Stay close. Let's go."

Harrigan led them into the water, eyeing Kora nervously. No one panicked, even when water began to cover the suits' shoulders. They all remained dry, linked, and making progress.

Sixty feet into the river, almost halfway, the ground sloth squealed. It dropped back onto all fours over Kora. Harrigan did not understand why the sloth had moved until it bolted north along the riverbank. Then he saw it — tan, muscular, and almost nine feet long — the biggest cat he had ever seen.

This silent, ten-inch-fanged *Smilodon* was half again the size of any Harrigan had ever seen. It padded down a ravine toward Kora, who lay unconscious thirty feet from it.

"Do you see it?" Lloyd screamed.

"I've...I've almost got it sighted. I'll shoot it!" Freund quavered.

Harrigan saw Freund trying to raise his suit's arm out of the water to target the cat. But it was too deep. He experienced the same. Harrigan began to run through the water but the soldiers, tied last in the line, started retreating. He fumbled for the Arabic phrase for "cross the river." Unable to recall it, he yelled, "Mannie, Bart! Pull them across. I've got to get closer."

The cat now crouched twenty feet from the girl. Harrigan knew it would fight for its meal. He grabbed his tranquilizer pistol and pounded the access panel's latch. The robotic bear's chest immediately flooded with silty water, momentarily pinning him to the rear of the compartment. He watched the cat flex its muscles and extend its deadly claws, preparing to pounce. He thrust himself from the water.

Harrigan raised his weapon as he swam, now only six feet from the shore. The *Smilodon* leaped just as Harrigan's dart punctured its right front paw, harmlessly squirting its contents in the air. Immediately the cat tucked its paw under itself and landed on its chin—inches from Kora—with a muffled crack. Frenzied at the distraction, the animal shook the needle out of its paw and drew back to pounce again.

Almost out of the water and within twelve feet of the cat, Harrigan aimed his weapon with shaky hands. The beast snarled, bearing its two neck-slashing canine sabers and its meat-cleaving carnassial molars deeper within murderous jaws.

It pounced again at Kora and stabbed its front claws into her thigh, pinning her in place. Then its sabers disappeared deep below her brown and white pelt smock. She did not stir but sagged belly-up as the cat lifted her off the ground. Harrigan gasped, despairing, and fearing now for his own life.

The smock tore and Kora fell to the ground with a thud. The bite had only caught her clothes, but the cat crouched over Kora's body, snarling, and looking up at Harrigan. He fired, pinning the cat's tongue to its lower jaw. Again, the round had pierced the flesh and delivered its payload into the air. The cat tossed its head, dislodging the needle. Harrigan nearly panicked as he fired two soaked duds, which plopped ineffectually to the ground. One round remained. He fired between the animal's furious eyes. The needle penetrated the cat's forehead.

Harrigan sighed as the *Smilodon* hung its head lower, drooling. But it remained standing, its serrated sabers directly above the girl's abdomen. Even if it passed out and dropped, it would stab her fatally.

Harrigan leaped into the air, cocking his knees back to his chest and aiming his boot heels directly at the needle still embedded in the cat's head. The cat raised its head and opened its mouth to sever Harrigan's lower legs. His boots hit the left saber and wedged momentarily against its right. The wrenching impact snapped the tooth at its base, sending the jagged saber flying to stick upright in the dirt. The *Smilodon's* jaw clamped shut on Harrigan's high-top boots and jeans, slicing shallowly into his skin, and halting his leap in mid-air. He fell to the ground beside Kora, the cat still holding his foot—and its other saber—above her unprotected stomach.

Harrigan kicked his feet, forcing release from the cat's jaws. Quivering with rage, the cat struggled to rise above Harrigan. The broken tooth socket dripped blood on him. The cat grunted, closed its eyes, and collapsed forward, its intact tooth plunging toward Harrigan's own gut. He could not stop the deadly fall.

Harrigan saw a swift lateral blur above, Lloyd's robot hands grabbing the tooth and yanking the cat's massive head far enough aside for the saber to strike the dirt beside Harrigan's ribs. The cat lay motionless, asleep.

"Get another round in before it wakes up!" Harrigan blurted.

Lloyd jumped from the bear suit with his pistol. He fired one round into the *Smilodon's* shuddering thigh. "Never saw one like that, here or at Megiddo. Huge." Lloyd paused for a moment and addressed Freund. "Good thing you jerked those blokes' chains to bring them across, or I'd have never gotten close enough to join the fray."

Freund walked up in his heavy lift suit, dragging Harrigan's behind him. He dismounted, checking Kora and Harrigan for wounds. The guards followed, offering some excuse about not knowing Harrigan wanted to keep crossing once the *Smilodon* came into view.

Harrigan rose, stumbled toward one of the guards, and swung a fist wildly at his face. Freund pulled Harrigan back, then released him as the other guard reached for his pistol.

"Oh, you wanna use that gun on me?" Harrigan shouted. "Come on, you cowardly scum. I can handle you, too!"

Freund disarmed the guard with a wrist-wrench and brought him to his knees.

Harrigan, still yelling, grabbed the first soldier by his throat and thrust him to the ground by the other guard. "You two miserable... *soldiers*... will return to the motor pool *now*. I'll deal with you later."

Harrigan raised his hand to slap both guards, but they ducked and scurried to their suits. They immediately retreated across the river and disappeared into the forest.

Najik had been called away. So, the guard's unit commander in the

Control room radioed to offer two more guards.

"Keep your worthless soldiers away," Harrigan growled. He caught his breath and turned to his friends. "You two saved my life. Thanks."

Freund treated Harrigan's and Kora's cuts and abrasions. He even packed antibiotics into the *Smilodon's* tooth socket. Then Harrigan had Lloyd lift the girl into Freund's suit and the expedition trudged off to her cave. The party moved uphill, just inside the thick forest, to reach two surrogates waiting on the sloped rock below the Neanderthal caves. They mouthed excuses as they received Kora. Harrigan replied with only a glare, turning his party around for the return trip.

A half a mile south, they witnessed an eight-foot-long *Geochelone atlas* tortoise being devoured by seven monstrous dire wolves, *Canis dirus*.

"Whoa," Harrigan exclaimed, "what bite force those wolves have to rip scaled legs and neck of a six-foot-tall, armored animal like that? Surrogates report *Geochelone atlas* is nine percent of the sapiens' diet. They set traps, then bind their beaks and claws."

"Lots of evidence, guys" Lloyd added, "that early humans as far back as *fifty thousand years* used boats to populate the Pacific, even the Americas, spreading *G. atlas* as a food source.

"Hey, can get the shell out for my kids?" Freund asked.

"Are you kidding?" Harrigan replied, "Najik would go ballistic. It's against the contract."

It was late, already dark, and the three turned and headed toward the river at a tired trot. Harrigan radioed back the report that they would have to cross the river to camp on the east side, then cover the ten miles to the exit in the morning. They were no longer in the mood for recreation. They reached the river, checked the still-sleeping, *Smilodon*, and put the river between themselves and it before it awoke.

All three dismounted and were about to set up trip-wire alarms in the misty forest when Tykvah's voice blared over the radio.

"Kevin Harrigan! You have a screaming child here who's scared to death his father is going to be eaten! What kind of stunts are you three pulling out there?"

Harrigan rolled his eyes and hung his head, receiving smirks from his friends. "Is an answer possible for that question, Tykvah? We're fine and we'll be back by noon tomorrow."

"You're in trouble, Kevin. Where is your judgment? You are a husband and father! I love you…and I couldn't stand it if something…"

A brief series of distant, low-pitched howls gashed the conversation. The men stared at each other and tried to present confident smiles and postures. Each gripped his weapon more tightly.

"It's all right, Tykvah, everything's okay. Really. I'll see you tomorrow. I love you. Ben's not at the mic, is he?"

Ben's small voice came on, quavering. "Daddy, I love you and I'm scared. I'm really sc— Daddy, *please* come home!"

Chapter Nine

At dawn, Harrigan crawled out of his heavy-lift suit in the temporary camp to a chilly zephyr whispering across his skin. He felt stiff from bumps, bruises, and cuts.

He stepped to the river's edge. The wind was clearing the fog, but a tall wisp reminded him of the cathedral in Boston and the hallucination that had so shaken him twelve years before. Guilt and sorrow tugged, and he could barely swallow. He stripped and dived in his underwear below the cool river's surface. Suddenly the memory of an odd admonition he had received from Ranger instructor Gaines pierced his complacent calm. *Distinguish between friends and enemies.* Harrigan inhaled water as he surfaced. He coughed violently and climbed onto a rock, where he collected his wits and dried. He found himself contemplative yet very much in need of his companions, who now rose to greet the day.

"You're crazy jumping in there alone," Freund said, clamping his hands like jaws.

"I checked it out first. It was okay. I just needed to get clean. I...Never mind."

Harrigan turned toward Lloyd, who was wiping sleep from his eyes.

"Bart," Harrigan asked in a quiet tone, "do you believe in God?"

Freund perked up and regarded the other two with interest.

"Well, yes. I suppose so. Don't give it much thought, really. I guess the whole subject makes me uncomfortable. Doesn't it you?"

"Yes. I didn't mean to make you uncomfortable."

"No. That's not what I mean. It's just, well, I knew a bloke once at Oxford. Bloody pain in the derriere, he was pestering people with guilt trips 'nd having to 'get born again.' That sort of thing bothers. Not your query. Why d'you ask?"

Harrigan now included Freund directly by a glance. "We study the mechanisms of life. But we still can't figure out what makes personalities; what makes people able to choose while animals act on instinct. Well, I'm drifting, I guess. The reason I asked is that I had an unsettling dream, night before last."

"You don't put stock in dreams, do you? I mean, a hard-headed bloke like yourself."

"Well, I know what Mannie would say about this. So, I'll ask you,

Bart. Then you can both tell me if I'm just stressed or what."

Harrigan paused, looking out at the fog-cleared and shimmering river. "It started...I was staring at the bathroom mirror. As I continued to look, I began to feel a gloating, powerful feeling. Intense, even enjoyable. Then, rapidly, my face became grotesque, evil-looking, and more so with each passing second. I began to feel really scared. And I don't scare easily. But this feeling of power was increasing right along with the fear. In a few seconds, I began to suspect it was a trap.

"My reflection reversed, becoming normal, and the feelings dissipated. But it felt like it could return at any moment. I turned from the mirror, and everything was black. It was so strange. I felt I was infinitely, agonizingly, alone. Then I saw a saddened face, like the pictures of Christ back home." Harrigan's eyes began to water.

"Whatever it was, it was not a picture. I felt—if you laugh, I'll throw you in the river—like I was a kid, being hugged by my parents." A tear fell from Harrigan's cheek.

"I know this is far-fetched. But I woke up crying, totally unsettled. Even had to check the mirror. I felt I had to make sure my family was still there; make sure the world I was used to was still there. Is that weird or what?"

Lloyd just stared at Harrigan, incredulous to see him cry.

Freund raised his eyebrows. "Was this 'hug' thing last in the dream?"

Harrigan looked down, feeling drained just from relating his story. "No, actually. I pulled away. I don't know why. And I sensed that the figure was crying, somehow feeling more intense sadness than I could comprehend. I felt responsible. Then I woke up, as I said."

Freund persisted. "If it's just nerves it'll go away with stress management. If there's more to it, you'll sense the whisper subtly yet unmistakably. And, if you're open to it and sacrifice your own judgment to it, it brings inspiration and joy."

"You've been telling me that stuff for years, Mannie. I'm not totally rejecting it but..."

"You need a vacation, old boy," Lloyd interjected. "That's what I think. In any event, if we're going to see much more and get out by noon, we'd better get back at it, eh?"

Harrigan smiled, embarrassed to have related such things. He wanted to get back and comfort his family, but he too felt eager to continue exploring. The men rose, cleaned up the area, and remounted.

A quarter-mile south, a bristly-haired, carnivorous boar— *Metridiochoerus*—leaped from a thicket, blocking their path like a giant guard dog. It stood five feet at its hulking black shoulders and snapped ravenously at them, brandishing two-inch fangs and ten-inch tusks protruding left and right from its snout. Beyond, a female without tusks eyed them from amidst half-grown, three-foot-tall piglets ripping a six-foot-long catfish apart and fighting over the remains.

The group backed up, rerouting well around them farther downriver. At the edge of the falls, they filmed a real *Ursus spelaeus*. The twelve-foot-long cave bear was trying to snatch fish in an eddy. As their stomping suits approached, it turned, stood erect, clawed the air, and roared.

Harrigan spoke slowly. "All right. It's not mating season, so it won't attack. Just walk *way* around it—and don't do anything fast. I'll watch him and follow you shortly."

As the bear rose and bounded at Harrigan, his stomach clenched.

"Holy sh-...Run!" Harrigan screamed into his microphone as he turned toward his friends. "I hope," he called between thuds and jarring, "these suits...are faster...than the...real thing!"

Easily outdistancing the bear, Harrigan began to feel safe, almost invincible in the awkward but enjoyable robotic suit, and finally purged of the previous day's angst and this recent scare. The three stopped near the riverbank, laughing.

Freund breathed heavily from the run. "I've never had a better time in my life!"

"Same here," Lloyd said. "They'll make a mint when this place is converted to a park."

Harrigan drew away from sucking on his water siphon. "Well, we'll never see any of that money once Iraq can do this on its own." Harrigan hesitated, remembering that Lloyd barely spent three months of the year at the preserve while Freund kept shuttling back and forth from Megiddo. "When will you go back to see Gertrude and the kids next, Mannie?"

"I suppose in a week or so. You and I have a lot to do Monday with Gregor, then at least a week of analyzing data after that. How about you, Bart? Where are you off to next?"

"Najik has me off next week to the South Pacific. He wants a fossil *Varanus priscus*, often called a *Megalania*. *V. priscus* is easier. He wants more material, not Komodo cousins, to add to what an Iraqi team found. And another 'charmer' rumored hiding in the outback of southern and northeastern Australia: *Thylacoleo carnifex*. The wombat from hell, I gather."

Harrigan perked up, angered. "*V. priscus*, the giant lizard?"

"And *Thylacoleo*, the buck-toothed, marsupial lion? Wrong! Nobody goes on expeditions or starts projects without *my* say-so! What the hell does Najik think he's going to do with killers like those? A *priscus* would eat one of these robot suits for a snack and thylacs would be as vicious as *Smilodons*!

No go, Bart."

"I was given to understand by Najik that he—"

"I'll deal with that…Najik, are you monitoring this?"

"Yes, Dr. Harrigan, this is Lieutenant Colonel Najik. We discuss when you return."

"Get this, Najik: Keep crossing me. I'll have you relieved."

"When you return, Dr. Harrigan. When you return."

"Don't let it ruin the day," Freund said in a calming tone. "You'll square him away."

"I didn't mean to cause a problem, Kevin," Lloyd called.

"I know, Bart. It's okay. I'll have a word with Mon. That is, if he will take time from his presidential campaign to deal with this. Well, let's salvage *some* fun this morning!" Harrigan looked at his console and noticed that it was approaching nine. "Let's pick up the pace if you guys want to see the rest of the east half by noon."

"Off we go, then, wha—" Lloyd turned and ran into an oak tree. "Ooff! Watch out for that tree, chaps!"

The other two smirked and chuckled. They began to trot, leaving the river and crossing the band of forest, almost into a magnificent herd of red and black tufted Imperial Mammoths. Each man stopped and flipped his telephoto lens into place.

Three adult males were converging from different directions on the usually exclusively matriarchal group. These loner-bulls were each about fifteen feet tall at the shoulder and had thick, curling tusks. They towered above eleven scurrying females whose tusks were only half the length of the bulls'. They began to joust, sounding more like freight train blasts than elephant bleating.

"We shouldn't get any closer," Lloyd warned. "It's mating season, and Smythe tells me the bulls are known to charge. They're faster than elephants, as fast as our suits."

"Fine. We'll go around no closer than this." Harrigan ordered, adjusting his camera. He knew Ben would love this. The combatants' blasting roars grew louder, more frequent, and threatening.

As Harrigan watched, two males jabbed at the largest male, ripping its trunk at the base. The old mammoth reared up, his tusks entangled with those of his rivals. He thrust sideways then pulled backward, freeing himself but cracking his twenty-foot-long left tusk. Blood gushed as the youngest bull rushed the elder and jumped upon the sagging tusk, snapping it off. The old bull shook his head violently and retreated eastward for forest and mountain ridge. It was chased relentlessly by the next oldest but escaped, vanquished.

"Control!" Harrigan shouted into his microphone, "There's an aging mammoth moving toward the ridge east of us. He's lost a tusk. Send out a vet crew and fix him up, please."

"Yes, Doctor. Control out."

The youngest bull now turned and caught the female. The other pursuing bull attacked and ripped a nearby tree.

"Magnificent creatures!" Lloyd shouted. "Absolutely unparalleled."

The men trotted southward, putting the roughest of the hilly ground behind them. As they scaled one last rise, a four-foot-tall gray cone pointed directly at Lloyd from a thicket. The image did not immediately register in Harrigan's mind, nor Lloyd's, apparently.

"What's this here? By Jove! It appears to be an—"

The *Elasmotherium* sprang from the bushes at Lloyd with a loud, growling snort, its single volcano-like horn raised menacingly. Then the imposing beast halted and turned its grotesque head sideways. The rhino-like creature's thick, gold fur covered the upper third of the giant's eight-foot-tall body and contrasted with the long burgundy wool below. The creature was nearly as wide as it was tall. Now its massive head swung straight again on hulking shoulders and its feet furiously kicked clods of earth behind it. Harrigan gasped, knowing the horn's impact would knock Lloyd unconscious if it did not pierce the armored suit. The Englishman jumped right, then inadvertently slipped left. He leaped high and twisted in an apparent attempt to right himself. The maneuver landed him face-down atop the bewildered beast.

"Ride 'em, Bart!" Harrigan, astounded, shrieked with laughter.

"Bart, stop!" Freund yelled. "You've been watching too many American rodeo films."

Up and over the rise Lloyd rode the beast, clutching its neck and loins with his friends in close pursuit. After a moment, it seemed to realize that it had nothing to charge. It stopped short, sliding Lloyd forward hard into its horn. It shook its head furiously as Harrigan and Freund hemmed it in between them. It bucked like a horse and threw Lloyd, who landed on his back with a mighty thud. The *Elasmotherium* fled into the brush still snorting and kicking.

"Are you okay, Bart?" Harrigan knelt beside his fallen comrade.

"Oh, my head! But, yes, I suppose so. What a ride!"

"Is your back all right?" Freund asked loudly.

"I'm fine, old boy," Lloyd reassured. "If I can survive that beast with a minor bump to the bean, I can take on anything! Not to worry. Let's move on, chaps. Where's your sense of adventure? Oh, oww!"

Freund dismounted to examine Lloyd's head anyway. Harrigan

posted as guard while Freund administered first aid to the overconfident British cowboy before the group continued.

The explorers neared the east escalator entrance around noon and called for an all-clear check. The all-clear was not issued, however. Something moved, obscured in foliage beside the access door. A recorded saber-tooth snarl and artificial scent were emitted to repel two immense tan *Ancylotheriums*, which thrust gargantuan horse-like heads out from the canopy, revealing brawny necks and raised-up claws. The herbivores immediately faced the source of the sound and scent. Adult 'ancies' were known to crush *Smilodons* with their wide, three-clawed hooves powered by two-foot-wide, muscular legs. A belligerent male approached for a fight.

"Control, open the hatch now! There's an ancy up here thinking we're *Smilodon* because of your stupid repellent—he'll stomp us!"

The grass-covered hydraulic hatch opened. They rushed in, just avoiding the feisty giant.

After spending time with Tykvah and Ben, Harrigan walked to Najik's house and invited him down to the lamp-lit street, where he stopped at a corner bench and stared Najik directly in his cold eyes.

"You've been copying my ciphered files, and monitoring conversations. You've kept my people's scientific papers out of journals, yet we've honored the contractual secrecy on the sapiens research. Several of my staff have been tailed on furloughs. File transfers never reached their destinations. Now you're usurping my authority with Dr. Lloyd. I am going to discuss these issues with Minister Mon. If I get my way, you'll lose your command."

"Dr. Harrigan, you are most cor-rect. I have been afraid that you or your people would try to smuggle valuable commercial secrets. I fear I will be held per-sonally responsible for patents lost. I offer you and staff apologies. Please do not cause discipline from my superiors."

Harrigan was taken aback by Najik's admission and conciliatory tone. "You have said nothing about assigning Dr. Lloyd without my approval."

"The contract states that, ahf-ter the sixth year, species selection is the pre-ro-gative of the Preserve. I thought you knew that."

"The Zoological Preserve is supervised by the Project Director, which is me."

"Of course. But anything not specifically listed as a responsibility of the Project Director becomes a pre-ro-gative item and, hence, controlled by a go-vern-ment representative—me. I do regret any misunderstanding, Dr. Harrigan. Truly."

"Why the hell do you want a *V. priscus* and a *Thylacoleo*, anyway?"

"The first usable specimen of *V. priscus* was recently found in an unidentified dynastic structure in this country. Minister Mon believes this reptile was Bel-Marduk, once our people's symbol. I and Colonel Hassan hope to be in his graces by helping revive our heritage. As for marsupial lions, these will keep herbivores from overgrazing our pristine plateau."

Harrigan did not see Najik's idea as even practicable. "*V. priscus* is cold-blooded and doesn't hibernate. How will it get enough nourishment in winter?"

"Like the turtles, in arti-ficial-ly heated burrows. They will retain enough heat to hunt in the cold for hours from gi-gan-to-thermy and they can live weeks on one deer."

"Listen, Najik: Two *priscuses* and six *Thylacoleos* — max. And I have veto power over your safety precautions when they affect experiments or the other taxa. That's in the contract too. I want your animals to have shock chips implanted and signal emitters placed at the sapiens caves, water supplies, and hunting areas to repel them. Speaking of safety, I want Kora's surrogates disciplined for lack of supervision. I also want the rest to be more loving to those children!"

Harrigan paused, wondering if he would have said this only a few years ago. He felt his judgment had at least improved.

"Very well, Dr. Harrigan. I agree. Now we understand each other better. How do you Americans put it? Our fences are mended between good neighbors! Right. Perhaps now we can come to trust each other, yes?"

Sunday morning, Harrigan watched with anticipation the whirlwind of preparation his staff was making. The Genetics and BC labs buzzed with activity as hundreds of accelerated-growth human embryos from around the world, and the Preserve's own ancient stocks, were in meiosis. He inspected the forming of the twenty-three chromosomes of would-be baby girls' eggs. He delighted in his team's inventiveness that enabled him to monitor and manipulate the otherwise illusive chemistry of life. They were making history, tracing human genes from early Cro Magnons through moderns.

Very few of the three hundred thousand eggs in each embryo could be harvested and observed in the time window provided by nature.

First, it was not visually obvious which cells were undergoing the fleeting process at any given moment. Second, the chromosomes formed in under an hour beginning at slightly different moments in each of the embryos' eggs. If extracted too early, the process would not take place. Too late and it would have been missed. Harrison leaned over the closest lab table, relieved that one new tool helped them overcome these obstacles. The lab had developed a retrovirus that, stripped of its deadly genetic codes, could invade the embryo. It followed chemical pathways to the developing egg cell and "read the molecules" on its surface, which signaled that meiosis was about to occur. Once cued in this manner, the virus released a spring-loaded "molecular hook." This hook pierced the cell membrane; snagged and retrieved the nucleus with its still-assembling chromosomes.

A scanner indicated when that molecular hook had sprung. When it had a nucleus hooked, the virus was withdrawn from the cell. The DNA strand formation could then be observed directly. The process also revealed RNA formations and their activities as regulators. The short-lived "primary" meiotic RNA assemblages, now referred to as M1-RNA, acted to either suppress or express DNA segments. All of this activity took place during the linking together of DNA strands to form the chromosomes that would have become half of the coding required for a human being.

Chromosomal formation observations were tricky. Only some of thousands of simultaneously occurring linkups could be tracked at a time.

This viral incision method was first developed at the lab as a way to detect and repair genetic errors, usually caused by the inevitable inbreeding of animal stocks. It could also insert DNA segments into a selected point on any chromosome, but now the technique was used to reveal how certain traits were transmitted or archived between generations of humans.

By late afternoon all of the staff except Dr. Gregor Ruliev were assembled to view the results of their investigations of meiosis. Dr. Ruliev had insisted on continuing Freund's behavior trait DNA project nonstop.

The scientists were gabby at this phase, culminating in the Genetics Lab. Harrigan especially hoped it would be a breakthrough in this, his life's work. All hushed as a wall monitor displayed tabular information about the M1-RNA of more than two hundred ethnic groups.

The group names were arranged in columns and rows, lines connecting them as in a family tree schematic. Below each name, the frequency of occurrence of one of several types of RNA molecules was reported, M1-RNA in red. Beside each frequency rating, a "confidence interval" of plus or minus some number of "standard deviations" was reported. Ethnic groups with the greatest prevalence of the M1-RNA appeared in the left-most columns. The far-left column listed only one group labeled "Hebrew-extracted." Columns in between included Celtic, Arab, European, Central American, African, and Asian groups.

Harrigan's face was pink, and his jaw hung open. "I'll...be...dog...gone! And so small a margin of error."

Tykvah had anticipated that he would question the results. She reassured him. "We've run this several times. The data from the meiotic process scanners don't lie."

Harrigan was not yet satisfied that the analysis was sound and, so reserved any conclusion. He needed to check on Tykvah's modeling and analysis. "Tykvah, did you run a debug on your model as well as a logic structural check constrained by both the modern and ancient genetic databases?"

"I knew that would be the first thing you'd suspect if we got any dispersion patterns at all, let alone one as clear as this. I ran both twice. The model is correct. This analysis is sound."

Freund grinned and exclaimed, "I always suspected it. Especially for a few groups like the Irish, and now there's proof. It's just amazing."

Harrigan looked surprised. "Why would anybody suspect that the entire world's population carries Hebrew genes coding for the production of an RNA molecule that only shows up during meiosis?" He jabbed a pencil at Freund. "Answer me that."

"I didn't mean the molecule, *per se*. I mean that I always suspected that the Hebrews, dispersed to every corner of the globe, assimilated with all ethnic groups. This may even be a clue to why they have always been referred to as the 'Chosen People.' There must be something about M1-RNA that mankind needs, something wonderful from a better past... Eden."

Harrigan still did not have his answer and frowned. "Whoa, Mannie! Why did you have this suspicion? And I don't want any 'chosen people' or mankind-before-the-fall nonsense."

"Historians have long suspected this, first from the Bible then archaeological and longitudinal studies of cultures. The Celts, including the Irish, were the only people of their time to use the same chariot and war tactics as the Bible describes of the Hebrews."

"Coincidence."

"And there's the fair skin noted in descendants of one of Hebrew forefather Ephraim. Such a description of complexion is consistent with that of Nordic peoples like the Celts."

"So?"

"And the prevalence of blonde and auburn hair — like yours — in both Ephraim's descendants and the Celts is noteworthy."

"A few similarities, Mannie. You can find coincidences in any two populations. Your hypothesis would fail any rigorous tests of correlation."

"Well, there's also the use of the surname prefix 'Ben,' meaning 'son of' in Hebrew names. Just like the Celtic 'O' and 'Mac.' Few other ethnic groups used surname prefixes with that meaning. It's found in Greek and Slavic names — but the results show those lineages as also having a high prevalence of M1-RNA. There is scant record of this surname prefix before the Assyrian invasions dispersed the Northern Hebrew Tribes — around seven-twenty-two B.C."

"There's just not enough evidence."

"And there's the fact that they shared similar, otherwise unheard-of, taboos about food and the like. Wait. Do I see you fidgeting, Kevin?"

Harrigan glared at him.

Freund continued. "Then there are the Greek history tablets that describe a people called the 'Kimmeri' who invaded the Balkans from Turkey. Historians have long established that the Kimmeri left the Balkans to move to points north, including Ireland, around five hundred B.C."

"Anything else?"

"Yes. Numerous Assyrian wall hieroglyphs peg one of the lost tribes of Israel as being the Kimmeri — the same written about by the Greeks."

Harrigan looked at Tykvah who just grinned. She faded and the vision invaded his mind, a glistening woman warning him to choose wisely.

He shook his head and turned, irritated but still good-natured, back to Freund. "You're testing if I'll get mad or show I'm bigoted or something, is that it? This analysis only shows that the Celts have the second greatest prevalence of M1-RNA. Let's have a look at the generational interpolation analysis. That will show whether there's any more evidence that the Irish and the rest of the world inherited Hebrew genes. You do the honors."

"I didn't mean to put any distinguished leprechauns present on the spot!" Freund ribbed. "Okay, I did mean to! And I think your reaction is a riot! Let's see if I'm right. System: Display generational interpolation analysis. Put geographic mapping on screen two."

Both screens flashed. The first displayed a family tree linking all modern peoples but now in chronological order of M1-RNA transmission.

The second screen showed a world map. Its moving arrows showed a geographic pattern of transmission emanating from the Middle East.

All jaws dropped again. Harrigan was incredulous. "Astounding!"

Each stared at the other. Then Harrigan ordered one more screen to display. "System: Display regression on screen three."

The confidence intervals had to widen to show any links, indicating lower confidence in the regression analysis. Nevertheless, these intervals indicated that the output was reliable. The molecule was shown to have passed into and then dispersed out from the Hebrew-extracted line.

Harrigan solicited interpretations. They batted theories, excited declarations, and "what ifs" around. Freund had to admit that, even though the origin and transmission were now in little doubt, he had no evidence for his belief in its purpose. Then Harrigan noticed that Dr. Ruliev had been ignoring all, despite his gregarious and talkative nature.

Suddenly, Ruliev jumped up from his workstation and turned. He shouted at the top of his lungs to the crowd of fellow scientists, forcing everyone to be silent and listen to him.

"I've have found eet! Dr. Freund, Dr. Harrigan, e-ver-y-one! These strands are not 'junk DNA,' as people have thought for decades! Most of these haplotype codes for personality traits and related propensities, like aggression," Ruliev continued. "They're hun-dreds of times the complexity of those we have mapped even in primates! Each one is sl-lightly different…and one new set is added each generation!"

Harrigan walked over and nervously placed his hand on Ruliev's shoulder. "Shh!" Then he called to the staff, "He's excited our genetics give validity to the next two-year phase of anthropological studies."

Ruliev ignored the diversion and continued, exuberant. "In meiosis — everyone must see this — half a new set of traits is formed, and the previous sets are rendered dormant by this M1-RNA! It does more than prevent speciation. It preserves — potentially expresses — special haplotypes, records of parents back to…whoever was first! Fellow pioneers, we have found the basis of per-son-hood — and we can read that of each of our ancestors!"

Chapter Ten

Northern Plateau Marshlands, Al-Rajda Zoological Research Preserve
1653 hours, 2 December 2034

Dark clouds were imposing night upon the evergreen-dotted terrain.
A north breeze further chilled all. Twelve sets of human eyes peered through
snow-draped pine boughs, which hid the hunters like a mother's apron over
young bullies. Warm and camouflaged in fur clothing, they eyed fourteen
elephant-sized, brown, and black woolly rhinos grazing just to their west.
The Cro-Magnon males, now the equivalent of fifteen- to twenty-year-olds,
thrilled in their trespass.

The two winded surrogate fathers, Ali and Harun, followed too far
back to see that the line of hunters had halted and spread out. They clomped
through icy mud trying to catch up. The pair only now realized where they
were: The objects of their loose supervision neared a spear-lined pit dug
months earlier by Neanderthals.

Harun neared the Cros, crouched on their haunches under trees just
ahead. He caught his breath and yelled in Nostratic, "Pit! Do not leave trees!
Stupid bastards! No fall into —"

Mo'ara, the Cro's de facto leader, glared back at his assumed father,
now running noisily into view. "Shhh! *Coelodonta!*" He turned and continued
to study the herd.

Three *Coelodonta* raised their shaggy heads and squinted at the tree
line. A large male stood three feet from the camouflaged pit. Grass blew off
the creature's four-foot-long snout horn but, still caught on the base of the
smaller horn behind, fluttered and tapped against its fist-sized brown eye.
The rhino threw its head up into the breeze, ejecting the grass tuft, then
resumed pulling bundles of grass into its undulating mouth with downy,
gray lips.

The surrogates fell silent, stripped of pride for having twice today
alerted potential quarry. The pair advanced quietly and knelt on either side
of Mo'ara, who ignored them and swept his left hand slowly forward, then
held it horizontal. The young Cro waited for the bull to step closer to the
hole's edge before he would order an attack. As the bull stepped, Mo'ara
dropped his hand and shrieked. His comrades rushed wildly from the woods
with multicolored spears.

The herd bolted away to the southwest. The old bull thrust his
fearsome head up and lifted his front legs to jump and turn. The hoof-like
toenails stomped and crumbled the rim. The beast faltered onto its chest at

the edge, shaking the ground, and rolled sideways. One kick of its mighty hind legs sent the giant leaping ten feet out over the center of the trap. It fell across the opposite edge with a thundering rush of breath punched from his chest. The pit wall collapsed inward, bringing the panicked beast within a foot of spikes set upright in the floor.

The Cros rushed at the pit hurling spears, most of which bounced off the woolly titan.

Frantically gouging dirt, the *Coelodonta* thrust itself out and onto its side on the grass, then leaped defiantly to its feet. It bucked, hurling dirt rearward, and turned to face its attackers.

The Cro did not run. Mo'ara ordered his kin to hurl two spears, retain a reserve, and shout menacingly. One spear hung momentarily in its jaw while another bounced off its front horn. The *Coelodonta* roared and raced away to rejoin its herd. The Cro looked to Mo'ara, who glared momentarily at Harun and Ali and then held up his spear in salute to his hunters.

"You all have courage of fire," Mo'ara growled, ignoring the surrogates. "We defeat *Coelodonta* another day."

Ali's voice was shaky but loud. "When you do not follow us, you fail! We hunt tomorrow. Now you follow us back to trail."

One of the younger Cro piped up, surly and indignant. "No! We follow Mo'ara. You are weak. You warn prey."

Harun slapped the adolescent hard across the mouth. As he raised his hand again to sharpen the lesson, Mo'ara gripped it.

"No! Strike me," Mo'ara challenged him. "I disobeyed. You strike me...*now!*"

Harun stared into the Cro's eyes and felt frightened by his own alarming thoughts. *What would you do if you knew you had been deceived for so long? If you knew how we sap your blood and study you, would you kill us in our sleep or face to face?*

All sixteen of the Preserve's surrogates had been increasingly plagued by such worries. Frustration, too, had mounted over their own primitive living conditions, brief furloughs, and the defiance of their "children" and "grandchildren."

Deep, gruff howls sounded in the distance as snow began to fall in heavy, wet flakes. Harun placed his left hand on Mo'ara's shoulder and spoke softly. "Release me...son. Soon you see me never. Respect me until you may lead."

The Cro grinned at Harun, releasing his hand only to brazenly spit, and turned to his kin. "Gather spears. We follow Harun back."

The troop proceeded north toward their caves, led by Harun and trailed by Ali. Soon, the expert trackers found six-inch-wide paw prints in the deepening snow — cave lions, at least five. Harun led the Cro past several hillocks to a brushy ridge where they heard a deafening lion attack in progress around what appeared from a distance to be a five-foot-tall dome. Stealthy and camouflaged, they moved in.

A motley brown, egg-shaped *Daedicurus* swung its deadly mace-tail wildly. With sharp claws on stubby legs, it slashed back at the tenacious lions. The armored mammal contorted, squealing like a deep-voiced pig, and scrambling for cover between trees and in ruts. It alternated between hugging the ground, legs and head tucked inward, and active combat. But the immense black-maned lions far exceeded the herbivore's remarkable speed and agility.

The male lion leaped upon the glyptodont's shell to get at the base of its lethal tail. Like a huge scorpion, the aging *Daedicurus* jack-knifed its tail and clubbed the great cat in its thickly muscled right shoulder. The big cat's deafening bellow threw the lions into disarray. The snarling females backed off as their male thrashed about. It managed to sink its fangs into the thick mace-tail. The *Daedicurus* returned the gouge by severing the lion's own tail with its rear claw.

This confusion was Mo'ara's signal. He grabbed two of his kin and dragged them forward, shouting and screaming at the animals.

"No! Must wait!" Harun ordered but was ignored.

The hunters followed Mo'ara without hesitation, forming an intimidating cascade of hunters descending directly upon the shocked cats. The boys knew to thrust their spears like pikes, rather than to throw them. The Cro hurled rocks and wood as they charged.

The lions turned in every direction, unable to reason which enemy threatened them most. The wounded male jumped up and faced the attacking humans. The *Daedicurus* crouched to the ground and waved its bloodied tail in every direction, splintering trees. Mo'ara thrust a spear at the male, wounding its cheek. The females crouched low, muscles bulging and ready to spring into a counterattack, as the male recoiled onto its haunches, roared, and clawed the air.

The line of hunters advanced, jabbing and shouting, their faces as contorted and enraged as those of the cats, which roared and feigned attack. This final, snarling attempt to intimidate the humans having failed, the male lion turned and fled, followed by the females.

Without hesitation, Mo'ara turned to the *Daedicurus* and pierced its neck. His fellows followed with spear jabs to its tail and legs.

Harun, astounded, looked from Mo'ara to Ali and back. The Cro victors took only the animal's legs and tail for meat. The mace at the tail's end was removed for a trophy. The Cro knew well the dangers of tarrying at a kill. Dismemberment took only minutes. Everyone smeared blood on their faces.

Mo'ara looked coldly to Harun. "Lead us home, great father," he said with a cynical tone.

Harun could barely meet the young man's eyes. He resumed leading the northward trek through deepening snow. Unable to find the trail, he decided to walk along the base of the rock ridge. Soon a distant glimmer of fire appeared: the Neanderthal caves.

Ali came forward to Harun to speak in Arabic. "We are not permitted to let the Cro-Magnons and Neanderthals meet. That is for more than a year from now."

"Each clan is aware of the other. Do you want to walk through the forest around their caves seven extra miles? We can walk just inside the tree line when we near their caves. They will not see or smell us until we're well north of them, if at all."

"Fine. It is on your head!"

The group neared the Neanderthal caves, avoiding the pungent odor of sloth. They heard Nostratic speech, so Harun guided the Cro deeper into the woods. But after a few moments, he noticed that he was alone with Ali, who was trudging sleepily behind.

At the base of the rock ridge, directly below the two Neanderthal caves, Kora and her mate, Rhahs, sat talking. Abdul, their surrogate father, sat nearby shivering despite the drugs that enhanced his blood's heat retention and body hair. His barrel chest, muscular physique, and cosmetically altered skull allowed his "progeny" to believe that he was one of them. But Abdul had grown to hate this charade. He even hated Kora's pet sloth, Yom, which now nosed at him for attention and licked his arm.

Just then two spears struck the sloth's shoulders, narrowly missing the three humans. A blood-curdling whoop burst from the darkness. The giant ground sloth squealed and fled.

Kora screamed for her clan as Mo'ara ran into the midst of the three, pursuing Yom. Rhahs stood and extended his great, muscular arm. He caught Mo'ara in the chest, knocking the wind out of the tall Cro-Magnon, who gaped at the Neanderthal's foreign appearance. Mo'ara reached for Rhahs's throat, succeeding only in yanking hair. The two were quickly surrounded by eleven angry Cro. A dozen Neanderthals streamed out of the cave and the two groups faced off, screaming, and threatening each other with clubs, fists, and spears.

But they allowed the leaders to battle alone. Rhahs snatched Mo'ara's spear and thrust it viciously into the Cro's face. It penetrated a quarter of an inch into the tip of Mo'ara's nose before he managed to reverse the thrust. The two struggled and Mo'ara finally yanked Rhahs toward himself to throw him tumbling backward.

He kicked Rhahs in the stomach and the big Neanderthal fell in the snow. Scrambling to his feet, Rhahs grabbed Mo'ara's long hair and cocked his thick arm for a devastating punch.

Abdul's strong arms blocked the blow as Harun, breathless, rushed between the belligerents. Ali joined him and, along with all eight Neanderthal surrogate parents just arriving, gained tenuous control. Mo'ara, temporarily humbled, was made to admit his wrong. As reparations, he agreed to relinquish two *Daedicurus* legs — but actually surrendered only one. The surrogates, tired of the entire affair, acquiesced to this as sufficient.

The Iraqi men sent the Neanderthals back to their caves and sat the Cro-Magnons at the edge of the woods. Then, all ten moderns present trudged up the ridge to speak privately.

Abdul contained his own irritation at Harun, who addressed his grumbling countrymen and women in Arabic. "As the Americans say, this is the last straw on the camel!"

The others looked puzzled as he continued. "I will *not* put up with this place and these surly, disobedient freaks another minute…At the most, no more than another few months. I mean that they are ready to be on their own *now*. Are we scientists or babysitters?"

Ali expressed the same sentiment. "I've had enough too. Even though the Cro are almost a year younger, they are ready to be on their own. The willful bastards think they are in charge and I'm sick of it! And I'm sick of Najik!"

"I'll tell you what I'm sick of —" Faqizade, a Neanderthal surrogate mother, interjected. "I'm sick of these muscles and hair and only two weeks away each year. And I just know — I can sense — that someone is monitoring us when we are outside the Preserve."

Lishazad, another Neanderthal surrogate mother looked worried. "At least they don't monitor us through these walking stick communicators."

Harun slammed his fist on a rock. "Do you really know that they don't? Najik is a slave driver! Look, we *must* act together. You have a year to go and we on the Cro side have eight months beyond that. Both clans are good at hunting and have everything they need. To these ignoramuses, this place is…Eden. To me — and I know you all feel this way — this is hell!"

Abdul found himself in agreement. "And our work is no longer of scientific value, in my opinion. All they want anymore are blood samples, brain tissue extractions, eggs, and sperm. What do they need us for? Let the

Westerners take over!"

Ali almost spoke loud enough for the Cro to hear him. "We deserve our bonuses now! Harun and the rest of us on the Cro side have already decided how. Tell them, Harun."

"I've already spoken with the other Cro surrogates. They are ready to go on strike. Najik and his superiors are afraid that premature publicity about the sapiens portion of this project will cause them international embarrassment, all kinds of trouble. All we have to do is threaten to tell the press if they do not shorten our service and accelerate our bonuses. I say that we should send the Cro back alone via the north ridge. The rest of us should take the raft to the escalators and give Najik our ultimatum. We'll be in civilization by the end of Ramadan! Who is with us?"

Abdul rolled his eyes. "I am. But what do you—or anyone else here—care about Ramadan?"

"Why do you mock me? I just meant that we should negotiate getting out soon! Now, who is with us?"

Abdul looked around and found himself joining the nodding, nervous faces.

Harrigan and Tykvah drove toward a darkening Baghdad.

"Did you see that sign back there for new homes at Nineveh?" Harrigan asked.

"The place has been dead almost three thousand years. Now they're reviving it. No thanks! I don't like oil heat, the commute's too long, and it gives me the creeps," Tykvah huffed.

"Why the creeps?" Harrigan protested, "They've got some really nice houses going up there."

"Saved from destruction only to betray that mercy generations later, and now it's rubble."

"You sound like Mannie pushing me about right choices. Hey, hon, call the sitter please."

"Sure. Kevin, thanks for listening to Mannie and me about the sapiens. I was afraid you had lost respect for my opinions."

Harrigan smiled at her. "Where would Ben and I be without Mannie and Superwoman?"

She squeezed his neck and called the babysitter. "He did? Copies his incorrigible dad! We'll talk to him. Good night, Shedi." Tykvah tapped the phone and placed her hand on Harrigan's wrist. "Ben's fine. You need to talk with him about things only Dads get to do to Moms."

"What did he do?"

Tykvah chuckled, "He pinched Shedi's bottom, is what he did!"

"Okay, we'll sit down with him when we get back. But you start!"

"Kevin, did you know I love you?"

Harrigan placed his hand on Tykvah's. "I'm amazed, and very much in love with you."

Throughout the state dinner, he glanced warmly at her. When the gala finally ended at 2300 hours, he left for a side room to confer with Mon. Hassan tagged along, grimacing.

"Ismail, it is in your interest to preclude injury to the sapiens. We are learning so much about genetic influences on immunity, neurology, and behavior. But they are essentially us. We don't need to subject them to so much danger and such Spartan living conditions."

"Have any of the sapiens complained, expressed a need for closets or food pro-ces-sorrs? Or the embryos either, for that matter?"

Harrigan stared irate, surprised at the cynicism and this only instance of non-support. "You must agree that the sapiens need a sense of family to develop societal structures for a valid study."

"You could be correct there, and Najik has appraised the surrogates' performance as unsatis-factorry. But experts agree that most parents are psychologically violent, controlling of their children. This is an insight I personally experienced when my parents fled Egypt for Iraq. Yet I have developed well enough."

Harrigan felt oddly distracted. His eyes floated past Mon's to a small photo on the wall. It showed a bearded, stern-faced man in his fifties with mesmerizing eyes. Its brass placard read simply, 'Belial Asry Mon.' Suddenly Harrigan felt inexplicably uneasy. The room disappeared and his 'sinister reflection' from dreams flooded his vision. He blinked hard to lose it, snapping his attention back to his host. "You had a tough childhood, Ismail?"

Mon's stare was almost hypnotic. "You and I are the tough ones of this world, Kevin, we are those who shape this world. There has never been a substitute for stress in developing strength. Would the sapiens studies be valid, especially as to physiological and genetic results, if we removed stresses that actually existed during the time of these sub-species?"

"No, I...I guess not. Well, it's...hard to say, actually."

Harrigan debated within himself, questioning which was more important: his research, his life-long passion to explore and create, or the humans. He felt tired and had a headache. He was mustering the strength to contradict himself when Hassan's cell phone chimed. Hassan left the room and returned within moments to address Mon.

"Sir, it is Najik. He reports that the surrogates have left scant supervision with each clan and have confronted him to demand early bonuses and dismissal."

Mon raised his eyebrow and then frowned as Hassan continued summarizing Najik's call.

"Najik stated that they have threatened to expose the sapiens research to the press if their demands are not met. He reports that an unsupervised Cro hunting party is now five hours overdue at their cave. Monitors show the Cro headed southwest toward the yeti caves. I feel we must send a platoon to recover them."

Mon glared at Hassan.

Hassan's probably going to try to redeem himself by disciplining Najik for allowing mutiny, Harrigan thought with increasing alarm, *and blow the validity of our sapiens research!*

"Kevin, I have complete confidence," Mon said still, frowning at Hassan, "in *your* judgment. How would you handle rescue and the surrogates?"

"One moment, Premier," Harrigan said, examining the weather pattern on his phone. He returned Hassan's scowl. "We must not allow sapiens to know about the outside world yet. Grant the surrogates' demands in exchange for returning the Cro, hopefully before reaching the yetis. Send Lloyd in now with a few troops in heavy-lift suits to rendezvous and escort the surrogates. The backup is me leading a *squad* in a helicopter. There's no way to land in that terrain, so I need a small squad of airborne — your best. Rappelling gets us closer, but rotors would be heard, and we'd be seen. One 'copter and chutes will be concealed by low cloud cover and falling snow. We'll stop at the complex, don skins and 'chute packs, get tranquilizer weapons and take off again." Harrigan noticed the time, 2336 hours. "With any luck, the Cro'll turn back, yetis stay snoring."

Harrigan felt proud, having shone brightly while Hassan and Najik were impotent.

"Colonel Hassan," Mon growled, "Dr. Harrigan is in command. I want him equipped and just one squad of your Ready-jumpers airborne in five minutes. Arrange for Dr. Strauss' return to Al-Rajda. You could learn from Dr. Harrigan's courage and swift thinking."

Hassan glared. "Doctor, use your swift thinking to not get killed."

Harrigan inspected the last of his fur-clad soldiers, then crowded them into the whirring helicopter twenty yards south of the lab. His voice vibrated strongly on the intercom to the pilot. "No lights. Sound dampeners on. Drop us south of these coordinates."

"No," the pilot replied. "That's over rock, too close to trees, and too low for reserve chutes to open. There's a flat area to the north—"

"I'm in command here, Warrant Officer. The yeti would smell us there and the wind could disburse my squad if we jump higher. Been through this, young man. Have some faith." Before climbing into the back, Harrigan watched the pilot control the craft's take-off. *Good to learn what I can. Works just like the ones I saw in the States.* The flight took seven minutes.

"Stand up," Harrigan ordered. "Hook up. Check equipment." Men fastened tethers from their packs to a ceiling cable, traced the line and inspected each other. The trooper behind him tapped his forearm with a thumbs-up. Harrigan opened the door to snow and dark, obscured ground. "Go!" he commanded as he leaped first. Tethers yanked, deploying chutes, and snapping rubber connectors just below the craft's skids.

Harrigan rocked sideways like a banana upon the inclined rock, just missing trees. All unsnapped the risers and struggled to coil them about their triceps, progressing to collapse wind-inflated canopies. He turned. The cave was dimly lit a hundred yards northward.

He saw it as he turned again to wrestle his canopy: a reddish blur leaping from behind a rock, tearing into the opposite side of the puffed-up nylon. Huge, furry claws pierced several spots and it screeched identically to that in Lloyd's old video. Harrigan fumbled to draw his tranquilizer gun as a new rip revealed the yeti stumbling to extract itself. A gust tore material to fully expose it, and it rushed at Harrigan through the cone of risers. He could only throw the tangle at the beast, now a few feet away and reaching out at his face. As the jumble of cords snared the beast, Harrigan heard Lloyd yell something from behind.

The yeti extricated itself and shoved Harrigan aside, tangling the gun in risers and stumbling at Lloyd. Lloyd tripped backward to the ground. Harrigan leaped onto its back, tightening his arm around its throat by pulling on his wrist with his other hand.

"Shoot!" Harrigan screamed as the yeti clawed through the pelt at his arm. He looked around desperately, seeing his squad fumbling with their tranquilizer weapons. Lloyd rose and ran toward the cave yelling, "Thought we gassed them! Getting the bear-suit."

Harrigan sensed the yeti was losing air and strength. He choked its neck with all he had as it stumbled backward, crushing Harrigan against the ground. Unable to breathe, Harrigan's vision narrowed, and he perceived surrealistic gunshot reports and darts' clanking off rock around him. The yeti flailed its arms and legs weakly now, unable to penetrate the leathery parka. Harrigan's grip melted away as he passed out.

"Thank God!" Harrigan gasped as he realized he was alive at the rear of the cave. He looked around at Lloyd dressing his arm wounds and soldiers injecting the yeti he had just fought. Then he saw the terrible pile. "Did you have to kill them or—"

"The Cro, my friend," Lloyd responded, frowning. "Not a scratch on the young warriors."

"How did they manage to kill five yetis twice their size?"

"Harun tells me they always approach game stealthily, throw half their spears, then charge in a line to surround and spear survivors. At least we know they can bloody-well hold their own with the animals here. We'll have to replenish the yetis and keep an eye on these Cro blighters."

"Oww! Can you stop stitching a sec! What the hell is that by the fire?"

"It's a dug-out yeti head. Our 'helpless teenagers' ate.... Bloody retched when I saw it."

Harrigan glared at Ali and Harun. "Look: If you don't stamp out this helmet-making and brain-eating, they might just try it on you. Understand? And where are they?"

Harun answered for the two. "Yes, Doctor. We understand this. They are camped with two surrogates a half-mile north of here."

Harrigan confirmed for the still-agitated surrogates Najik's promise of early release. He instructed them to return north via the safer and easier ridge route once the guards and researchers left with the yetis' remains. The surrogates were ordered to avoid Cro contact with the Neanderthals on the return march.

As dawn approached, Harrigan and Lloyd departed with the soldiers for the walk back to the research complex. Tykvah, in tears, scolded Harrigan but lavished kisses on him. He promised to follow her back home shortly but needed to debrief Lloyd. He sat with Lloyd, exhausted and drinking coffee, in the research center break room.

"Bart, thank you for regaining control of the surrogates and the Cro, and for gassing and weakening that yeti. Things could have been far worse. I owe you."

"Thanks, old boy. If you had you not led the charge, that beast would have—"

"Mon thinks I have great judgment, better than his officers. But sometimes I wonder whether I'm on a leash of my own making. I wonder whether my choices are for good or evil."

"Everyone here respects you, old friend. We'd all follow you to hell and back."

'And back.' Can that even be? Harrigan lowered his eyes to the floor.

Chapter Eleven

Al-Rajda Motor Pool
0721 hours, 5 February 2035

Harrigan and Najik exchanged grimaces as Najik exited the west escalator with Corporal Abrih's six guards. The group cleaned the robotic suits and turned them over to Harrigan's science team. "What were you doing on the plateau last night?" Harrigan demanded.

"Good morning, Dr. Harrigan. Control alerted me yesterday that the *priscuses* were underr-nourished. So, I took out some deer for them. And we made surety the shock chips to work."

"You personally? In the middle of the night in a tractor...dirt and blood on your pants!"

"Yes, and such work is dirty indeed! I too am personally fas-ci-nated by these animals but almost never exper-rience the plateau. Surely you can appreciate—how do you call this?—camp out with buds? And I did not want to be in that bulky heavy-lift suit all of the time just to keep any straying sapiens from observing us."

Harrigan's eyes narrowed. "*Were* any sapiens far from the ridges? *Did* any see you?"

"Not to have worries. I had men to use heat-sensor goggles, being certain to be not observed. Your work today will be in the north, yes? Quite dangerous there unless you will be only on the ridges. Are you observing both clans?"

Harrigan ignored him and asked his second in command for the results of her inspection.

Her Bombay accent was not too thick. "*Megaloceros* pelt costumes, walking stick communicators—tranquilizer model three, standard loads—water, med kits. The entire packing list is here. We're all up, doctor." She pressed a box on her collar, starting a video log. "Present for this day-long observation are Project Director Kevin Harrigan, geneticist James Fong, zoologist Stefan Woj, veterinarian Carl Smythe, Paleo Lab Director Claude Olivier, and myself, anthropologist Ina Singh. Dr. Freund has been excused as his son, Hans, is in hospital with appendicitis."

Harrigan spoke privately to Singh. "Thank you, Ina. Later, please strike the personal part." Then he addressed the group. "Since I and a couple of you do not speak Nostratic, let Dr. Singh handle most of the talking. Okay, mount up!"

The east half of the plateau was the only route avoiding the *Varanus priscus* burrow. Harrigan approved. They all climbed into the tractor with the Iraqi driver and guard, received clearance, and ascended the east escalator. Soon they emerged onto the foggy, evergreen-spotted plateau. Crows and wind gusts were the only sounds on this snowless winter morning.

They passed fascinating animals — and a few vicious kills — to reach their destination of tree-lined and scruffy foothills at the base of the crux between the two ridgelines. The scientists tied the gift pelts to their furry parkas, left the guards inside, and trudged west toward the Neanderthal caves. Harrigan walked point, his tranquilizer "stick" held at the ready.

They trudged two miles through brambles and wet brush to get within sight of the caves. Visibility was at least sixty feet in this environment of leafless trees and saplings, until they entered thicker evergreen areas. The caves lay a hundred feet up the bare ridge beyond the last of the pines. They had almost reached the flat, open rock near the caves when they heard a low, bubbling sound like a small gas engine at idle. At first, the sound emanated from rustling trees between them and the ridge, then it seemed to be behind them as well. Out of both the north and south, they heard branches snap followed by light thuds upon the ground. The bubbling grew louder and seemed to surround them. Harrigan drew everyone into a circle.

The growls grew closer. Suddenly the bushes rustled, and a rabbit dashed past them in the undergrowth, followed by an immense black and gray blur.

The marsupial, easily two hundred pounds and almost five feet long, sported black, tiger-like stripes on thick, and gray fur. It bounded like a kangaroo past the group but halted, turning to eye the humans.

Harrigan stared at the dark, front-facing eyes and two adz-like buckteeth curling downward from the center of its angry snout. Muscly arms ended in four-inch thumb claws and inch-long finger claws on thick, ape-like hands.

"It's a thylac!" Harrigan breathed. "And it's coming back!"

Harrigan scanned from the beast to the canopy and back. His stomach tightened. *Arboreal pack hunters. Can this one be alone?* He grabbed for the emitter to activate the animal's safety chip: the holster was empty.

Suddenly high branches all around the group began to bounce. Barking yelps preceded each predator's drop from trees, and the swift repositioning of some now on the ground, as gaps in the fast-forming encirclement closed.

"They're coordinating positions!" Harrigan warned. "Weapons ready, but don't move!"

Four now bounded from the thicket on two sides of the expedition. Then the pack slowly crept as one to within five yards of the humans.

"Backs tight to one another. Like this!" Harrigan pulled Smythe from his forward, aggressive stance backward into his comrades to tighten the circle. He swallowed hard and struggled to control the panicked scientists. "Fire!" he suddenly commanded.

The stick-shaped weapons each were fairly quiet weapons. But together they made a resounding "Bbbbang." Three thylacs fell. The rest leaped up, bounding away tree to tree. But one launched itself through the air at Woj, just beside Harrigan whose reload jammed. Woj fired again as the marsupial lion slammed into Woj's chest. Harrigan blanched at the hideous, alien face and gouging front teeth. As Woj and the beast struck the ground, its muscles went as limp. Woj lay still, pale as death.

Woj woke to concerned faces. "I yam dead?"

"No. Yor not dead, mate. Can ya move?" Smythe felt Woj's ribs and nervously looked around for other *Thylacoleos*.

Woj rose and grabbed his rifle. Smythe pointed to a pair of female thylacs carrying pups away in their pouches. "Thought I fixed the females, so they'd only be inseminated and brought to term in the lab. Obviously, I was wrong. Now, there's no way to tell how many are out he-ah."

Harrigan shivered, finishing for Smythe. "*Or* which lack safety chips in their skulls. Hey, anyone see my emitter?"

Everyone ignored Harrigan's question and nervously watched the mothers retreat deeper into the canopy. Harrigan huffed, then radioed Control and the group's base that there were no casualties. "Get to the ridge, now," he ordered.

But as they reached the rock, the scientists blanched and halted. Racing toward them on slightly bowed stubby legs was a mob of club- and spear-waving Neanderthals.

Harrigan whispered to his team. "Kneel! Hold your heads down."

The Neanderthals quickly surrounded them, slamming their weapons on the ground, and screaming out into the forest and down at the frightened moderns. Suddenly one of the thylac mothers appeared behind the group at the edge of the forest. The animal snarled and gashed the air with its deadly claws but retreated when the Neanderthals charged.

The Neanderthals turned their attention to their guests. The researchers stared up at the sweaty, hairy crew for several minutes. Singh studied the Neanderthal faces and whispered assurance that they held no anger.

Olivier broke the silence in Nostratic. "We — our clan — come to trade. We want peace!"

He held out a pelt. "Friends! We give you pelts."

Harrigan glared at him, asserting authority. He gave up his spare pelt, as did the rest. Each scientist was picked up bodily and taken to the clan's main cave, where the Neanderthals set them down. It was smelly and cluttered, connected to a second, similarly shabby cave. The walls and parts of the ceiling bore rudimentary paintings of black, red, yellow, and green animals. The hand outlines were accurate, however, for these had been made by placing hands on the cave walls and spitting or dabbing paint all around.

The community now consisted of thirty-eight adults and young adults and thirty-one children — "Two more," Singh told Harrigan, "than are known from the surrogates' notes."

"Time for your people skills, Ina," Harrigan queued her.

Singh advised all to smile, and they received grins back. But jostling from inquisitive Neanderthals and the surroundings made things difficult. "That's Rhahs, their leader," Singh told the team. "Pay him respect." She bowed to Rhahs. "We visit. We are friends. You like pelts?"

Rhahs' voice was husky and his shallow vowels sounded nasally. "Pelts? You are black-hair, long-leg woman. You are like Khayni. They will come, will attack for you!"

"In context," Singh told Harrigan, "Khayni means Cro. But I've not seen anything in the surrogates' records about Kora repeating words from her subconscious to her fellows, including this word. I'm unaware of a clan name adopted by either the Neanderthal or the Cro-Magnon."

Singh turned to Rhahs. "No attack. No one comes for me, or us. We are not Khayni. We will visit Khayni soon. We like to visit you now."

Rhahs looked confused as he touched his guests' differing complexions. "I am Rhahs. We are friends to you. We are Abli. You have many colors? Name your clan."

Woj spoke out of turn. "We are *Friendli*, our people's name is! Friendli have many color skins. Many colors; one clan."

The researchers shot Woj a look of exasperation.

"The label and explanation may help." Harrigan suggested. "But how 'bout we let Dr. Singh run this part!"

Rhahs smiled again, sang something unintelligible to his people, and split up Singh's group to be physically dragged around the cave and introduced to every member of the clan. Kora smiled and climbed down from her rock ledge to greet them.

Once pleasantries had been exchanged, the researchers were hauled back to the center and given cooked meat. As the Abli handed out bowls of water, Singh pointed Harrigan's attention to their hands. Several had fingers severed at the first or second joint. Rhahs himself was missing the tip of his small right finger.

"Rhahs, finger short. Why?" Singh asked.

Rhahs jerked Singh to her feet and dragged her outside, Harrigan and others in-tow. He pointed to the sun and then to a blood-stained boulder outside. "As-sun shines, speaks like fire inside us. Fire warm us, save us from animals, clean meat. We give ourselves back."

The scientists made as congenial an exit as they could, receiving more smiles than frowns on the way out. They reached the sloth-tractor with sighs of nervous relief and fatigue all around. Harrigan found and carefully secured his signal emitter. The group rested, conjecturing what the finger sacrifice and "As-sun" could mean.

"Obviously," Fong offered, "it's a natural fascination. A precursor to religion sparked by the most constant and unreachable thing these people can conceive of, the sun. It might even be some subconscious effect of their last set of physical exams a year ago, or of our periodically gassing them in their sleep."

Woj disagreed, his Polish accent barely noticeable. "No. Rhahs indicated daht the fire spoke to them. More than one had that experience. Rhahs associates fire with the sun. Maybe they have — or think daht they have had — religious experiences. They're only able to liken it — symbolize it — to something they know exists yet cannot touch. The sun may be only a symbol of their god. The sacrifice of a finger at least shows sincerity."

"It's no great leap of thought to associate foyah and the sun, chum," Smythe countered in his outback Aussie accent. "This is the most common primitive worship, something we moyt ought to expect. You can't conclude these people are in touch with some deity!"

"I didn't exactly say daht!" Woj protested, obviously irritated at the criticism. "I just said they are sincere in their beliefs. And the sacrifice is no — what is in English? — shirk."

Harrigan halted them. "We'll discuss this and accumulate more observations later. Now, we have to get up to the Cro-Magnon caves or we will find ourselves unable to return by dark."

The group tied more gift pelts to their own and trudged uneventfully three miles east to the Cro-Magnon caves.

———————

As his team approached the northernmost of the clan's two caves, Harrigan saw two Cro sentries duck inside. Soon, his group was surrounded. The Cros were uniformly black-haired, with prominent cheekbones and jutting chins. The males had sparse beards and the females had a little more body hair than modern women. Their complexions were tan, and they had detached ear lobes. The Cro pulled at Woj's blonde and Harrigan's red hair, scratched at Singh's dark skin, and poked Fong's eyelids.

"Friends!" Singh called out in Nostratic. "We give you pelts. No hurt you. No hurt us!"

This elicited a barely civil response as they ushered the researchers into their cave. The pelts were confiscated and placed in the rear of the tidy cavern, where fires illuminated detailed, colorful wall drawings. All stared at the rich artwork, including stencils of hands—not mutilated. The Cros seemed more advanced in art and dexterity than Neanderthals. The best animal and sapiens pictures were the highest up. *Children must have practiced on the lower walls*, Harrigan surmised. But there was also a painting of a spear being thrown by long, thin figures into a crowd of clearly short-legged figures. Harrigan wondered what Singh might discover, asking the Cros about the Neanderthals.

Singh pointed out Mo'ara to Harrigan. "You are Mo'ara? Leader?" She inquired. "You know short-legs, yellow-hairs?" She translated for Harrigan and others as quickly as possible.

"Short-legs, yellow-hairs? Abli, bad. Take our animals."

"Are you Khayni?"

Mo'ara's brown eyes narrowed. "We are *strong* Khayni! You, many faces. You are what?"

Singh glanced at Woj, then back to the Cro leader. "We are Friendli. Friendli have many faces but do not fight. Friendli trade, grow food."

Mo'ara frowned and dragged Singh to a fire enclosed within wicker skirting, Harrigan guarding. "No! Fire make food grow. Ash and scraps make green grow. *We* make fire happy!"

All hushed as the Cro leader took some dried meat from outside and a rotting piece from a pit. He held the fresh meat, skewered on a spear, to the fire and threw the spoiled morsel onto coals. After a moment he withdrew the skewered meat, blew on it and chewed it as he spoke. "Fire make all animals; give *all* to Khayni. Fire make Khayni. We give back to fire."

Harrigan was intrigued but neither he nor Singh could make sense of this. She played along for a few minutes more until the whole group was abruptly put outside the cave.

"Keep a friendly attitude nevertheless." Harrigan reminded his team.

As they left, Olivier bent to examine a spoiled spot on one of the drying strips of meat. Immediately their lone escort struck the back of his head with his spear. Olivier rose, his face contorted. The escort rushed him, but Olivier caught him by the hide tunic and threw him head-first into the rock ledge.

Harrigan and Singh turned to try to calm them, but the entire clan picked up weapons and rushed from the cave. Harrigan yanked a smoke grenade from beneath his tunic and yelled, "Run!" then on the radio: "Base!

Drive out here with a sound gun. Now!"

Smythe and Fong deflected spear thrusts to knock the approaching outside guards to the ground. All six fled down the ridge as the grenade burst thick black smoke behind the team. They reached the forest with a quarter-mile lead on their pursuers; three quarters of a mile to the tractor. All gasped for air as they ran.

Harrigan directed them over a small ridge and glimpsed the tractor crawling toward them in the distance. Some stopped to rest but Harrigan tugged them ahead. "There are four with spears with your names on them fifty yards back and closing fast!" he growled.

They jumped and tumbled down the spur. Again, Harrigan shouted, "Go left. Down left!"

They maintained their lead and rounded to the less-steep end of the next ridge. There, thirty feet ahead, was the disguised tractor. "Cup your ears," he ordered.

Harrigan yelled into his collar radio. "Sound blast! Do it!"

All held their ears. The high-pitched blast dropped the four closest pursuers, who went rolling into briars. The other Cros stopped short and held their ears, screaming.

They clambered into the tractor as it pivoted and raced south. Smythe caught his breath while dressing Olivier's cut head. The researchers gulped from canteens provided by the guards.

Olivier was livid. "I hope those barbarians die and rot out here!"
"We have to win them over, Claude," Harrigan said wearily. "Over the next year or so, those 'barbarians' might teach us more about ourselves than we may want to know."

Chapter Twelve

Freund's Residence, Megiddo, Israel
1809 hours, 13 April 2036

Harrigan and Freund sat with iced tea on Freund's veranda, relaxed in the warm evening breeze, which carried the scent of Gertrude's roses and the chirp of grasshoppers. Freund's slight paunch pulled at a button, but Harrigan, still muscular at forty-two, felt no superiority. He hoped that a month's vacation, spent with the Freund and Strauss families, would relieve stress, and give him time to devise and present a saner research plan to Mon.

Freund yawned. "Ben's growing up fast. Tough lil' guy you've got."

Harrigan sighed and lowered his gaze to his glass. "I need to spend more time with him. Tykvah read me the riot act yesterday on that, sapiens treatment and trusting Mon. I felt like shit."

"She's the best thing ever happened to you, bud. What are you gonna do? Quit, cut your hours? Keep at it and teach the Cro to love Neanderthals?"

"I might quit, or consult, but not until the current contract's up...and I can ease both clans into society. Shit...I don't know how...freakin' Cro...like a mirror! No wonder countries keep going to war. Anyway, Tykvah's right about Ben and this sapiens issue."

"And, Kevin, your pride keeps you from seeing Mon for what he is."

"I just can't agree, old friend. There's reason to trust Mon, if not Hassan and Najik. After all, he trusts me!" Harrigan grinned. "But— seriously—there's only so much I *can* do."

Harrigan stared silently at the pink, post-sunset clouds above the houses. For a split second, they looked like roses. He squinted and rubbed his tired eyes. "Thanks for taking me along to reconciliation and Mass, Mannie."

"Did you get anything out of them?"

"No." Harrigan laughed, revealing slighter crow's feet than Freund's. Freund joined him. "Would you admit it if you did?"

Harrigan smiled wryly. "No, guess not."

"Dreams still bothering you?" Freund held his glass to his mouth.

Harrigan grimaced. "Yes. Let's not discuss that, okay?"

"Just asking. Touchy!"

"I need a rest, but I have to keep on. You know, Mannie, sometimes retiring sounds all right. Mon owes us his life and trusts me more than his staff. He responded to my note about a new contract and work after the park conversion but didn't address my other concerns."

"I don't trust him, Kevin. At all."

"Well, the Iraqis would steal whatever of our work they could, but they're no military threat. Even so, I've been tinkering with ways to mitigate our military work's value and increase security. I'm getting really tired of Najik's sneaky monitoring to impress superiors and arguing with me over safety and sapiens issues."

"I appreciate you fighting those battles, Kevin. Am I hearing things or are you trying to say that you might just hang it all up? Tell Mon and his bureaucrats to take a leap?"

"You kidding? We've only scratched the surface! You wanna quit?"

"No. Got the fever. Every time we discover something new, it raises more questions."

The two sat silently contemplating the fantastic mysteries they and their team had tapped.

"Mannie?"

"What?"

"I'm sorry I cut you off about my dreams. I think I've been spooked, subconsciously, by some of our discoveries and sometimes I think I see—" Harrigan cleared his throat, "strange pieces of evidence that keep falling into place, like Kora's memories and everyone getting M1-RNA through the Hebrew diasporas. And yet there's no proof of God or anything spiritual."

"If there were proof of God, you'd never ask for faith. And you need faith to open the eyes of your heart, to endure to the end. If he were overt, you wouldn't feel free to *choose*, defer your will to his. You would view sacrifice and repentance as a requirement, not an act of love."

"Mannie, I really did try this faith thing. There have been... times... when I thought I felt that 'whisper' you talked about. But I can't accept a few...unexplained occurrences or dreams as evidence of this spiritual world you say exists. Have you ever seen it, touched it, experienced it?"

"*It* touches *me*. God helps me accept it. Just ask for faith. He'll give it. But for that to be genuine, it must be a sacrifice of one's own imperfect will to God's. You cannot gain new life if you will not let the old one go."

"Too deep! New subject. I wanted to tell you: Tykvah helped me refine my genetic progression model."

"What does it predict?"

"It extrapolates our future genome, based on data we've assembled. It predicts that personality microsatellites cannot be added to each generation endlessly. Q-arms, especially, get so long the chaperone protein bonds lose stability. There's a definite number of generations before archived strands can no longer be added to the lengthening chromosomes. Past that point,

M1-RNA stops adding new personality codes and starts breaking them down."

"Break down? As in random, freak-like mutation?"

"No. It triggers expression of the already-archived personality sequences, starting with the oldest and most fragile, cascading one generation after another."

Freund dropped his tea and did not reach to pick it up. "Do you mean to say that future generations could start producing copies of ancestors in the order of original occurrence?"

"That's the chemistry. Ended lineages regenerate because the process progresses from the most ancient sequences forward, creating all combinations similar to the prior generation but which did not already occur. It's just a computer projection."

Freund smiled nervously and reached for his glass.

"But there is one thing," Harrigan said, "that checks out perfectly with my lab trials."

"What's that?"

"The regeneration cascade can actually be triggered with the right vector and coding."

Freund stared at Harrigan. "Triggered? *Mein Gott!* What do you mean, 'triggered?'"

"I mean it produces a zygote. A targeted virus shell penetrates an egg, releases its instructions and sufficient M1-RNA to assemble genes from available nucleotides in the host and the virus. Once forty-three chromosomes are assembled, regular RNA gets produced. That shuts down M1-RNA, but the zygote keeps growing."

"Conception without sperm? How are archived personality genes targeted?"

"I've observed excess amounts of M1-RNA homing in on the archived gene markers that have the weakest bonds, the most ancient. M1-RNA expresses the oldest personality genes first."

"But wouldn't the cascade activate too many personality genes in one child?"

"No. Once those genes express, that segment of the chromosome produces hormones that neutralize the M1-RNA near that segment — like an egg shutting out other sperm at the moment it's fertilized. Then the remnants of the M1-RNA mark that newly expressed gene for dormancy again. So, an M1-RNA cascade starts with baby number one, expresses the single most ancient set of personality genes, and halts. When that baby grows up to have kids, the *next-oldest* personality gene set gets expressed in *its* first child because that next set now has the weakest bonds. Progressive generations are all ancestors, and this starts from the most ancient."

"The Resurrection of the Dead! Kevin, this could endanger the whole human genome."

"Hey, stop worrying. Not just *any* tinkering with longevity genes would start this. Someone would have to put massive amounts of M1-RNA into partially denatured viruses that had the capability to both replicate and target the reproductive tract. Then they'd have to get a woman to breathe or ingest it. Sure, elevated M1-RNA would be a trait she'd pass to her descendants, and the virus itself could spread to people around her. But the placental barrier would keep the virus from infecting successive generations, so daughters would get pregnant in the usual way. Male progeny would develop a resistance and grow up normally. But initially, if men are exposed to too much... It's just that adult levels of testosterone change M1-RNA so that it shuts down longevity genes and codes for fast aging."

"It could kill the world's existing generation of men? Do the Iraqis know?"

"No, neither of these effects. Just you and I know its effects...even Tykvah hasn't seen this work. They want to steal the monopoly on prehistoric reproductions...Mannie, stop staring at me! The odds are so small...it just couldn't happen."

The next morning, Harrigan parked his rental car several blocks from the U.S. Trade Consulate in Megiddo and fumbled nervously with his phone. "Zip," he said in a level tone. He got out and walked circuitously uptown to enter the small concrete and glass office building. He was escorted to a windowless office where he requested a new phone. "They're still probing," he reported, "and they have a vector similar to what I use to target animal meiosis and—"

The agent leaned forward. "Can they mass-produce it?"

"Not possible. But they made a human-targeted version offsite, just not specific to any race or genetic group. I can't copy it for you. So, it's still not clear they want a weapon. Still, you'd better get eyes and ears more closely on my lab and Hassan's people. If they decode my human gene pool databases...they'll be able to target specific peoples and immunize their own."

"Any indication they're getting at that database, or working on mass production?"

"Well, neither. But that doesn't mean they're not."

"Leave analyzing intelligence to us, Dr. Harrigan. Next time, skip the cloak and dagger visit and use the phone. I'll file your...report. Thanks for saving the world, Double-oh Seven."

—————————

The following morning in Baghdad, Hassan's young Computer Science Chief had come in early to gain his attention. Hassan sat at his desk, read the report, and gazed up smiling. Hassan stood up and walked over to shake the visitor's hand.

"Thank you," Hassan said softly. "You have worked long and hard and this will not go unnoticed. You may go."

Hassan was on the phone before the young man had even left.

"This is Colonel Hassan. Give me the Premier."

A dark, stern face flooded the monitor. "Yes, Hassan, what is it?"

"Congratulations on your restructuring of the government, *Premier* Mon. The Congress and the presidency were worse than useless."

"What have you called me for, Hassan? I am quite busy."

"Sir, we have found and eliminated the deception that Harrigan has been using to hide his meiotic research. We can now identify and produce aging genes, genes for strength, intelligence, all of the traits you require! FGR is now available for our researchers to employ in genetic trait identification, removal, and insertion. By constructing and mass-producing virus vectors, we can even send programmed gene sequences into any host. We are very close, also, to being able to genetically immunize our own people so that their progeny will avoid recessive traits. Harrigan's coding has extra base pairs at some locations, like the Y chromosome's SRY gene. We are working to discover their functions, but we have had success with two female test subjects who had babies with defects we coded and two males who died of rapid aging."

"Excellent, Hassan. Are these delivery systems practical?"

"Yes, sir. But it will take refinement. We have debugged the duplicate FGR program and equipment here in Baghdad. We are on the verge of mass-producing the virus vector. It will kill males by fast aging if they are producing testosterone at adult levels. It also responds to several female hormones to seek and effectively fertilize any newly ovulated egg. These fetuses will mature rapidly, and with any of the several traits we desire. It can produce workers for your new order."

"Hassan, you have accomplished your assigned goals well, *if late*. I will remember you when the time comes. In your judgment, is there a reason to keep Harrigan and his staff?"

Hassan was about to thank Mon for what he misinterpreted to be an order to kill Harrigan and his staff. Before he could do so, an aide approached Mon and whispered into his ear.

Knowing not to listen in, Hassan depressed the volume button on his keyboard almost to mute and shouted exuberantly at his ceiling, "Yes! You dogs are *mine* now!"

Mon nodded at the aide and addressed Hassan. "I want Harrigan and his team kept on, just in case more useful discoveries can be obtained, and to avoid Western suspicion."

Hassan looked back at his monitor. Noticing that Mon was addressing him, he increased the volume slightly. Mon seemed distracted and impatient, so he repeated phrases he had understood.

"Yes, sir. 'Useful discoveries.' 'Avoid Western suspicion.'"

"Pay attention, Hassan! I must go. Well done!"

Mon turned and spoke with his aide as Hassan called after him, the volume still set low.

"Sir, I will move in anti-aircraft units since Al-Rajda's cover may be compromised without the foreigners."

"Uh. What? Yes, a fine job—though you *did* need the foreigners. Fix your phone before you call me again! Goodbye."

The screen went blank. Hassan grinned widely, satisfied that he had heard what he wanted. His voice took on a smooth, self-satisfied quality as he made his next call. "Al-Rajda Facilities Commander, please."

Najik greeted him. "Good morning, sir. How may I serve you?"

"Harrigan and his staff are no longer required. My people were always able to do this research. Finally, the Premier respects me! He wishes that they be disposed of. Permanently."

Najik's expression brightened. He leaned forward to the lens, causing the image of his face to fill Hassan's monitor. "Excellent, sir! It would be most practical to deal with the staff tomorrow. The Harrigans and Freunds, however, are being monitored in Megiddo. They will return in four weeks. I trust the Communications Section will intercept and handle any calls they might make to their staff…until I have the Harrigans and Freund back here?"

"I will alert the Communications Section. You may conduct the operation as you wish and report success to me."

"Yes, sir. Will there be any change in the operation of the facility?"

"Maintain it as usual. Your technical contingent will grow, and the sapiens and animals will be useful. Also, I am posting an anti-aircraft battalion just south of Al-Rajda. Remember that you do not command it!"

Late that evening in the Neanderthal caves Kora glanced from her sleeping mate, Rhahs to her two young children in their grass-stuffed pelt beds. She noticed the familiar scent of roses outside and crept silently out, almost up to the cliffs. There she squatted on her shins, facing the forest. Her reddish blonde hair fluttered in the light breeze upon her furry shoulders and protruding brow. Starlight glinted off Kora's eyes as she began to tear, smiling and reaching outward toward the sparkling mist forming above the trees. The woods became silent as red roses appeared in a radiant fog just above the trees. A woman in a white dress and blue shawl emerged from the glistening vapors, holding out her palms as if embracing Kora.

Kora's eyes rolled back into their sockets. Her breathing became shallow, and her face began to reflect the shine. She listened inwardly to words that graced her, then responded in a tremulous whimper, her smile disappearing. "I fear! These ones I know not. Pain. Killing. Who are these? How could—"

Kora fell silent. Her smile began to return. Her shaky voice recovered and built into a sanguine proclamation. "You do the will of As-sun. I do as you ask: One last call to Friendli. This other witness I am to meet, a 'Temple Mount' I know not. There we will prepare the way. I will be not afraid."

————————

Harrigan had been asleep beside Tykvah in Freund's guest room a mere two hours when his eyes shook wildly beneath their lids and his arms twitched. Sweat beaded on his forehead and intermittently rolled off into his slightly thinning hair. The image in his mind was simultaneously fearful and comforting. His lips began to move, and his shaky, gruff tone woke Tykvah. She listened, becoming more unsettled with each word.

"Must not let this be! So many will die. I can stop— I *will* fight this. Don't underst—" Harrigan was silent and his muscles relaxed. His eyes remained closed as suddenly his hands cupped his face, and he almost woke himself. His voice softened. "Another chance? I must choose...so soon mankind will...? I'm so blind...weak." Harrigan's eyes fluttered open.

He looked at Tykvah through the blur of tears and sat up into her embrace.

"Kevin, you're drenched, you're shaking! Bad dreams. It's okay now. I love you. Be calm, now. What was it?"

"Death," he whispered, pausing as she wiped a tear. Then words poured out. "Some horrible choice, and what we are, and the sapiens, and whether I can see..." He paused. "I can't remember," he said with resignation.

"I've nagged you about the lab work and the—"

"No, it's not you. It's faded. Gone. But everything is *not* fine, Tykvah. Not at all."

Harrigan's phone lit, 2307 hours, 14 April. It flashed an access alert he had programmed his office computer to send when his files were accessed. He jerked his head up, then texted Freund and his CIA handler. "You and Ben stay here. I need to get Mannie and see what's going on at the lab. I'll return in a few days."

The next morning, the ten Al-Rajda staff members, eight children, and four spouses awoke to a loud announcement from Najik's adjutant, Major Bhaszdi, on their home intercoms. "Attention staff and fam-ilies! A Kurd terrorist attack has been interr-cepted."

Within minutes, Bhaszdi rushed all foreign staff and families to the garage, forced them into the cargo holds of two tractors, and headed up the west escalator for the grassy plain. Two miles north, along the edge of the greening forest, the vehicles halted just within sight of the *Varanus priscus* burrow. The soldiers kicked the civilians out of the vehicles and dismounted.

From the concealment of the control seat in the sloth neck, Najik tested his signal emitter and received a hissing roar from the burrow. He had Bhaszdi line up his men facing the sobbing, frenzied group. The crowd began to slowly back away from the soldiers until they realized that they neared the monstrous reptiles. Suddenly someone in the back of the group fell, dropped down into the earth as if swallowed by it.

Najik grinned as the roar came, muffled at first, then loudly. The earth underneath the screaming civilians burst, tossing them outward from the eruption of soil. Soldiers stumbled backward as a *Varanus priscus's* head thrust from the sod. The civilian who had dropped from sight onto its scaly neck was now ejected onto the grass with a thud. He scrambled to his feet and dashed to rejoin the others. The lizard sustained multiple gunshots but continued to clamber from its hole. Now its scaly tree-trunk legs and ripping claws pounded the ground as it rushed the soldiers. Najik cursed Bhaszdi as escaping captives yanked every child into the concealment of the trees.

The drivers jammed their tractors into reverse gear. The *Varanus priscus* swung its massive bulk, knocking a soldier down and then impaling him through the chest with a rear claw. It hissed and writhed as Najik tortured it with the signal emitter. The other soldiers trampled each other as they followed Bhaszdi into the tractors. The pair slammed the hatch against now-Sergeant Abrih and another pleading soldier and sped south.

Najik quivered violently, watching, and listening through a portal as now two of the giants yanked a soldier in opposite directions, bifurcating him. *How will I…Mission report…I'll put Bhaszdi's signature…. His…his mission accomplished. Records? I was on leave, yes, when he got the mission.* His mind raced, plotted, and silently planned a fabricated report. *How long can these people survive defenseless on the plateau? As for the Harrigans and Freund, they will come right to me in a month…just like the gloating surrogates! I can take my time sending out patrols to kill off all of these 'mice.'* Najik finally smiled and calmed, relieved to descend into the darkness of the west escalator.

The air taxi debarked Harrigan and Freund at the residential complex and headed southward toward Baghdad. Alarmed to find homes deserted, Harrigan led Freund on foot to sneak into the motor pool. Najik and his men were just exiting to their conference room. The two donned robotic bear suits and followed dirty tracks up the west escalator.

"That bastard must have killed the staff," Harrigan said through the mesh as they exited into the mid-morning sun, "but we have to check." They progressed northward, stopping to inspect the *Varanus priscus* area.

"Big group of footprints leading back into the forest," Freund called, pulling Harrigan from the bloodied dirt clods and torn up grass. The pair made quick progress and reached the cheering, rag-tag fugitives.

Harrigan quickly verified that all were present and fit to travel, set Freund and Lloyd as second and third in command, and directed two women with children to operate the robotic suits.

"Listen," Harrigan briefed the group, "I believe that Najik and Hassan may be taking over, a coup against Mon. I can't fully trust him either. As you've noticed, your phones don't work and neither does mine. American intelligence…started monitoring my phone…recently, so they know it's jammed, and they may respond to that.

"Anyway, here's my plan: We can't descend the cliffs and there'll be patrols outside the ridges. We'll go north. Join with the Neanderthals — the Cro are too violent — until I can get help. Dr. Singh, it's up to you to secure Neanderthal protection in case Najik sends patrols. Dr. Freund and I will take the robotic suits south and bust unexpected into Najik's set-up. From there, we'll either get help from Mon or link up with American authorities."

Simone Kairaba pulled on his shirtsleeve. "What about predators?" she asked, quavering.

"No worries, love," Lloyd interjected. "Threatening noises, superior numbers, and club-wielding aggression will intimidate predators, I should think. And we have able leaders."

Harrigan smiled. "Some of us are familiar with the terrain, but we'll follow the river so we won't get disoriented."

"We'd betta hope nothin' tracks us — or is waiting beneath its surface," Smythe said.

"If anyone can get us through this," Lloyd growled, "it's Dr.

Harrigan. And I'll thank you to respect Dr. Freund's and my leadership too, if you want to survive."

"Everybody get rocks and clubs," Harrigan ordered. "One bear suit behind me and one behind Dr. Freund at the back. Dr. Lloyd's group in the middle. Follow me and stay together!"

They stayed close to the river, growls of *Smilodons*, shrieks of a *Phorusrhacus*, and unidentified noises warning them away from the concealment of deeper forest. Changing his mind mid-way to the caves, Harrigan turned west, nearly reaching the savannah, and noticed fresh boot tracks in the mud. He halted the group and passed word for Freund to come forward.

The pair left to reconnoiter northward a quarter mile. Cresting a hillock, they halted under bushes. Forty feet away knelt Sergeant Abrih, filling two canteens beside a reddish pond, apparently a spring feeding a wide, swampy creek that meandered northeastward through undergrowth.

"Must have been left behind by Najik, or assigned to find the group," Freund whispered.

"Look out!" Harrigan yelled as a submerged green image raced at Abrih from his left.

The *Meiolania's* armored face and temple-horns broke the surface. The monstrous turtle's triangular jaws opened a full twelve inches. It sliced off Abrih's jaw almost ear to ear, leaving the upper larynx dangling. Abrih groped frantically for his lower skull as water and blood spouted with each wispy cough.

The eight-foot-long horror twitched its spiked tail then thrust itself on land, tossing the gangly jaw past Abrih's own eyes. As Abrih scrambled to escape, it sliced its claw into the soldier's heel. He fell, hinged at his skewered foot, and dropped his sidearm. His head jerked as if screaming, but the void that had been his jaw emitted only bubbling noises and whisper-like puffs of air. In a second, the *Meiolania* lurched forward upon Abrih's impaled leg, tore off half his right buttock and gulped the meat unchewed. Relentlessly and continuously, it thrust its beak into Abrih's thigh, raised its head up to swallow and reiterated the bites.

Harrigan and Freund both retched: The thorny head continued gashing and snapping, now into Abrih's gut, while the tormented sergeant's arms thrashed the ground. In a moment, his arms only twitched, then lay still, then were devoured. The beast disappeared into the pond.

"You're our lookout," Harrigan yelled, sprinting to and from the corpse and recovering Abrih's ballistic pistol, spare clip and knife. "We gotta leave, un-ass the area now before scavengers—" Harrigan scanned northeast along what he knew to be a mile-long marsh. Over a dozen more *Meiolania* approached, doubtless many more beyond view. "Note to self: unsafe area...Twenty rounds. I'll save 'em for Najik," Harrigan said, handing the knife to Freund. They returned in silence to the group.

As daylight waned, Harrigan nervously approached the foreboding northern swamp and turned west. He knew they would have to cross its dark streams and thickets—patrolled by thylacs and other lethal beasts.

As he crossed a creek and began to ascend the next bank, he turned to watch three children in the rag-tag column crest the bank behind him. He scooped a drink and was about to encourage them to do the same when he noticed the approaching water. *Extraordinarily muddy water! What could've —*

Gruff panting murmured through rustling bushes to the west, up the hill, then more clearly and louder.

"Get across," he whispered forcefully. Hurry! Hey, Woj, Smythe: get them up in trees!"

As the children began to cross the stream, Harrigan saw the giant wolves crest the hill twenty yards upstream. Half leaped down into the water and ascended the northern bank, creating a two-pronged attack racing toward the humans.

Olivier popped up over the hill at the rear of the group, running west through thick brush to club what he thought was a lone, adolescent wolf. "I saw a wolf! I will kill it. Back me up!"

Harrigan yelled, "Claude, get down here. Are you out of your mind?"

Thunderous barks and growls erupted as Harrigan frantically tossed a child up the bank into a tree. Both halves of the pack raced through the undergrowth, gashing the air with hideous fangs. Converging downward into the ravine, the lead wolves vaulted toward the children.

"Wee-oop! Eah!" came bone-chilling screams from the north.

Ffft. An arrowhead and shaft jutted from the right side of the lead wolf's neck as the beast cried out hoarsely and tumbled into the creek, dead at Harrigan's feet. The other wolves, silenced, veered north, crouching low and snapping at the unseen archers. Spears rained down upon the wolves, felling another as the banshee shrieks grew swiftly louder. The pack fled southwest through the creek in a storm of splashes and howls.

Six Cro hunters, stone-faced and armored with giant green scales linked by leather straps, stood in a line staring down into the creek.

Struggling to regain his composure, Harrigan extended his hand in gratitude. The young man spat in his hand, tore his arrow from the wolf, and gave orders in Nostratic to the other five Cro, who ignored the researchers and began skinning the two dead wolves.

"Well thank you nevertheless, young man," Lloyd said in English. "Let's get out of here, chaps, before we end up like the wolves, shall we?

From the reports I've read, I don't think these Cro will take kindly to us if they know we prefer to stay with the Neanderthals. Bloody shame."

Harrigan whispered to Singh, "Wha'd the leader tell the others?"

"He said Friendli — that's us — weak, can't fight. Food for his prey."

Harrigan frowned. "Not any time soon! Everybody back on the path. It's getting dark."

The Cro left abruptly with the wolves' heads and hides.

"That reminds me," Harrigan said, regrouping his people. "If we get in a scrape, kill sapiens only if absolutely necessary, but the Iraqis are armed so there'll likely be no choice. Move out." He had all jog northwest toward the Neanderthal caves, almost a mile away. As they neared the darkened ridge, they could hear and see rustling high in the trees.

"Thylacs," Harrigan roared. "Sprint for the rock!"

In the panic, both robotic suits tumbled and could not be righted.

"Don't open it. We'll be back for you," Harrigan yelled, pushing others uphill. But the mothers, each with a child, popped the doors and scrambled toward the group. Harrigan and Freund each slung a child in the fireman's carry and sprinted to rejoin the group.

Bursting from the foliage onto the rock a quarter mile south of the caves, the pair wheezed, scanning for thylacs. The black gulf between them and the cave fires was foreboding. As they approached the caves, bobbing torches streamed out and Neanderthals quickly surrounded them, poking and handling the modern clothes. Neither wolves nor thylacs followed the researchers to the caves, but Harrigan suspected that — very soon — other, more vicious animals in uniform would surely pursue them there.

Chapter Thirteen

Al-Rajda Motor Pool
0534 hours, 17 April 2036

Major Bhaszdi impatiently accepted the captain's troop inspection report of "Ready, sir" and bellowed, "We are already four minutes late departing the escalator. But if you follow my orders, we will be back for breakfast by dawn tomorrow. Follow the tractors and begin!"

He wished he had the confidence he had just faked. But he reassured himself that at least he was not a coward like his commander. He knew Najik feared having to explain the destruction of five out of seven robotic suits, and the discovery of the false report that the researchers died. He entered the lead tractor, which was followed by fifty-eight riflemen on foot and one trailing tractor, and soon emerged from the east escalator.

Driving and trampling through thick weeded grass and bushes along the Rajdakim, the parade flushed hundreds of noisy quail. Foreboding caws from ravens further taunted the nervous troops who fired at every fleeing animal they saw. Five miles into their march, however, the line of tense troops fell into disarray, surprised by a pack of wolves. The canines immediately bolted out of sight of the vastly larger group of soldiers.

Bhaszdi decided to take no chances, even though he could no longer see wolves from his open tractor. "Slaughter the pack! Fire into the woods," he shouted. "Over there…somewhere."

The infantrymen's forty-five automatic rifles managed to wound just one wolf. Bhaszdi launched a concussion grenade that deflected off a tree, eastward into the savannah. The deafening explosion echoed off ravines, hillocks, and ultimately the east ridge.

From the east, the soldiers heard a rumble. Most assumed they had triggered an avalanche. As they marched northward, it increased. Brown dots became visible, bobbing up and down, to the far right of the patrol. The rumble grew thunderous. The dots became clearer. At least a hundred black and brown blurs appeared below the morning sun. The blotches got larger, gray dust lines appearing out to their sides. The ground began to vibrate.

Bison latifrons, some seven feet tall at the shoulder, stampeded at full speed toward the troops. The panicked men could not be kept in formation. Soldiers sprinted north to escape the mass of animals, now fifty yards away and closing. The bison careened toward them at almost forty miles per hour. The animals spread over a hundred-yard front to accommodate the six-foot horns extending from each side of their locomotive-like heads.

The immense beasts changed direction, now rushing along the low ground southwest toward the forest and the river, south of the men. For a moment it seemed to Bhaszdi as though the entire military formation would escape being trampled. But suddenly the herd veered again, northwest, directly into the panicking soldiers. Screams and shots rang out as bison and soldiers alike tumbled, wounded, crushed, and dying in the grass. Surviving soldiers dashed into the woods and away from their tractors. Barely slowed by tree limbs, bison crashed into the woods. Horns snapped on tree trunks and became splintered clubs as the beasts thrust toward the river, decapitating, goring, and trampling men. Pained and frightened bleating from the herd mixed horrifically with soldiers' frantic screams and wails.

In seconds, the bison were through to the river and away. The woods and grass were strewn with dead and expiring men and beasts.

A shaken and nauseated Bhaszdi radioed Najik. "Sir! I...I request to withdraw my patrol. You must have monitored the stampede. Colonel, most of my men are dead! The wounded are suffering so that I cannot..." The patrol leader could no longer contain himself and vomited over the side of the tractor. "Hmm, ahh. Sir, please!"

"You will put yourself and your patrol back together, Major!" Najik replied. "I must now send you men whose loyalty you will have to enforce through iron discipline. I will send two more tractors of men as reinforcements. You will send back one tractor at the scene now...with the dead, wounded, and their weapons. Do you understand, Bhaszdi?"

"Yes, sir. I am loading the casualties and weapons into a tractor now. B-but it would be unwise to send them back before replacements arrive, sir."

"Very well, Major. Najik out."

After a few hours, the reorganized patrol drove northward, three tractors with thirty-seven demoralized troops tightly huddling inside. They reached the hilly forested area at the marshy headwaters of the river and halted for a map check. Heading west across tiny gurgling creeks and small wooded ridges, they passed the foreboding site where Najik's previous, unsuccessful recovery crews had dragged the last patrol's damaged heavy-lift suits and bodies, now skeletons. Drivers halted and the soldiers jostled to peer through the tiny portals.

Approaching the Neanderthal caves, Bhaszdi saw smoke issuing from both entrances. From inside the tractors, his men lobbed tranquilizer gas canisters, then donned gas masks and dismounted. Bhaszdi tossed his last few grenades into caves. The troops heard nothing after the explosions. Knowing the cavern to be extensive, Bhaszdi made the decision to enter.

"You ten privates and you three drivers post here, outside the caves. Lieutenants Harif and Karut, take your men into those caves. The rest of you follow me inside."

The officers and men stared silently at Bhaszdi, as if about to refuse the order. Then, one by one, they all turned on personal searchlights and crept inside. With no resistance at the entrances, the two groups merged back into one in the main cave. The rear of the cavern had at least three main extensions. Impatient, the patrol leader assigned eight men to each and moved in. They followed fresh tracks and bloodstains, for over half an hour, so deep within the rock ridge that radio communication became impossible.

Bhaszdi thought he heard something crack several times but was unsure. What was beginning to irritate him, though, was that by now he and his men had been inside for forty-five minutes and had seen no researchers. He felt doubly uneasy when he realized that he had neglected to set any rendezvous time for his three groups, now separated from each other in the cave. His stomach knotted as it began to dawn on him that all of this might be a trap.

He turned, barking a command on the run. "Out of the tunnel now!"

As his own group emerged into the main cavern, Bhaszdi heard a hiss behind him. He turned and saw fire in the three passages. Then three explosions in quick succession knocked his group to the ground. Dust and debris burst out of the tunnels. Small boulders rolled out, barely missing his prone troops.

Bhaszdi's squad frantically checked the two passages with soldiers.

"Harif? Karut? I order you to come out now!" Bhaszdi collapsed on his knees on the cave floor, sobbing. "I said, I order you! Come here!"

Two of his men grabbed Bhaszdi and raised him to his feet. Fear and shame slapped him back to reality and he knew that sixteen men had been sealed in permanently. Bhaszdi shook with panic as he ran from the cave followed by his surviving seven men.

Outside the cave, Bhaszdi's stomach turned, and his bowels wrenched. Every man in his outside contingent lay dead with the tractors engulfed in flames. Each corpse had been speared or shot, presumably with captured rifles. Heads had been bludgeoned into unrecognizable, soppy lumps of bone chips and brain matter. He could see no weapons or ammunition boxes anywhere.

Harrigan, four other researchers and six Neanderthals were running into the woods below — but this was no consolation. Bhaszdi and his small squad were alone and outnumbered.

Bhaszdi's mind whirled and he could not keep his voice stable. "East! Run east! F— Follow me into the woods."

As the Iraqis darted off the sloping gray rock, Harrigan emerged from the forest below and to the Iraqi soldiers' right. The troops veered left, fleeing north toward the tree line there. As Bhaszdi and his men scurried, he glimpsed Harrigan assembling a line of several researchers back out on the rock where they took careful aim. Bhaszdi flung himself at the ground, yelling for his men to do the same. One soldier caught a bullet and fell silent. The remaining seven Iraqis crawled desperately twenty more feet to the forest. Inside its concealment and partial cover, they ran headlong eastward.

Bhaszdi fled the swift pursuit. He now recognized Harrigan's rifle-equipped comrades. Freund, Olivier, Smythe, and Woj — plus the spear-toting Neanderthals — sprinted along the rock to where he and his soldiers had entered the woods. In moments, the researchers were outpacing the Neanderthals, gaining on him and his squad.

A loud cheering rose in the forest to the south. The whoops and shrieks intensified. Bhaszdi realized he had no choice but to turn and fight. "Get behind that log," he yelled, winded. "There! At the top of the ridge ahead! Train your weapons at the bushes to the right. The researchers will attack from the bushes south of us!"

Bhaszdi glimpsed Harrigan and his men running from the brush west of him. He knew they had seen his trap when they flung themselves into a ravine. Three of the trailing Neanderthals tumbled sideways, inexplicably stuck through with arrows in their sides. Then came screams and chants out of the south. A mass of twenty or more Cros in tanned loin covers chased the remaining Neanderthals, badly wounding three, then quickly hiding.

The Iraqis watched as Harrigan's men surprised the Cro attackers, bludgeoning two and scattering the rest through the woods. Bhaszdi and his men ducked as Harrigan and Lloyd directed slow, constant fire on the Iraqi position, allowing Smythe and Woj to evacuate wounded and unconscious Neanderthals to the caves. Bhaszdi could not stop this maneuver and had his men save their ammunition and simply observe. Harrigan and Freund alternated firing and retreating as they followed the rest of their group back toward the caves. Soon, the woods were quiet.

Bhaszdi had no intention of counterattacking the researchers and Neanderthals when he might be able to win over the Cro-Magnons. He had been only vaguely curious about these sapiens before and now recalled that the surrogates had taught them language. As the only language the researchers had in common was English, he reasoned that the Cro-Magnons spoke English. Bhaszdi could speak English fairly well himself.

He radioed Najik. "Colonel! Colonel, we cannot fight in the manner of these people and the Neanderthals, but the Cro-Magnons apparently hate and attack them. I can show the Cro-Magnons that our troops also wish to destroy the Neanderthals and scientists. Then, we can launch one — final and effective — attack with fresh troops in a few days. The Cro-Magnons will be happy to be fodder for us, I feel certain."

"Yes. Do that. Do it now, Bhaszdi. Offer them one of your weapons and win them over. Promise them food and supplies if they will help. I will send a tractor now with food and to pick you up at their caves. You may withdraw *if* you have their support."

Bhaszdi led his men due east, where the Cro-Magnon caves lay some three miles distant. They encountered only one animal attack, from several *Thylacoleos*. He nearly panicked when his signal emitter failed to repel two of the beasts, but his men were able to wound and scatter them.

His squad reached the ridge just as night fell, but Cro warriors jumped and disarmed them. The Cro spoke no English or Arabic; Bhaszdi and his men spoke not a word of Nostratic. The soldiers were bound hand and foot and dragged into the ornately painted cave. There, a young Cro-Magnon boy painted in wide yellow and orange stripes was also bound, nearly immobilized. The boy lay sobbing and squirming on a pelt-covered ledge, surrounded by brightly feathered adults holding stone axes. A few Cros cried while the remainder of the clan chanted excitedly.

One Cro-Magnon voice rose above the rest. It was Mo'ara. As clan leader and shaman, he wore a feathered *Phorusrhacus* skull as a mask and red straps draped across his chest. He silenced his clan, commanding the boy's release.

Though unable to glean Mo'ara's meaning, Bhaszdi felt optimistic that he and his men would be released, since the boy was being untied and tension in the Cro's faces was dissipating.

Mo'ara rendered his judgment of recent events. "We warred again today. But two Khayni died! Our sacrifice...angered fire. Boy make fire happy. Now, no kill boy. Now, make fire more, more happy. Sacrifice seven Friendli!"

———————

Harrigan and his men followed screams toward the Cro caves, then watched from behind trees as moonlight illuminated Bhaszdi's and his soldiers' lifeless bodies being piled just outside. They returned silently to the Neanderthal caves.

"Either the attack was part of a coup," Harrigan told his people as he and Freund said their goodbyes, "or Mon and the West are at war. Either way, Dr. Freund and I will get help by exfiltrating the plateau and Najik's control to assess the situation. This whole thing could result in Mon removing bad elements in his army so those of us who want to continue our work can..."

Most frowned and shook their heads.

"Look," Harrigan pleaded, "we're the ones who should ease the sapiens' entry to the modern world over the next a few years. We still *must* minimize the sapiens' awareness of what's beyond this plateau.

"And if this attack was ordered by Mon, we'll alert the West to send rescue. Dr. Freund and I will take the robotic suits south and give Najik a surprise visit."

The pair tied rawhide pouches to their belts, shook peoples' hands and turned to leave.

"It's after midnight," Lloyd urged. "You'll need sleep and breakfast!"

"No," Harrigan smiled back, "can't give Najik any more time, and we need to move in darkness. See you soon, old friend."

———————

Harrigan and Freund reached the east escalator well after seven a.m. due to animal encounters and avoiding their previous routes. They emerged into an unguarded motor pool that held a ten-ton truck and a utility jeep. They removed motor cables from the robotic suits, truck, and jeep. Harrigan stood guard at the door to the lab complex while Freund pocketed the jeep's keys, and verified that its tank and spare gas can were full.

"Motor pool phone's turned off or jammed," Harrigan whispered, now leading Freund through the lab to Najik's office. "And Najik can't have more than twenty soldiers left."

"Twenty? Piece o' cake."

Harrigan placed his ear to Najik's door. "Thank you, Colonel Hassan. Finally, your rightful place to head our nation is within sight, sir! Congratulations. Goodbye."

Harrigan translated the gist for Freund. "Mannie, they *are* executing a coup. We have to get to the American embassy or warn Mon. We'll rush him and call both. Ready?"

The pair readied their weapons and burst through the door at the lone officer. Najik immediately activated a communications shut down from his computer. They gagged and tied him. When he refused to order his troops to rescue the researchers, Harrigan knocked him out cold.

He locked the door as the pair snuck back to the motor pool. They took the jeep to Harrigan's house instead of the south highway and feverishly threw a change of clothes and the spare gas can into Harrigan's sedan. Then they sliced tires on all other vehicles and raced toward Baghdad.

After ten miles, Harrigan's phone began to operate again, and he sent the status to his handler, who approved of his contacting Mon. He got through to Mon's secretary, who explained that he could not put the call through because Mon was in conference with American President Cox, but he promised to immediately report the matter to Mon, personally dispatch a rescue party from the west by hovercraft—landing unseen, west of the north ridge—and even set an appointment for the next morning for a meeting with Mon. Harrigan sighed with relief as he relayed the news to Freund, who slowed to the speed limit.

"Mannie, a rescue craft will be scrambled. It's safe to stop when we reach the Baghdad Hilton by nine tonight. We meet with Mon at seven a.m."

"No pistols in Mon's building. Hide it in the room but don't check out...I smell a trap."

Harrigan nodded, frowning. "We have to do this. Our staff and their families—hell Mannie, nations—are at risk. But, you're right. In case both south highways have roadblocks, head for Sulaymaniyah, then south to Baghdad on back roads. Shit, that's an extra five and a ha—We'll get there by two-thirty for a few hours' sleep. We can call our wives—Don't let on and worry them. We'll catch an early breakfast and dress to see Mon. This may be fortuitous. I can use the incident to pressure Mon to transition the sapiens to the modern world. I think we just headed off two disasters and can help the sapiens to boot!"

"Thank you," Hassan told his Communication Section officer. "That interception was crucial indeed. I will take it from here."

President Sheryl Cox glanced at the time atop the map of Iraq on the White House Situation Room wall monitor. It showed 1942 hours EST, 20 April 2036 and 0242 hours, 21 April in Baghdad. She studied each face at the situation room's long conference table. Expressions were grim. Secretary of State Wayne Crystal shifted in his chair as the President's glare met his eyes.

"Are you *actually* telling *me*, Wayne, that the Israelis are so intimidated that they will not assist us...and that surrounding countries—"

Crystal swallowed hard, now paying the price for his earlier boasts.

"Madame President, the Israelis feel Mon should not be antagonized since the Mediterranean could easily be closed off from North Africa. He has a subtly dominating influence in every Arab nation and several others. We have no allies in the area from which to stage military operations, and the nuclear option is not realistic. Under the circumstances, I'd say that Mon's got us by the ba...ah...b-by the way he has manipulated even our allies."

Crystal's *faux pas* did not escape Cox. She ignored it, though. "I decide whether the nuclear option is realistic, Mr. Crystal."

The Secretary tried to regain credibility. "We *could* offer to buy oil," he said with a shrug, "while having the U.N. threaten Mon with sanctions if he fails to hand over the facilities, software, and hostages. Use *both* the carrot *and* the stick. He *has* shown a willingness to negotiate spats in the past."

Cox shot him an incredulous glare. "Crystal, do you not realize that this man could destroy the genetic stability of the entire world? Mon could kill millions — perhaps billions — while leaving his own and his puppet regimes to sweep the rest of us off the planet. Do you think someone who'd develop the capability to subjugate the world would negotiate that away?"

"S-so, are you advocating a military threat?"

Cox was so angry she could no longer look at Crystal. She stared at the wall as she answered him. "This nation lost credibility of threats long ago. Let cowards issue threats."

She focused on her CIA Director. "James, we're lucky Harrigan's a patriot. Or *is* he, given that his ego started this and Mon funded his work?"

Flush-faced CIA Director James Fording stood and activated the wall monitor. "Madame President, our agency has been monitoring everything continuously from the start," he quavered, reddening, and clearing his throat. "We've got satellite surveillance, plus eyes on Harrigan in case he leads us to any new information. We don't think he's knowingly on board with Mon. But he's duped by his own confidence that Mon's his benefactor and his *critical* files can't be penetrated."

Cox pointed menacingly. "Bullshit, James. If it hadn't been for Harrigan, we'd have been blindsided here. And we still don't understand FGR! Now, are you *certain* Al-Rajda is the only place where these genetic weapons can be manufactured — and that Mon has no stockpiles yet?"

"Yes, ma'am. Our assessment from Baghdad sources is that the Iraqis have only *just* developed vectors. They've had no time to reconfigure FGR and equipment for mass production of virus weapons, let alone configure them to avoid Mon's people and allies. Harrigan knows meeting with Mon is risky. He meets with Mon in five hours. We need whatever he learns, like whether an additional facility exists. There's no choice but to let him go in."

National Security Agency Chief Dixon Merriweather interjected, "Satellite imaging shows that the researchers are holed-up in one of the caves above the plateau. Iraqi patrols went out after them...never came back. But we think it's just a matter of time before the researchers and children are killed. As for the Iraqi scientists, they're still working at the lab."

Cox turned to General Frederick Mepps, Joint Chiefs of Staff Chairman. "Fred, I want *every* hostage, *every* child, *every* Iraqi scientist; *every* piece of hardware and software removed from Al-Rajda and brought back here. Who do you have and how soon can it happen?"

The officer's stern expression never changed. "We prepped the mission days ago when we suspected Harrigan was captured with his staff. It's called 'Operation Mars Scope' to enhance secrecy, Madame President—a composite of men from the Seventy-Fifth Rangers and a few civilian specialists. They are rehearsed and ready.

"The Air Force has a classified second-gen space shuttle, the *Quest*. Triple the first-gen size for troops and cargo. Belly armor and onboard fuel enable a second, horizontal takeoff. It'll land on the plain south of the lab, approaching too fast and too low for the Iraqi SA-23 missiles. This mission cuts it *really* close on fuel, razor thin margin if they have to use the contingency landing site on the plateau. But it's doable, ma'am. Fly guys can launch on four hours' notice, boots on the ground a half hour later."

"Fred, there is no margin for error. We'll get—*humankind* will get—exactly one shot at this, short of a nuclear exchange. Gentlemen, if Fred's people want any item of support, I want it provided before you draw breath to say 'Yes.' You have a 'go'. This meeting is closed."

Chapter Fourteen

Cape Canaveral, Florida
2335 hours, 20 April 2036 (0635 hours 21 April in Baghdad)

The *Quest*, poised vertically upon its launch pad, appeared as a giant version of its predecessor. At T-minus fifty seconds, Army Lieutenant Colonel Bryce Fulton surveyed the seventy-four Rangers and technicians under his command. He was a no-nonsense African-American of six feet, five inches in height; two-hundred-sixty pounds of cool but dangerous muscle and brain. As a West Point cadet, Fulton had been Harrigan's Cadet Battalion Commander. It galled him that an alumnus had, knowingly or otherwise, endangered America—and the world. As the countdown sounded T-minus thirty seconds, fear at being launched into space gnawed at Fulton—though he hid it behind his square-jawed, self-disciplined expression.

Fulton's Executive Officer, Major Ronald Jasper, was every bit as tough and ready. Jasper commanded the reserve team, Team Foxtrot, and its communications and other equipment.

Fulton, excited by the opportunity to attack the enemy, activated the microphone under his green-camo helmet and gave his trusted NCO In-Charge, Command Sergeant Major Joe Di Nucci, a private call. "So, Airborne Joe, are you ready to get 'space-borne'?"

Di Nucci grimaced, then forced a smile. "All the way, Colonel!"

The passenger bay had no windows. Troops stared at the large monitor at the front of the passenger hold and tensed as the countdown was fed into their helmet communicators. The monitor displayed most of what the pilot, Air Force Colonel Ed Richmond, could see. For now, the audio was limited to the countdown sequence. The screen showed a tiny sliver of moon in the east of the partly cloudy sky, and lights on the vehicle tower's retracting gondola.

Pre-ignition at T-minus twenty seconds brought the thrusters to deafening power, rocking the vehicle, and making everyone on board except the Navy and Air Force crew jump in their seats.

Four. Three. The noise and vibration increased, further shuddering passengers. Two. One. The *Quest* thundered off its pad.

Nothing could be heard above the din of the engines. The whole cabin vibrated as all were pinned forcefully back in their seats. As the shuttle began its slow roll to topside-down, the commandos gripped their seats and took the anti-nausea pills they had earlier refused.

After about five minutes, the vibration and roar began to abate.

Di Nucci looked at his men from his vantage point at the rear. "Anybody who's sick or got a problem, sing out—and don't be shy!"

The tense troopers began to stir but none replied.

As gravity lessened, the feeling of being upside-down diminished. Pulses began to decrease to almost normal and tense muscles relaxed. They were moving at eighteen thousand miles per hour. The screen showed the dark black of the Atlantic Ocean and light sparkling from behind the earth's curvature ahead. Because the camera was also upside down, the inverted image gave the men the impression that earth was above them. After ten minutes, the only sound was their breathing. In a half-hour, they began to recognize the dim, glinting lights of cities in Europe and Africa. The thin corona of earth's atmosphere became visible, and the horizon brightened.

Soon they could see that they were over the eastern Mediterranean coast, where it was dawn. The shuttle rolled slowly over, replacing their view of the planet with star-studded black. The roller-coaster feeling returned.

Fulton encouraged his troops. "Men, we're now approaching Iraq. Reentry is imminent. No enemy aircraft have been scrambled. We're gonna hit 'em too fast for the slow fighters they've got in this northern sector to catch us. We'll hit 'em hard and get out double-quick!"

Sequined black space on the monitor gave way to wispy blue caused by reentry—of necessity a steep descent. Fulton checked Baghdad time: 0649 hours. He realized that, in pieces or intact, they would be on the ground in fifteen minutes.

———————

Harrigan had left a voicemail for Tykvah just before leaving the Baghdad Hilton for Mon's office, five blocks away. "Hi, babe. We're safe but, as I said last night, things are...complicated. You and Ben sit tight. Then we'll extend our vacation! Love you. Hug Ben. Bye!"

The pair took a cab to the Office of the Premier of Iraq. They cleared security and took the elevator eighteen floors down to the executive offices. The doors opened to Hassan, grinning.

"Ah! There you are, gentlemen! So glad to see you."

Harrigan suppressed his alarm as he eyed Hassan and quickly brushed by him.

"Excuse us," Harrigan said flatly, "we have an appointment with the Premier."

"You think me a fool, Doctor? At least you can be useful!"

Hassan stepped back as two soldiers rushed the scientists and sprayed gas in their incredulous faces. The guards caught and carried the men down the hall to a lab adjoining Hassan's office, where they set the unconscious bodies into seats and confiscated their phones. One guard opened a steel box, drew clear liquid from a vial using an eyedropper, and placed a drop into each of Harrigan's eyes. Then he placed a drop into Freund's nasal cavities.

The soldier fumbled with the vial's cap and dropped it. Hassan cursed in Arabic. "Idiot! Get the sterilization foam and clean that up!"

The guard bolted out and returned with a small canister which emitted white foam over the spilled substance. Hassan left with the other soldier to prepare for his seven-thirty meeting with Mon. Within seconds, Harrigan and Freund's eyes began to flutter open as the remaining guard cleaned the floor. The guard at Freund's feet never knew what hit him. A bloody brass lamp dropped from Harrigan's hand as Freund reached for the man's pistol.

They bolted for the door, then Harrigan hesitated. He sat at a computer marked "Director" and quickly logged in.

"How did you just—?"

"Tykvah taught me this. Only works if it thinks you're the administrator. Oh! Holy *shit!*"

"What?"

"Their virus vector is different from ours. The only defense would be to purge these local files or get a copy of their algorithm model to make a vaccine...Can't copy or destroy these files. Even a bunker-buster bomb couldn't penetrate down this deep, and the hallways look like tunnels beyond this building. Best I can do is set a limited firewall opening for properties labeling. American intelligence might— Hey, shh! Someone's in the hall."

Freund stepped behind the door. Just as the guard raised his pistol at Harrigan, Freund knocked the soldier out cold, then dodged a shot to slam and lock the door to Hassan's office. "One's coming through Hassan's office," Freund yelled. "Damn, our phones! Run!"

The pair slipped into the elevator and took it to the roof. They tried to appear unflustered as they approached the helicopter pilot standing with a guard at the aircraft stairs.

"Good to see you again, Raj," Harrigan greeted the pilot in Arabic. "The Premier needs you to take us to Al-Rajda."

As the pilot entered his helicopter to verify, Harrigan and Freund decked the guard. They took his pistol, rushed in, and tied up the co-pilot.

———

Fulton touched a control button on his wrist. Menacing, ominous classical music built inside every helmet. The men began to grin, clench fists, and make threatening grunts.

The civilian computer team leader poked Fulton and cocked her head. "What the heck is *that*, some 'attack' music?"

Fulton smiled, noticing with pride a look of confidence, even ferocity, on every face. "It's by Holst. 'Mars, God of War.' Very effective. Watch the troops as we begin to land!"

"Yes. Those are about the most intimidating expressions I've ever seen," she replied. "Wait, I remember that piece now. Colonel, that's 'Mars, *Bringer* of War.'"

"To each his own god, *Civilian!*" Fulton snapped, frowning at being corrected.

The shuttle banked right to approach from the less-guarded north as mountains jutted up onto the screen and the music's volume became thunderous. Music combined with the video image of their steep approach to the plateau to give the men a powerful impression of swooping like eagles upon unsuspecting prey.

Indeed, they were on no radar screens and had a scant vapor trail, but the prey was not unsuspecting for long. The *Quest* had been tracked by infrared optics, and heat-seeking SA-23 missiles were now being trained directly on it.

Hassan could scarcely contain his glee as he finished his morning report to Mon.

"...and in addition, Premier, it is an immense pleasure to report that Harrigan and Freund have become subjects in our virus trials!"

Mon glared at Hassan. "What did you say, Hassan?" His stare told Hassan that something was wrong or misunderstood.

"Sir," Hassan pleaded for confirmation that he had done the right thing, "I thought that, since these useless, usurping irritants had come to waste your time — perhaps do worse — their deaths should at least be useful in testing the new vectors."

"You thought *what?* They could have helped continuing research. Who knows what we might have gained? The West might even.... What have you done?"

"But...Premier, did you not ask me to dispose of all of the researchers, now that—"

"I most certainly did not, you imbecile! How many have you killed? Do Harrigan and Freund know you have tried to kill the others, or them?"

Hassan's voice came weak and throaty. "All of them are dead, sir. I think Harrigan and Freund are unaware of their comrades' deaths, or that they have just been infected. There is… We have a serum. At Al-Rajda. Traces of the agent can be eliminated."

Mon's aide ran in holding a tablet. He whispered into Mon's ear and spoke a command to activate the screen. Mon's expression moved from alarm to a smile.

Mon snatched the device from the aide and spoke to an adjutant on the screen. "Prepare my jet and a company of guards. Tell Joint Forces Commander Akkad that I want him to scramble two squadrons of fighter-bombers — armed to bomb troops — to Al-Rajda. Send in Sahgrim's parachute brigade. Then have Akkad join me in my plane."

Mon turned to a guard who stood in the doorway. "Harrigan and Freund must receive this serum without delay. Put them on my helicopter and make them comfortable. Escort Colonel Hassan, who is now under arrest, to my jet and handcuff him to his seat. Alert my chauffeur."

A bloodied guard stumbled through the anteroom to Mon's office. "Sir, they escaped!"

Mon slammed the intercom button on his desk, transmitting directly to the helicopter pilot. "Premier Two, this is Mon. Where are you and are Harrigan and Freund aboard?"

Mon's intercom crackled with only the muffled sound of helicopter rotors, then the pilot's quavering voice replied. "Sir, I have not seen them."

Mon cocked his head but replied "If you do, tell them that I have arrested Colonel Hassan and that you are to take them to meet me at Al-Rajda. Mon out."

Mon's aide spoke up. "The pilot is under duress, sir. Shall we have them shot down?"

"No. Have them intercepted when they land at Al-Rajda. I will speak with them there. Now, let's get to the plane."

A red light and alarm signaled in the *Quest's* cockpit and passenger bay. Richmond's voice boomed over the music in Fulton's ear, "Missile in route! Brace for evasive flight!"

The *Quest's* nose lurched upward, pinning everyone weightily in their seats. The plateau on the screen dropped suddenly from view, replaced by clear, blue sky.

The tech grabbed Fulton's arm, screaming. "We can't take hits! We have no countermeasures! We were supposed to have surprise!"

Fulton was far from unruffled, but he extracted his arm. "Relax!" he growled. "The best they've got here are SA-23s. One of those can't penetrate the belly armor. They'd have to hit us with at least *ten* simultaneously. And the Iraqis aren't that smart!"

Beyond the plateau, a dozen puffs of smoke stretched into lines toward the center of the screen. An alarm blared as the monitor displayed the time until impact, twenty seconds. Fulton held his breath as one missile began to trail, waiver and head off the screen. Eleven more held their course, now fifteen seconds away.

In the cockpit, Colonel Richmond reached for the oxygen and fuel purge controls. He gaped in horror, barely enough oxidant and JP-13 to reach orbit. Purging even a small amount would likely strand them all. The pilot jerked the levers down once then quickly back up.

Heat streaming off the shuttle's underside ignited evaporating oxygen and fuel from the engines. Every missile fired directional correction retros. Seven veered horizontally, under and past the *Quest*'s dormant engines. Four missiles struck the craft's belly at an oblique angle, all in a row near the aft. The shuttle tipped violently forward, almost vertically careening toward craggy mountains just north of the plateau's rock perimeter. A split second later, seven near-simultaneous explosions thundered behind the diving aircraft.

Richmond strained to control rudders and retro thrusters to right his craft. It was leveling out but heading straight for the jagged northern edge of the plateau ridge. He ignited all three engines, further depleting fuel. Scraping over the top, the *Quest* sent shock-pulverized stone bursting off the ridge. Now he heard troops gasping as all beheld the sight of the merciless terrain thrust onto the screen. He squirmed in his seat as the plateau and its river landmark came into clearer view. Then Richmond and the co-pilot surged forward in their seats at the tug of parachutes slowing the shuttle's approach onto the plateau.

The copilot called on the intercom, "It's okay! But we land by the lab. It'll be a bumpy landing at the contingency site, middle of the plateau."

Richmond repeatedly punched the landing gear button and wrestled manual controls. Only fronts wheel responded. He retracted it and glimpsed the fast-approaching ground below. Trees jutted up out of a dissipating fog that blanketed the northern semi-swamp. Alerted by the blast, herons soared up off the marshes, eagles fled the trees. Strange animals ran south. Screams distracted him as all witnessed the plain punch up and down violently.

Richmond yelled into the intercom. "Brace for collision! Hold on!"

The shuttle struck hard on its belly in the hilly, lightly forested, and marsh-dotted north. Dirt and tree limbs flew up beside the shuttle. In seconds, they emerged from the wisps of fog and skidded beside the wood line two miles to a halt on grassy, level ground. The *Quest* had landed oriented southward, just northwest of the center of the plateau.

The commandos yanked their seat releases to get up and begin their tasks. But their attention was suddenly caught by the video monitor, still active. Panicked animal snarls, screeches, roars, and grunts blared in a deafening cacophony into each helmet. From left to right, the screen was filled with animals stampeding, bounding south and west away from the shuttle. Some fell as they ran, flailing to get up or avoid trampling by mammoths and *Coelodonta*. The troops were shocked despite the advance briefings about this place.

Fulton addressed his men forcefully. "Men, you were briefed on this contingency. If this aircraft cannot get out, we blow the research facilities and attempt to exfiltrate with the hostages. I will evaluate whether we get out together by air or dispersed in teams on foot. For now, put your faith in the crew of the *Quest* and assume the aircraft *will* transport us out. Let's move!"

He was issuing teams their orders when Colonel Richmond addressed him on a private circuit. "We should be able to launch off this plateau, Colonel. Just not sure how far we can get. If there is to be any chance at all, you'd better send a team out to kill that SAM site."

"Covered," he said tersely.

Fulton punched a wristband button and the roof opened to the sky. Di Nucci was already directing movements and crews which, in turn, were opening large lockers, handing out black, canister-like rifles and other equipment. The large crane that ran the length of the shuttle's cargo bay shot up and began hauling out two folded-in helicopters and two boat-like pallets from the aft cargo compartment. The right-side door slid open ten feet.

Everyone quieted as Fulton pointed with his hands and barked out the contingency plan they had already rehearsed. "Copter assembly teams: assemble your aircraft and carrier pallets.

"Air Team One: Drop off Bravo and Charlie Teams, and me and the technicians, on the roof of the research complex. Blast a hole in the southern tree line in case this crate can't get fully airborne before reaching it, then knock out the SAMs.

"Air Team Two: Drop off Delta and Echo, then stand by to assist Air Team One.

"Foxtrot: Handle loading, off-loading, and maintain security and air defense here.

"Alpha: You and Command Sergeant Major Di Nucci get to hoof it to the caves on foot."

Then Fulton grabbed his rifle. "Let's do it!" he shouted and stepped through the hatch.

It took five minutes for the two helicopters to be unfolded and completely assembled. Each Air Team had a gunner and a pilot as crew. The Air Teams flew off, each towing a boat-shaped, armored pallet full of men. The twenty-four troops and technicians in each pallet stared and held out their weapons, amazed at the hundreds of frightened animals beneath them.

Air Team Two dropped off six soldiers at each escalator entry on the plateau as Air Team One flew to the lab building. After using exploding rounds on a *Smilodon* that came too near the trap doors, the men of Team Delta focused on both escalator entrances. This team could operate a wide variety of foreign electronics equipment and vehicles. They unlatched and propped open the hydraulic doors and shot their way into the motor pool. Once Delta was out of danger from the cat and inside the escalator, Air Team Two lifted off southward.

The sheer, four-hundred-foot drop-off at the plateau's southern end passed thrillingly into Air Team One's view. The Americans had no time for sight-seeing, however, as they were already taking sporadic fire from Najik's panicked troops. The din of the helicopter's rotors now became interspersed with automatic gunfire and the odd explosion. The Iraqis outside the research building fell to the commandos' wide-arc flechette rounds.

Air Team One dropped off its five civilians and the seven Team Bravo soldiers on top of the research building. These men set focused-blast cutting charges along the edges of the roof of what intelligence briefings stated was the Genetics Lab. They would enter on Fulton's command, once the front offices were secure. Air Team One's helicopter moved off to pound the building's front with rapid fire from its chin turret. All windows and doors were blasted, preventing Iraqis inside from threatening Charlie Team.

The twelve men of Team Charlie and Fulton jumped out of the low-hovering helicopter's pallet and stormed the building with amazing ferocity. Once the commandos were inside, the aircraft returned to the *Quest* and loaded up coils of advanced, tube-shaped explosives. Reaching the southern wood line, the deadly aircraft fired explosive rounds from its chin-turret into the trees, roughing out a path to the cliff.

Then its crew unrolled the explosive coils in two one-thousand-foot-long lines along that path. Moments later, a mighty explosion shattered what was left of the foot-thick oaks, forming a two-hundred-foot-wide avenue carpeted with shredded stumps and limbs. The helicopter raced southward, launching three metal-seeking missiles that destroyed the SA-23 sites spotted earlier.

Air Team Two now flew over the cliff and east, past the river. It set Echo Team behind the deserted houses and sent missiles crashing into the nearby troop barracks. Its chin turret mowed down those who were already running out. The helicopter returned to land behind the homes, concealed. Its pilot listened to the situation on the radio.

Iraqi troops on foot and in jeeps came streaming out of the tunnel to escape southward. These were killed to preclude their return to threaten Echo Team. The east end of the tunnel was the only covered and concealed entrance to the research complex, so Echo wired it for demolition. The team also set up several listening devices in the area and acted as guard against land assault.

On the northern plateau, Di Nucci and his Alpha Team moved swiftly toward the Neanderthal caves. The shuttle's violent landing had cleared nearly all the animals from the northern third of the plateau, especially on the west side, so Alpha progressed without interruption and reached the forest edge in just over twenty minutes.

The noise of the explosions and sonic boom, and then sight of the shuttle's landing, alerted Lloyd and his people in the caves. They realized the craft they had seen was their rescue. Lloyd ordered quick good-byes to their obviously confused and frightened friends. Most of the moderns left the cave in tears. As they did, an arrow shot from the tree line at the base of the ridge pierced Lloyd's arm. Kairaba screamed and tried to pull Lloyd down, but he threw her and several of his fellows back into the cave. He caught another arrow to the thigh. He returned fire but stopped, seeing only shaking foliage.

Rocks began to pelt Lloyd from overhead. The Cro-Magnons were both above and below them. They must have gotten past the sentry when everyone came inside after the shuttle was identified. He fell back into the cave and pulled the arrows from his flesh, screaming. Kairaba and Singh dressed the wounds.

After a while, Lloyd glimpsed the American soldiers running toward them through the trees. The Cro fled to the southeast, back into the forest— potentially along the route to the shuttle. Lloyd and the others rushed out to greet the Rangers.

"The best we can do is trot…" Lloyd said, "children, my leg."

"We can move faster than that, sir," Di Nucci said, motioning for his men to lash the children to their backs and help Lloyd. "Our orders are to evacuate *only* staff and family."

Rhahs was shooed off by soldiers. He turned, head low, to lead his clan back to the caves.

"No!" Kora ordered in Nostratic. She pulled Rhahs back forcefully. "We must go! We must teach Friendli; prepare the way. One final call to them. We follow now!"

Rhahs stared at her and squeezed her hand. "Kora trust flower-voice. Rhahs trust Kora."

Kora and Rhahs led their confused band of Neanderthals to follow their friends. Lloyd looked back helplessly, the thought that these primitive people were to be left behind — to Iraqi experiments or wrath — wrenching his conscience as he ran hard with the others. The Neanderthals' cries faded as they became easily outdistanced in open areas south of the swampy woods.

As two soldiers helped Lloyd hobble faster through the previously boot-trampled grass beside the wood line, he eyed the woods and fretted. *If I were a Cro, where would I...Oh no!*

"Sergeant Major Di Nucci," he panted, "are you sure the Cro won't have anticipated that we'd take the same route back?"

Lloyd got no answer, but saw alarm seize Di Nucci's face as he cupped his earphone.

"Jets!" yelled Di Nucci, relaying the warning. "Run faster!"

He called for a helicopter. "Mars Scope Commander, this is Alpha Leader. We're three miles from home. Need choppers! Over."

"Negative, Alpha Leader, you'll have to run. Choppers needed here. Commander out."

Harrigan jammed the pistol into the pilot's ear. "Too slow. Get us to Al-Rajda yesterday!" he growled.

The man looked puzzled at first, then pushed the throttle to full. The engines whined louder and the men were pulled back by the acceleration.

"No tricks," Freund barked, "or you die and we fly this thing!"

Thirty minutes later they saw the concrete landing site ten miles south of Al-Rajda. The adjacent hut looked deserted. The pilot started to descend, but Harrigan grabbed his arm.

"No, you don't. Take us to the research building. We're gonna pick up some passengers."

After a minute, a red light flashed, and a buzzer sounded in cycles. The pilot spoke calmly. "Our missiles deactivate near the Premier's personal aircraft. Electronic recog-nition."

Seconds later the missile was visible, a smoky arc hurtling at them from the left front. Another red light flashed and the buzzing became constant. The pilot became frantic.

"Foreign missile," the pilot cried. "It will hit!"

"Foreign?" Harrigan and Freund blurted in unison.

The pilot jerked back the controls and climbed the craft in a dizzying vertical loop. The engines shut down as the helicopter finished its maneuver, plummeting from rotors-down to wheels-down. It struck in the center of the river, the cockpit underwater instantly, just as the missile plowed into the river's east bank, blasting up mud.

Harrigan fought the pain in his strained back and grabbed Freund, unconscious, in the rushing water. The pilot was dead, his chest pierced by a control lever. Harrigan yanked hard at the copilot, but the unconscious man's legs were pinned. As water flooded the cabin through the destroyed windows, he swam out pulling Freund.

Harrigan reached the bank and began mouth-to-mouth resuscitation until Freund rolled over and violently coughed out pints of water.

"Hih-ummm! Ck-cuhh! I don't k-h-hiss on the first date!"

"Fine with me! Come on! We've got to get vehicles or radios or something. Get our people out somehow, maybe north to the Kurds."

They climbed to level ground where they found the smoldering remains of a shredded Iraqi anti-aircraft launcher truck. Dead soldiers lay around a drab green jeep. Harrigan jumped inside and started the jeep while Freund recovered rifles, ammunition, and binoculars. They sped east to the low, rocky riverbank. Less vulnerable to fire from their flanks, they drove north along the water's edge toward the research complex. Freund stood looking ahead.

"Kevin!" he shouted, "Two small helicopters at the building! Never seen ones like that. Soldiers on the roof and—"

The roof of the research building exploded as he spoke. The sound of the blast followed in seconds as the smoke cleared.

"I can't tell if they're Iraqis or..." Freund said. "They're going down through the roof!"

Harrigan continued driving, steering hard to stay covered by the riverbank. As they drove within a mile of the damaged building, rifle fire began to ping off the jeep's grill and then shatter the windshield. Harrigan spun the jeep almost sideways to a stop. He and Freund scrambled out and peered northward from under the bumper.

"Where's that shooting from?" Harrigan asked.

"That water drain up ahead!"

Najik's men knelt clearly visible and without helmets in a rut.

Harrigan grabbed Freund and whispered, "Do you remember the first Florida patrol?"

"Yeah. There's nothing else we can do."

As Freund laid down slow, continuous fire at the five, keeping them ducking, Harrigan crept back from the vehicle, up the bank, and into thick grass. He continued low to the ground until he was behind the Iraqis. From the edge of the deep grass, he had a perfect line of sight on the men, who continued firing sporadically at the jeep.

Harrigan considered his options. *Do I really need to kill these guys? We worked side by side for years. And we're not even sure what's going on here!*

Harrigan fired at the men's feet and yelled in Arabic, "Stop!"

Now in an untenable position, the soldiers froze and slowly turned, weapons down. Freund moved in on them from behind, and the pair disarmed them and stashed their rifles in the jeep. They got no answers as to who was fighting whom, so they made the hapless soldiers run into the cold river and swim away. The two returned to the jeep and sped off toward the research center, where small arms fire and explosions continued unabated.

Chapter Fifteen

Al-Rajda Research Preserve, two miles north of the *Quest*
1107 hours, 21 April 2036

Di Nucci and his men slowed as some of the adults had faltered and had to be carried. The Neanderthal clan, also carrying their children, struggled to keep pace some forty yards behind. The jets had become more than just dots in the southern sky, making Di Nucci nervous — but he dared not panic his group by sharing his fears. *Jets could blast the Quest!* He fretted. *What if the intel was wrong and there are enemies in the woods? Where did those Cro-Magnons Lloyd warned me about go? What if some predators weren't flushed from this area? We're running right along these woods and can't see inside!*

A shower of spears, arrows, and bullets erupted from his left. One of his men fell as the others threw their passengers to the ground. The Neanderthals dove into the grass. A bullet struck Di Nucci in the side of his armor-textile uniform, stinging as if it had entered his chest.

"Near ambush! Fire! Attack through it!"

His men's well-conditioned counterattack was immediate. Alpha Team fired left and charged at the knoll.

The Cro kept low behind the hill and trees, but Alpha's automatic fire and explosive rounds were shockingly overwhelming. The soldiers reached the hill before half of the Cro-Magnons could escape. Three of the seven Cro fell wounded. Di Nucci led his men crashing through the Cro's assault line until he saw three warriors being dragged away, rifles abandoned.

"Halt!" Di Nucci shouted. "No time to chase! Check casualties! Quick, stack those rifles and blow 'em. Everybody back!" he ordered.

"Fire in the hole!" came a sergeant's warning as the troops chased off more hidden Cro-Magnons and piled rifles to rejoin the cringing civilians. The grenade exploded as Di Nucci reached Lloyd and other adults, who were checking wounds and comforting screaming children.

"I'm not sure about your people, but none of mine are bad," Lloyd called to him.

Di Nucci turned to his men for the hoped-for signal that none were seriously hurt. A sergeant was swiftly dressing a wound at the back of a fellow soldier's neck.

"Alpha is 'all up,'" the trooper yelled. "Penquist's cut good, but no casualties."

"Load 'em up and move out."

Di Nucci forced himself to ignore the Neanderthals, who were closing the gap, and continued the rapid trek. He hoped that, somehow, the Neanderthals left behind would fare well. The modern children cried out continuously for the adults to wait for their primitive friends.

Di Nucci scowled nervously at the southern sky as he raced onward.

───────────

Harrigan rolled the jeep to a stop just south of the waterfall and slumped forward against the steering wheel. Freund could just see the top of a helicopter half a mile westward.

Freund looked over at Harrigan and pulled him upright. "Why are you stopping?"

Harrigan responded slowly. "Tired. Vision's cloudy, that's all."

"We're getting too old for this stuff. Let me examine your eyes."

Freund held Harrigan's eyelids open. He found his own attention slipping as he inspected Harrigan's right eye and momentarily forgot whether he had already examined the left one.

"Nothing I can see without a scope. You okay to make it to Najik's office? Maybe we can use his monitor to find out where everyone is."

"I'm fine. Good idea. If soldiers are anywhere, they'll be in the labs or the control room, not Najik's office. You know, this shoot 'em up stuff was fun twenty years ago. But now —"

Freund finished the sentiment. "Now people are really dying. Let's go."

They leapt out, crouch-running then crawling through the grass to reach Najik's window. Suddenly they heard a 'whoosh' and the jeep exploded in flames.

"Geeze!" Harrigan gasped, "We'd have been —"

"Quick, get inside!" Freund warned.

They struggled to open the window, then cracked the panes with the butts of their rifles.

"Hawlt! Stop or I'll farr!" A southern U.S. accent shocked them. They froze in place. Two burly soldiers advanced from around the front of the building.

"There," Harrigan screamed, "Somebody's firing missiles!"

"Who do you think called in that farr, knucklehead? Shut up, drop your weapons, and put your hands up behind your —" The sergeant paused, squinting. "Well, well. You two look just like your pictures."

The NCO motioned for his corporal to quickly frisk the prisoners and rush them around to the front of the building.

"I say'd git yor hands up behind your head and git movin'," the sergeant roared.

Harrigan was angry at the soldier's inexplicable unfriendliness. "What the hell is going on? Where are my staff and their families?"

"You can speak with Colonel Fulton shortly. Shut up'n *move!*"

Inside the building, no lights shone at all. Concrete dust and sulfur odor filled the air. They could hear explosions and small arms fire from the direction of the motor pool. They moved through the gloomy halls to the Genetics Lab, joined by several other soldiers along the way. Rays of sunlight streaked down through a huge, jagged hole in the lab's ceiling. Broken tiles and shards of building materials were strewn everywhere. Men in white, rubberized coveralls were unbolting the FGR modules from the floor while others used acetylene torches to cut components free. The sergeant ushered them to a huge black man speaking into a microphone on his helmet. Fulton stopped speaking abruptly and grimaced at the pair.

"Never thought I'd see the day! Harrigan and Freund!"

Harrigan squinted. "Do I know you? What's happening here?"

"You ought to know me, you self-important son of a bitch! Always second-guessing the cadre. Always had the right answer. You were the tough Ranger-type. Gonna reform the world in your image. Well, *I'll* fight *for* you while you keep silent!"

Freund raised an eyebrow and started to defend Harrigan. "You're wrong! He's changed—"

A burly master sergeant stepped from around the half-dismantled FGR gene sequencer, grabbed Harrigan by the neck and growled, "Remember me, asshole? What goes around comes around. Can you say 'I'm sorry I tried to trash my Ranger Instructor's career?'"

Harrigan's esophagus was clenched tight, and he could not respond. His vision clouded. "Get off him, Jenkins," roared a captain.

Harrigan interrupted his own gasp as confusion gripped him. He thought he saw a fleeting haze around Fulton's smiling face, and he perceived vengefulness streaming from Jenkins' narrowing eyes as if it were a spirit. He still could not decide on the right response, so he took a swing at Jenkins, who immediately countered by wrenching Harrigan's arm and punching him squarely on the cheek. Harrigan collapsed, unconscious.

A guard threw a green field bandage over Freund's head and pulled it tight into his mouth, tying the ends behind his head.

Fulton grinned at Jenkins and roared, "Get them out of the technicians' way and out of my sight! Put them…What's the most secure room outside this one, captain?"

"The southeast corner office, I'd say, sir."

"Put them in there. Post one guard with them and one in the hall. Then clear these Iraqi *boy scouts* from the rest of the building!"

On a tall platform in the *Quest's* cargo hold, Major Jasper sat coolly eyeing a radar scope.

"Fighter-bombers," he said matter-of-factly, glancing up at the southern horizon.

Eleven soldiers stood out on the *Quest's* wings with long, green tubes on their shoulders and crates containing more at their feet. He peered again at his scope. Eight bright dots appeared on its edge. Jasper held his breath as the dots rapidly approached the screen's white ring, a computer-calculated estimate of the best engagement range.

"All launch!"

The high-pitched roar of eleven shoulder-mounted anti-aircraft missiles was almost deafening. The missiles flew thousands of feet up before any of the soldiers could even drop the spent canisters and reach for more. The men did not have to spot their target. Jasper quickly moved a tethered stylus on the scope to adjust the computer's allocation of missiles to targets. Wispy exhaust trails began to diverge in the southern sky — then halt, striking targets.

Jasper studied the screen: ten more targets approaching. He did not have to look at his men to know that they waited at the ready.

"All launch!" he called again.

Another volley screamed into the sky toward the south and east, chasing Iraqi jets.

Nine more jets appeared on the screen, moving toward the white gauging rings. As Jasper prepared for the next volley, the first ring disappeared from the screen. None of the last wave of aircraft remained.

"All launch!"

Missiles screeched yet again from the commandos' shoulders. Jasper's men swiftly prepared their next volley. Jasper noted nervously that only one box of four missiles remained at each post. The launching and destruction continued as the number of missiles dwindled. In moments, the empty crates were thrown off the shuttle onto the smoky, rutted clay behind. Grim faces looked up at their team commander.

Jasper jerked his stylus over the radar screen to allocate every last missile to a target. He carefully studied his scope and then glanced at his seat, the mission's last crate of eight missiles.

"All clear!"

He smiled as his men cheered and whooped, but he kept tensely eying the radar screen.

Air Teams One and Two swooped into sight with their gondola-like pallets holding confiscated lab equipment and a few soldiers. Jasper's men guided these into the cargo bays, opened the pallets' armored sides, and tipped out the contents. The choppers left and returned filled with soldiers and twelve bandaged-up Iraqi researchers, zip-tied at their wrists. Jasper looked at his watch and climbed higher, up onto the *Quest's* still-hot engine covers. Through binoculars, he saw Di Nucci and the civilians less than a mile away.

As he turned, his stomach filled with acid. The southern sky had filled with aircraft, many more than eight.

Jasper's men off-loaded troopers from Charlie and Bravo Teams, scrambled to secure the captured hardware in the cargo bays and clamped the Iraqi scientists into seats, gagged. The helicopters sped off to pick up Echo and Delta Teams and Fulton.

Jasper ordered distribution of the remaining eight anti-aircraft missiles while studying his radar screen. He saw five supersonic aircraft and fifteen large, subsonic jets. He called to his men. "Yentik, Ross, and Taft! Hold! The rest of you standby to launch...Launch!"

Five missiles thrust off, screaming at the jets. Jasper again worked his stylus. The five targets disappeared. He waited. The larger aircraft still approached. As seven of these reached the deadly ring on the scope, the helicopters reappeared over the cliff edge and sped toward the shuttle.

"Remaining missiles: Launch!"

The three streamers closed on the fifteen transports. Jasper knew that this revealed to the Iraqis that the Americans had spent their defenses, but there was nothing more he could do.

Jasper checked with Richmond. "We gonna have a 'go' for take-off, sir? Any more fast-movers?"

"A lot of ifs, Major. I can issue a 'go' on aircraft integrity. But I'm unsure we've got the fuel to make full orbit. Wait...transmission from Intel."

———————

Mon was not interested in the objections of his Joint Forces Commander. The two men sat before a situation monitor in the cabin of Mon's jet, which had flown in behind the transports that carried Colonel Sahgrim's reinforced parachute brigade of three thousand men.

"General Akkad, if you fail to drop Sahgrim's troops at Al-Rajda immediately, the Americans will escape. That would leave me less bargaining power with their government. We will also be uncertain how much they know about our work here. Losses from missiles or parachuting into trees are secondary considerations. Is this clear?"

General Akkad knew better than to disagree, let alone show anger.

"Yes, Premier Colonel Mon," he stammered. He turned to his microphone and ordered hundreds of his men to what he knew was certain death. "Sahgrim, your transports are to continue at maximum speed. There is no time to wait for more fighter-bombers. Acknowledge."

The speaker on the console was silent for a moment. Then came the response. "I...Yes, sir. I understand and will comply. Sahgrim out."

Mon turned from the console and had the guards move Hassan, who sat gagged, bound, and struggling weakly, to an aft cabin and shut the door behind him.

"You have one chance to live. Do you understand me?"

Hassan stopped wiggling and nodded.

"You may be able to redeem yourself. I would like that better than killing you for ruining my plans with your ineptitude, wouldn't you?"

Hassan nodded rapidly.

"We must defuse this crisis, old friend, or fight a war for which we are not yet ready. The Americans will surely not stop at one raid. And there may also be world opinion to consider if other governments feel we are a threat. We must allay their fears. Therefore, you must do *exactly* as I tell you...if you wish to live. Here is what you will do when we land..."

Colonel Richmond's voice blared in Fulton's earphone, "G-2 advises incoming troop transports, unescorted. Expect air assault. ETA thirty minutes. You have twenty minutes to board for take-off. The time is now eleven nineteen. Acknowledge."

Fulton acknowledged and turned to the civilian technical team leader. "Everything secure on those pallets?"

The man provided Fulton a response by telling the helicopter pilot to lift out the pallet. "Ready to go. Take it away!"

Fulton issued commands to his other team leaders. "All teams, pull in now. Guard detail, bring in Harrigan and Freund."

The guard detail did not respond. Fulton's expression changed to alarm.

"Guard detail, come in!"

There was still no response.

"Damn! Captain Marsh, you and four men come with me."

Fulton and the others raced to Najik's office, which reeked of sulfur and eggs. The hall guard lay unconscious as the room guard tried to get up from the floor.

"Where are they?" Fulton demanded, eyes darting to every corner of the room.

The room guard pointed toward the floor, choking. "Gas...canis-ter. Iraqis. Trap door!"

Beside the steel trap door, a rug lay half-rolled back. The door would not open. Fulton had his men blast the floor, first with grenades, then with their remaining explosives. It served only to chip into the thick concrete and mangle the steel.

Jasper radioed Fulton again. "Recommend you leave now. We'll be swimming in paratroopers, bombs, and air-to-ground missiles any minute!"

Fulton swore under his breath, then yelled, "Get out! Everyone get on the pallet *now!*"

"You should never have followed your husband to Bagdad," crackled the CIA operative's voice through Tykvah's headset as she sat in the Bagdad Hovercraft Company copilot seat. "And I shouldn't have let you convince me to get my Station Chief to okay rerouting to Al-Rajda."

"Why?" she grimaced left and back as Ben popped his head into the cabin.

"News on my sat-phone says, when we get there, we'll be in the middle of a firefight, that's why!"

Tykvah sat beside him in the co-pilot's chair, considering returning because of Ben. She fidgeted and finally opened the computer it had held.

"Hey, get away from that laptop!" he growled."

Tykvah glared back. "If you people are here, Mon is threatening something...and my husband and Mannie are in danger. The entire world may be in danger! Do you monitor Mon or his people on this?"

He took the computer, entered his password, and handed it back to her, smirking. "You wouldn't even know where to star—"

"Yes. I'm an airhead, very slow on the uptake."

Her fingers flew over the keyboard and the Iraqi Interior Ministry seal appeared on the screen.

"You can't get into their research files. Even we can't get through the firewa—"

The agent stared, incredulous, as Tykvah manipulated the device to shortly circumvent security.

"That's new. How are you able to access the registry for properties permissions?"

"I have no idea. Somebody left it editable. Look, I'm that far at least."

Two files, titled ASLI and MUHAWALA, flashed as partially accessible.

"That's what they stole from my husband, ORIGINAL. And now

they're making a series of versions of the genetic coding from it, and algorithm-model to create a weapon."

"We know that. Copy them before it closes you out!"

Tykvah tried to access the files and failed. Then her eyebrows shot up and her fingers flew again as the two file's created date changed. "But if they think these were sabotaged, they won't trust it — or their work — and that will at least slow them down."

"They'll never notice that," he scoffed.

Her fingers raced over her phone. "Kevin or Mannie will try to check their texts. This could be our only shot at getting them to scare Mon into at least slowing his research until you people can finish the job."

The Al-Rajda plateau appeared to the northeast. As they crossed its west ridge, she could see the plateau's north-south wood line.

"Get out of the cockpit and buckle in behind the cabin wall *now!*" the operative yelled.

The craft approached within a hundred yards of the *Quest*. Tykvah scanned south, out of the right passenger window and suddenly gripped Ben. A line of smoke stabbed toward them and exploded the engines beneath. The craft surged upward thirty feet, then plummeted fifty to the grass. Flames blasted into the cockpit and surrounded the craft like a corona.

"He's dead," Tykvah yelled, yanking a silvery blanket from a cabinet and wrapping herself and Ben. "Stay by me. We'll run *through* the flames. Readyyy…" She heaved the door lever. "Now!"

They burst from the flame wall, veering right toward the *Quest*. In the distance to the right, helicopters roared in, to their left, figures ran toward the shuttle. The pair vaulted through its door.

"Where's Dr. Harrigan, and Dr. Freund?" she demanded of the soldiers inside.

"Lost," Jenkins stated flatly from across the cargo bay. "You must be the missus and kid. Ah'm sorrih. The Iraqis got 'em. Git buckled in."

Di Nucci reached the *Quest* as Air Team Two landed just west of the shuttle with the remaining troops of Echo Team. The off-loaded soldiers ran to help Di Nucci's near-exhausted Alpha Team haul the civilians into the *Quest*. Lloyd, limping badly, was shoved into a seat and buckled in. He passed out, still bleeding.

Fulton called the pilot on a private channel as he flew in on the last helicopter load. "Colonel Richmond, can we make it out in this thing?"

"The simulations show we can get airborne if we can make four hundred ten or more miles per hour by the time we reach the cliff."

"Is that a 'yes,' Colonel?"

"Yes."

The Iraqi transports were already landing troops around the river and housing areas below the plateau. More transports poured out hundreds and hundreds of paratroops two thousand feet above the lower plateau. Parachutes and planes rapidly darkened the sky. Some soldiers' canopies collided, tangling some jumpers, and sending them plummeting to their deaths. In moments, troops were on the ground all over the plateau on both sides of the river. Paratroops who landed in the open managed to avoid the pandemonium of crowding, fighting animals in the southern wooded areas, but *Smilodons* and other predators crouched nearly invisible in the grass.

The shuttle bay door began sliding haltingly to close as soldiers feverishly pulled it. Engine fuel pumps whined. Nearly everyone was strapped in. Tykvah grabbed Singh and Olivier, who stood just inside the door resisting a soldier assigned to seat them. "With me!" commanded Tykvah, as the trio ran out to pull in the Neanderthals who had managed to run up to the wing.

"You can't take off!" Tykvah screamed. "You've got people in the engines' blast area!"

She yanked a young Neanderthal male into the shuttle. Then she and Olivier dashed back out to retrieve the rest of the straggling and breathless clan. Ben followed.

Fulton responded swiftly. "We have no time, Doctors. Get back in your—"

He could not believe his eyes as more civilians now exited the shuttle. Five others darted out past the Rangers. They ran back to pull more clan members ahead when a shower of Iraqi bullets cut their route back inside. Fulton rushed out with a handful of men and two Armor-piercing Automatic Weapons, or APAWs. The APAWs blazed from the operators' sides as other soldiers ran for more ammunition and fired grenades from their huge rifles. Di Nucci ran out onto the shuttle wing with five more soldiers and, along with those already outside, decisively silenced most of the nearby Iraqi fire.

"I will *not* let this mission fail!" Fulton shouted, grabbing an APAW to force Tykvah's group to abandon the Neanderthals. He fired just over their heads. "Get in now or you're dead."

Di Nucci believed that the threat was only a bluff and so did the researchers. He shoved another Neanderthal through the door and ordered the researchers to hurry.

Fulton fired again. Two Neanderthal adolescents being helped onto the wing by Singh and Kora fell, their arms shredded by Fulton's fire. Singh screamed as Jenkins shoved her back inside. Tykvah dove toward Kora as

Rhahs and four children retreated off the wing into the rut. Kora gaped at Ben, who approached from behind his mother.

Kora shouted in Nostratic, pointing at Ben, and hugged a bewildered Tykvah.

"Mom, what's she saying to me? She looks like the one in my dream. Is she a—"

Tykvah scooped up Ben and, with Singh, pushed Kora and her family toward the *Quest's* wing. But Fulton bowled the Neanderthals off and had his men drag Singh, Olivier, and Ben inside. The Neanderthals now retreated fifty feet off the wing, just west of the shuttle's engines. Tykvah jumped Fulton from behind, knocking him to the ground. The enemy fire renewed as she and Woj pushed and carried yet more Neanderthals back to the wing.

Di Nucci pulled Woj off of Fulton and threw him at his men. Finally hauled in, Tykvah fought to be between Ben and half-conscious Lloyd, as soldiers buckled and zip-tied all except Lloyd into seats. Now unable to free herself, Tykvah bowed her head to Ben's shoulder and joined his sobbing.

The clang of small arms fire and thundering grenades striking the craft's hull mounted to an alarming fury. As Fulton stood, an Iraqi bullet passed through his cheek. Two more struck him in the eye and nose. Di Nucci screamed for his men to get inside as he tried to pull his commander back into the shuttle. A bullet hit Di Nucci in the armpit gap of his armor-shirt. He lost his grip on Fulton's lifeless body as other Rangers dragged both leaders inside.

Now the engines' pre-thrust began to whine, slowly building and vibrating the craft. Its heat streaked just behind Kora and her stranded family. Inside troops thrust nineteen of the Neanderthals into seats, but that left twelve adults with no place to sit. Di Nucci had his men push them into the cargo hold and secured the latch. Then, with sweat and tears coating his face and blood trickling down his side, he collapsed as if dead into his seat, his arms sprawling upon the seat backs beside him.

But in seconds he mustered his strength and sat straight in his seat. "There was just no saving Colonel Fulton," he called out loudly. "That's just the way he was. Major...Jasper's in command now."

Jasper looked through the door and yelled, "That everyone?"

"All up, sir," Di Nucci returned weakly, and passed out.

The *Quest* was receiving powerful mortar fire now. The near misses threw plumes of dirt with every deafening boom. A few direct grenade hits were ineffectual but worried Jasper, as the engines abruptly ceased pre-thrust. *What now?* Jasper thought.

"Major," Richmond's voice boomed in Jasper's communicator. "You've got to stop the mortar fire now or they'll blow the ship apart!"

"Roger," Jasper replied as he leaped back out. "Alpha, assign four men with APAWs to Bravo up past the nose cone. Bravo, cover the woods to the east and south. Charlie, cover west and north. Taft, put the counter-mortar radar and the tubes forward of the wing. Yentik, Ross, hook up the smart-rocket launcher to it."

The area, already thunderous, now blazed with the Rangers' small arms and rocket fire. As the Iraqi mortars and rockets stopped, and small arms fire waned, Jasper gained confidence. He held up his binoculars, scanning from north to west, scattered rifle fire only. He swung his gaze a quarter mile south along the wood line. Fear struck him hard and his jaw fell open.

"Shit! Bravo, don't you see that case of missiles? Suppressing fire, now!"

"Where? I don't..." Bravo team's captain stopped. "Yes, there, and a machine gu—"

Machine gun fire raked Bravo team from nearer along the wood line, forcing heads down as the operator and assistant hefted a missile from its packing material.

Chapter Sixteen

Harrigan ran, almost breathless, in the bear-like mechanical suit northward through hazy woods. His view was obscured by the suit's wire mesh portal as he noticed Freund pull slightly ahead in his own robotic suit. Gunfire, roars, and screams rang like a tolling bell from the west.

It appeared suddenly in a clearing to his left—one of the gargantuan *Varanus priscus* lizards, its four-foot head jerking skyward to gulp a flailing soldier. Something rustled branches in front of them. A screeching streak of grey, yellow, and red feathers launched from a thicket at Harrigan and Freund. As the *Phorusrhacus's* three-foot beak and therapod talons opened, six gray tigers—marsupial *Thylacoleos*—fell from the trees onto the terror-bird. They ripped it with huge buck-teeth and recurved thumb claws.

"Left," Harrigan screamed. "Keep running!" The pair dodged the melee, swerving north again as the gun battle sounds grew louder. "There!" he shouted. "Our ride outta here."

Freund yelled back, "Look, they've got a missile! They're gonna blow it up!"

Jasper peered through his binoculars in horror as an Iraqi rocket launcher operator got the "fire now" tap from his assistant. He anticipated death within seconds. *God help us, there's no time!*

He gaped in awe as two gargantuan bears fell upon the operator and assistant, trampling them as the rocket ignited in a billow of gray smoke. It exploded thunderously a hundred yards to Jasper's right near a discarded helicopter. He exhaled to see the Iraqi launcher crew lying mangled and still.

Suddenly, machine-gun fire resumed from the tree line, raking the bear suits which went sprawling on their sides a quarter mile short of the shuttle. A belly plate popped open on the robotic suit and Harrigan emerged. He yanked feverishly at the other suit's belly. Finally, he tugged it open and hauled out Freund, who lay limp. Heaving him upon his shoulders, Harrigan dodged machine gun fire ripping the ground and dashed toward the *Quest*.

Jasper and his men ducked a flurry of rifle fire. Machine gun fire resumed from several yards down the tree line, peppering the ground behind Harrigan and overtaking his stride. Harrigan dove at a corpse, then rose firing back with his new rifle. Gasping, Harrigan pulled Freund, now conscious, among the Rangers who whisked Freund aboard. Jasper now studied his tablet, ignoring sporadic rifle fire.

"Radar shows two platoons headed our way, each a hundred meters out. Can't stop both!"

Harrigan examined it. "The one on the left, east, can't get to us. Concentrate mortars on the one south of us. Hurry!"

"Who do you think—"

"Monsters in that pond and swamp," Harrigan panted, "and a soldier's remains to boot. That platoon'll never get at us. Do it now before the south platoon destroys your craft!"

Jasper sent the coordinates of the southern platoon to the mortar computer. "Everything you've got, Jenkins!"

"Summ-beeyitch," Jenkins grumbled as he executed the order. In seconds, rapid thumps of the mortars sounded loudly.

Jasper gazed in amazement at his screen: The south platoon was a blur, indicating nothing standing, and forty or so figures were dispersing eastward away from the *Quest*. He grimaced at Harrigan, then returned to the screen. Suddenly a line sped across the screen from a burst of light to the southwest.

"Anti-mortar fire!" Harrigan screamed as four Rangers leaped from their huge tubes to just escape the rocket screaming in to blast the weapons into shrapnel.

As Jasper struggled to get the wounded into the craft, his radio crackled. "This is Richmond. Orders: Get out now. Can't risk the *Quest*."

"Give me a minute!"

"Negative."

"Alpha, Echo: every second man inside now, then close it up."

Jasper knew Iraqi units would be streaming toward him from farther out on the plain and along the woodline. He looked around and turned back to Jenkins. "Jenkins, get 'em inside."

Richmond's voice crackled again. "Closing the door now, Major Jasper. Get inside!"

"Love to, since I feel...can't see well. It's possible Dr. Freund and I were infected...a lab, got to be twenty floors below Mon's office building. You need our blood for analysis. Even then..." Harrigan trailed off, "might not be time to develop and distribute a vaccine." Then he grabbed Jasper's arm and powerfully spun him around. "But those Neanderthals," he growled, pointing behind the wing, "are not animals, and I want them inside!"

"Infected? No shit, seriously?" Jasper replied. "Jenkins! Get 'em in now. Get pressure suits on 'em," he ordered, "and blow that copter so Hajjis can't get it."

Immediately, a soldier knelt in the opening, carefully aiming a launcher at the helicopter.

Jasper's men tried to drag Harrigan and Freund toward the door, but Harrigan pointed toward Kora and Rhahs, who cried out with a scratchy scream. They broke from the soldiers and sprinted for the Neanderthals near the rear of the shuttle.

"Wrong! Your freaks die. Get in Harrigan, asshole," Jenkins growled, intercepting Harrigan's neck with his thick arm.

"Kevin!" Tykvah shouted, bumping Lloyd awake. Lloyd drew a knife and cut her ties. She rushed, breathless, toward Harrigan and knocked the grenadier, whose grenade blasted more dirt from the crater by the helicopter. He punched her and threw her, limp, into her seat.

Harrigan started toward her, then turned toward the Neanderthals. Jenkins blocked his path.

"Ooff!" Jenkins blurted as Harrigan's rifle butt rammed into his stomach, dropping the NCO where he stood.

"Get Jenkins inside and throw those two in *now!*" Jasper roared at the Bravo team captain.

The door slid slowly, leaving a five-foot horizontal gap as soldiers dragged Jenkins in. Harrigan and Freund bolted back behind the wing, pulled Kora and her family up onto it, and thrust them at Jasper and the three commandos remaining outside. Harrigan raised his rifle.

"You call yourself human?" Harrigan boomed, "Get them in now or I'll shoot."

"The door's closing!" Jasper shouted as the pre-thrust erupted. "All right. Get 'em in."

As the soldiers pulled the Neanderthals in, Iraqi rifle fire ricocheted off the hull. The door slid to within three feet of closing. Jasper shoved Harrigan and Freund toward it. The craft lurched forward, causing them to trip. A shower of bullets caught Jasper and he collapsed in the doorway. One of his men pulled him inside as he screamed, "No! Retrieve the scientists!"

The door closed as Jasper blacked out to the sound of bullets pelting the hull.

"Yo, Dr. Strauss-Harrigan," Jenkins cooed as he zip-tied her to her seat, "or whatever your name is: Your husband and Freund are alive...for the moment."

––––––––––––

The *Quest's* three giant engines roared, gradually increasing power and thrusting it southward. Richmond knew that just one enemy hit on an engine would slow them, causing the craft to lose lift and careen off the cliff and crash. A shot on key seams might blow the vehicle open, but Richmond's console indicated that the *Quest's* physical integrity had not been compromised. The craft and its passengers accelerated down the jarring, uneven runway.

He watched in terror as the craft approached and passed an Iraqi paratrooper sighting his small bazooka-like rocket launcher. Richmond did not hear the blast, but his stomach tightened when he felt the craft lurch slightly. Suddenly the words "Number 1 Fuel Pump Inoperable" shone in red on his status monitor. The copilot gasped. The arm-sized missile must have pierced the hull at the base of the top engine, blasting its primary fuel pump. Fuel flow to that engine had automatically shut down.

"We can't reach take-off speed without *all three* engines!" the copilot screamed.

Richmond flipped the auxiliary pump switch. It operated briefly, then shut down. "Dammit! Why would it shut down?" he growled.

They had only two more miles to reach the minimum speed of four hundred ten miles per hour. They were moving at less than half that speed, and the computer projected complete failure to attain it. Richmond noticed that he had failed to shut off the troops' monitor, but he concentrated exclusively on his instruments and throttle levers. He considered halting the craft before it careened off the cliffs, but he was not ready to give up and be captured. He teased more speed from the two remaining engines. Still not enough.

The cliff edge was now only a mile away and the *Quest* had only reached two hundred eighty miles per hour. The nose began to rise slightly. A half mile away, three hundred forty, three hundred eighty-eight.

"Too slow!" Richmond gasped, as his vehicle shot over the edge.

The ground dropped off, suddenly revealing scores of Iraqi soldiers and rocket launchers. Richmond heard some of the commandos scream to witness their fate burst onto their screen. He fought to maintain his composure, anticipating the imminent crash of his craft. His mind raced feverishly as they plummeted toward the grassy plain.

The electrical breakers! They made the auxiliary shut down!

Richmond could not reach the breakers. "The breaker!" he cried, "Hit Auxiliary One!"

The copilot fumbled to open the panel. But the shuttle, now a hundred feet from impact, was descending precipitously with its nose slightly skyward. Seventy feet. Fifty feet.

"Open it!" Richmond screamed.

The copilot's finger reached the breaker and reset it just before impact. The impact ripped open the soft earth beneath the ailerons and the engine housings. It spewed old, blackened bones and charcoal-dirt up from the research complex's lawn into the air in a grisly burst. But the softness of this re-opened ground at this sepulcher prevented critical structural damage. The pump warning on the monitor disappeared, just as the tail struck and deeply rutted the ash-filled ground. In that same instant, the number one engine ignited as furiously as the other two. The bounce did not appreciably change the shuttle's momentum or orientation to the ground. It skipped once and remained aloft. The altimeter read one hundred feet up, then four hundred and more. The *Quest* was soaring away, but Richmond could not yet breathe normally. He looked at the copilot for the fuel sufficiency recalculation report.

"With the clear weather and the weight changes, Colonel Richmond, I think we can — we might — attain a shallow orbit."

Richmond smiled back nervously, but as he did the radar alarm cut his confidence to shreds. "Incoming missiles," he shrieked. "The other jets Intel reported!" He increased the angle of the ascent, partially presenting the damaged armor to the threat that came from below and before the shuttle. The *Quest* now flew two miles high but moved at only fifteen hundred miles per hour. Richmond knew that the missiles could reach three thousand miles per hour if the fighter/bombers which fired them had been moving at two thousand.

"Incoming at fifty miles and closing, sir." The copilot was dripping sweat. "Airspeed…twenty-seven hundred. Not enough! They're going to hit! We're at full thrust now!"

"Steady. We might just be able to…"

The radar couldn't track anything within a few miles, but the readout extrapolated time to impact. "Impact in eight seconds, Colonel!"

"Airspeed?"

"Thirty-four hundred! We're gonna make i—"

The explosion came from behind and below the shuttle, cracking the engines' exhaust vents. For a moment, everyone thought they would tumble from the sky. But the exhaust vents held, and the *Quest* continued to gain speed. All fuel soon expired, silencing the engines just as they attained sufficient momentum to escape gravity. The light blue sky faded quickly to foggy black. The only remaining vibration came from retro rockets adjusting the craft's direction. The cloud-dotted Indian Ocean glistened calmly. Richmond relaxed his white-knuckle grip on the controls.

"Now I know how the last Israelite in line to cross the Red Sea felt," he murmured, grinning weakly at the copilot.

Cheers reverberated throughout the craft as the sight signaled that they were finally safe. They were in an unsustainable orbit but would reach an emergency landing site in Australia.

Harrigan raised his singed head just above the lip of the deep crater that the Army Ranger's tipped HE grenade had made and saw soldiers running south all around him.

"Run for the helicopter while they're chasing the shuttle," he whispered to Freund.

"We don't know how to fly it—just the demonstration stuff on different models twenty years ago!" Freund protested.

"Our only chance. You wanna wait in this hole for Iraqis or animals?"

They crawled along the ground and sneaked into the tight cockpit. Harrigan sat in the front seat and Freund sat behind him.

"No gas. No crew helmets. We can't use the radio," Harrigan said.

"It's got to have gas. The power's off, that's all."

They studied and poked at it for what seemed like minutes—too long. Rifle fire sounded, and bullets began to pelt the skeletal craft.

"Get your head down!" Harrigan yelled. "Hey, this is a start bu—"

The craft shook as the engine whined and its rotors spun to a blur. The craft bounced. Harrigan found the collective pitch control for the rotors.

"I'm gonna pull back on—"

The airship now hovered four feet above the ground. Harrigan tested the cyclic pedals under his feet as more bullets clanged off the hull. The craft swayed from side to side, then lurched forward.

"Trees! Pull up," Freund screamed, pulling on the two sticks before him. As he did so, the chin turret made a sound like a lawnmower and a line of trees before them blew to match sticks. Harrigan saw forest to his left, right, and in front of him. He yanked back his control stick and his stomach sank as sky appeared out of front and side windows.

"Ease up. Don't flip us upside down!"

"I've got control of this thing now, I think. We'll follow the river and head south and try to get to some embassy in Baghdad."

The helicopter leveled off. Harrigan banked it southward, skimming ten feet above the river to keep from being seen. Bullets harmlessly pelted the hull and windows, but Harrigan cringed at rifle grenades that kept exploding about the craft. The waterfall appeared two hundred feet away. Harrigan could see six men struggling in the water, perhaps not realizing what they were drifting toward. Then he saw two *Smilodons* leap from the woods to bowl over a pair of soldiers running toward the river. He passed a

Meiolania that was devouring a soldier at the riverbank and glimpsed an *Ancylotherium* chase two more men into the water.

"You see what I see going on down there, Mannie?"

"Yes. Just say a prayer and pay attention to driving."

"Oh, shit!"

"What?" Freund asked. "What?"

"Out of gas. Wait. We'll get some at the village if it's not guarded."

"I think this thing needs jet fuel or—"

The engine finally stopped, but the rotors still provided enough lift to slow their descent. They were now skimming just five feet above the water and falling toward the falls.

"Hold on. I think we're gonna hit!"

The river and terrain suddenly dropped from sight beneath them. The four-hundred-foot drop to the rocks yawned below. They caught momentarily on the submerged bars that combed the falls, keeping animals from escaping over the edge. Harrigan felt sick as he saw half-eaten bodies caught in the bars—then he panicked as he saw that the craft was slipping off them. The helicopter tipped forward and plummeted toward the river below. Rocks and foam rushed up at Harrigan. Then everything went black.

Chapter Seventeen

The Central Plateau, Al-Rajda Zoological Research Preserve
1213 hours, 21 April 2036

The battle over and the Quest's exhaust plume dissipating eastward, relative peace seemed to blanket the plateau. The Iraqis began collecting their dead and wounded.

One platoon's lieutenant called to his men to regroup at a tall cone of dirt around a hole. Standing atop, he began to signal them when hissing sounds gave him pause. He summoned his platoon sergeant to investigate. The NCO affixed a flashlight to his rifle and crawled inside. In seconds, he was back out, feet first. Feet were all that remained. The *Varanus priscus* opened its gaping jaws as it arched skyward, letting gravity pull the legs into its gullet. The lieutenant fell backward and scrambled for the forest, his men and hundreds of others following. It abruptly dropped back into its burrow.

Herbivores had stampeded north and westward across the plain, but predators tended to merely shift positions within the concealment of the forest close to the river and along the ridges.

The lieutenant, a fast runner, led the way to the river. Branches slapped his face with every step. As he passed a thicket, something large and yellow popped into his peripheral vision. The ground pounded heavily behind him. His men screamed out unintelligible warnings.

The *Phorusrhacus'* gaping beak and lashing tongue filled his entire field of vision as it screeched directly into his face. The officer dived, escaping the bite, but its talon pierced his back and exited his stomach. Bird and prey tumbled, and the talon withdrew.

For an instant, the lieutenant thought he might escape the fallen bird. But his ripped diaphragm would not allow him to breathe. The terror-bird rose to its feet. The lieutenant raised his head, unable to resist a look at the nightmare. Its beak enveloped his shoulders and crunched through his ribcage. A hail of bullets ripped the bird apart in a bloody, five-second explosion. Four men pulled the convulsing lieutenant from the raptor's jaws, but the officer suffocated within minutes. The men trained their weapons outward, afraid to move in any direction.

Other troops began to encounter beasts lurking in the grass. Roars of *Ursus*, *Smilodons*, dire wolves, cave lions, and others built to a maddening cacophony. Human screams echoed across the plain and throughout the woods. Twenty-eight hundred men in the southern half of the plateau now fired at anything that moved, inadvertently killing fellow soldiers.

Unit coherence evaporated as men cringed in ruts, ran headlong off the cliff to the barrier ledge or into the river. Predators on land pursued them everywhere and *Meiolania* simply waited for their meals to swim out to them. Pandemonium spread as bloodied, flailing humans were tossed, torn open, and yanked beneath the surface of the water. The submerged prongs at the lip of the falls were clogged with half-drowned men and body parts.

As soldiers cleared from the plain, the smell of blood permeated the atmosphere. Now the adult *Varanus priscuses* ventured out of their burrows — licking the air. The original pair had been periodically gassed and their eggs removed for study, but the extent of their burrows and nesting in recent months had been missed. Their babies had grown every bit as vicious as the parents that had abandoned them at the far end of their tunnels. These eight deep-green, twelve-foot juveniles headed for the river's edge.

The young lizards amplified the panic of men and beasts; their hideous bodies rocking left and right in a fearsome, surly gait as they sought prey. They raced for the water's edge and followed the river south toward the greatest concentration of soldiers. The troops quickly managed to kill one young *Varanus priscus*, then tried, ineffectually, to flee the others.

Soldiers at the cliff edge lost all nerve when the pair of adult lizards approached. The men cringed or fired wildly from the base of the five-foot safety cliff. Furiously counterattacking the source of the myriad stinging bullets, the giant monitors hurled themselves down among the men. Unhurt by the five-foot tumble, they eyed hundreds of terrified humans.

The two thirty-foot *Varanus priscuses* scooped up and tossed soldier after soldier to the ground or off the cliff. The lizards took a huge number of rifle shots and began to succumb, first retreating stubbornly then limping and floundering in the small arms fire frantically. The loss of blood left too little strength to scale even the five-foot cliff to escape back to their burrow. The pair turned suddenly east, trampling paratroopers, and whipping their massive tails. Both *Varanus priscuses* ran straight off the cliff, falling four hundred feet and landing thunderously between the crashed American helicopter and the river below.

Those soldiers who ran north, avoiding almost all the predatory animals, met ambushes set by the Cro-Magnons. The Cro collected their victims' weapons and regrouped at their caves.

Within two hours, most of the predators had been either chased north or killed. Of more than three thousand paratroopers, some two hundred perished during the assault, twenty-six from American action on the ground, and four hundred eight from animal attack. Scores lay desperately wounded and dying, hundreds more in shock.

Hours later, the remnants of the airborne brigade called for airstrikes, collapsing the mouth of the Cro-Magnons' cave.

While chaos on the plateau unfolded, Najik sealed in his bunker, struggled between escaping and fixing his sabotaged radio. "Najik to any Iraqi units. Come in!" he repeated, exhausted.

Mon perked up in his seat as his jet approached the research building. He grabbed his microphone. "Mon here. Najik, where are you? Where are Harrigan and Freund?"

"I am beneath my office, Premier. I captured both of them...just as I returned from leave. But, ah, they have escaped. My... I am unable to exit the shelter, sir. The trap door is damaged, and we cannot budge the passage's door to the motor pool."

"You are an imbecile, Najik. Do they know Hassan had you kill the researchers?"

"How...No, sir." Najik's voice began to crack. "I followed what he said were your orders. Harrigan and Freund have no knowledge of my conveying to Bhaszdi what I honorably thought were your orders...sir."

As Mon's plane landed, he ordered Akkad to have Hassan taken to Najik's residence, and Najik to be released from the bunker and questioned about the raid. Ignoring Akkad's boast about having restored electrical power, Mon stepped rapidly through the clinic's rubble-strewn halls.

Harrigan woke Freund when he noticed Mon entering their room.

"Gentlemen," Mon said. "I am heartened that you survived your crash with only bruises. But I must relate...affair is truly grave and tragic. Colonel Hassan, an officer whom we all trusted for years, has attempted to abuse your work by directing our scientists to develop genetic warfare research behind my back. The traitor has been unsuccessful in this, and in killing your fellow researchers."

"We'd like to see someone from the U.S. or German embassies," Freund quickly interrupted, frowning at Harrigan.

"Yes, and may we call our families?" Harrigan inquired, fatigue beginning to affect him.

"Do not view Iraq as an enemy. There will be no reprisal for this attack. But I regret that your request is out of the question temporarily because phone capacity has been destroyed. I will have this worked on. For now, we cannot spare the military communication facilities."

"I see," Harrigan said suspiciously, glancing wearily at Freund.

Mon resumed pressing his point, "I am as well investigating Najik, but it is Hassan's treachery that has triggered this American commando attack, so I have come now per-sonally to defuse the sit-ua-tion. Equally as heinous, gentlemen, he has injected you with hormones to cause rapid aging. You must be treated here at these uniquely equipped facilities, and quickly, my friends! It is for this reason that you are fortunate that you were unable to depart with the American spacecraft.

When and how, Harrigan wondered, *had the Iraqis developed such a medicine without being observed by me?*

"We have no time to lose to avoid war," Mon continued, "and to save your lives! You can help avert any further attacks upon us, or greater crisis. You must—I implore you—state before a video camera that there have never been genetic weapons developed at Al-Rajda."

The pair politely and repeatedly declined.

Mon spoke warmly, patiently. "Perhaps showing you a video—which I am told Hassan himself has made—will convince you of my honor, and convince you to reconsider. I will have it for you shortly. Your help is absolutely critical. I must go now."

Harrigan noticed Mon's shadow pass over a rose in a glass by the sink, yet the flower seemed to sparkle brilliantly as if repelling the shade. *Seeing things again,* he told himself.

After Mon left, Harrigan turned to Freund. "Mannie, what have I done? So many lives lost. I've been a fool to believe Hassan all these years, thinking I was in control."

Freund looked Harrigan in the eyes. "Don't trust Mon. He's making you believe what you want to hear. Hassan and Najik are his fall guys. Kevin, evil blinds us to its nature and intentions. It tries to make the wrong choice seem right. Make the choice to shut him down."

"Even if you're right, ol' friend. I don't see what more I can do."

General Akkad had set up a command post outside Najik's residence and was trying to regain control of the troops on the plateau when Mon arrived.

First, speaking privately to his aide and guards, Mon described how Hassan was to be rehearsed. Mon then reassured Hassan that cooperation would restore him to favor. Mon handed him a pistol and left. Next, Mon visited Akkad's command post outside, taking him aside privately.

"The Americans must be convinced that they have attacked us based upon incorrect intelligence," Mon told his general, almost whispering. "Have the Foreign Minister go to the U.N. with all the evidence we can make to demand an apology, the return of our researchers, and reparations. The world *must* remain convinced that we are no threat. I even want you to have Harrigan and Freund returned to the very doorsteps of their families — provided the virus becomes untraceable in them. We cannot afford to attack too soon or lose the genetic warfare option before it is fully operational."

Akkad nodded. Mon paused and then spoke more forcefully.

"We must nevertheless be prepared in case the West threatens or mounts any form of attack. Have each nation around Israel go secretly to a level one alert. Have the Syrians find an excuse to put mechanized units into Lebanon along the north-south highway we built. Have the Turks visibly revive the West's guilt over Balkan Muslims. They can then strike Greece if we have to go all the way. We can hold Israel and the Balkans hostage. In this manner, we can prevent or thwart any attack."

Akkad responded in a worried tone. "I will return to Baghdad and execute your instructions immediately, sir."

"You must absolutely ensure that our virus is purged. Give them aging hormones so that the Americans will believe they died by more conventional means, not genetic manipulation. Now, are you sure that our own kidnapped researchers will not talk?"

"The researchers have been conditioned to experience genuine memory loss of their classified work if interrogated, Premier."

"Hassan's people inform me that they need a year to complete a sufficient inventory of virus weapons, and to enable targeted infection. Let us hope that we can buy enough time to develop our destiny unmolested."

Akkad saluted, briefed his officers, and left for Baghdad. Mon remained at the command post awaiting the production of his video and continuing to communicate with his officers.

In the house, Mon's aide gave Hassan a paper and had him practice his lines as technicians emplaced cameras and fitted him with biometrics as evidence against a "deepfake" video. He even had Hassan fire one blank to reassure the nervous colonel that he was not being double-crossed.

"Look, Colonel, if the Premier had wanted to kill you, you would already be dead! Point it at my chest and fire if you do not believe me!"

Hassan hesitated, fearful and not trusting. He pointed the weapon at a lamp and fired. Red ink splattered the lamp, but it remained intact.

The aide smiled. "Now, can we get this done? There is no time to lose if we are to avoid an escalation of this crisis with the Americans."

Hassan practiced his lines fairly convincingly. The aide, however, made him practice several times more. Hassan tried his lines yet again, suspiciously pointed the weapon at the aide and fired. The obvious pain of the red ink capsule pelting the aide between the eyes was half of the sting Hassan felt when the privileged junior officer slapped him.

"Did you consider that to be funny? Perhaps I should inform the Premier of your chicanery!"

The aide wiped his face with a towel as Hassan groveled in apology, finally believing that the video setup was genuine.

He spoke his lines again, now with recorders on. The script called for him to look repentant and speak in Arabic. "I am Colonel Fezhil Hassan. I betrayed the trust of my country by unilaterally — without the knowledge of my government — attempting to conduct genetic warfare research. The research was only recently begun and has been completely unsuccessful.

"Inspections of the site raided by the American force will be permitted. I wish to show the world the depth of my shame at bringing undeserved suspicion upon my honorable and peaceful government. Of my own volition, I will now end my life."

Hassan raised the revolver to his temple. He flinched a bit, knowing it would hurt. He pulled at the trigger, telling himself to convincingly fall over when he felt the ink pellet burst.

Momentarily he perceived the bullet. In the split-second that remained of his life, Hassan received an insight he had long sought. He had a sense of falling into a clearer understanding of an unspeakable immensity — a seething and insidious malice — reaching up to claw and pull him further into itself. He felt this, oddly, accelerating.

Around 1100 hours, Mon returned with the video to the clinic for another attempt to convince Harrigan and Freund to help him. An accompanying soldier wheeled in a large monitor as Mon raised his hands in a grand announcement.

"Good morning gentlemen. I have learned that all of your friends survived Hassan's treachery and were taken on the American spacecraft. Unfortunately, some of my citizens were also taken, and the situation now worsens. So, I still need your help."

Harrigan watched his eyes as the Iraqi leader continued. "As to defusing the current crisis, please watch this horrendous, yet revealing video. It is soon to be released to the press."

As it played, they cringed in silence.

"I want to call family. Dr. Freund needs to do the same."

"I understand, but please forgive me," Mon replied sounding sympathetic. "Phone service is not restored, and we cannot risk military transmissions to be misinterpreted."

Harrigan mentally debated the facts. *Was I wrong all along?*

Mon interrupted his contemplation. "Gentlemen. Do reconsider my humble request. I implore you to tell the world that this is but a scientific and business venture. Hassan and Najik sought to take over Iraq by stealing your work in a fruitless attempt to develop weapons. You know that this is a true statement and that your tes-timony would help avoid an escalation of the recent tragedy. *You* will save lives."

The pair remained politely noncommittal.

Mon appeared not to be perturbed, his words even sounded reassuring. "Well, gentlemen. I must respect your wishes. Please do reconsider. In any event, I promise that you will be home in mere days, but now, gentlemen, I must leave you to return to Baghdad."

Around 1600, truck and medevac traffic increased. Harrigan and Freund could not leave the room. Its window was their only link to the outside world. They could not quite discern the gray objects in the gouged soil, though a light rain made them appear to be bones.

Harrigan was soon asleep, his meal uneaten. The two slept through most of the next day, receiving continued excuses about why they could not call home. It seemed that their bodies' degeneration was accelerating. Yet neither of them lost hope.

The next afternoon, Harrigan's eyes darted beneath closed lids. A feminine voice echoed the eerily familiar admonition, *Choose in humility,* as he awoke drenched in sweat.

He dismissed it, now focusing on the grave decision before him. *The raid took our work for analysis, but not Hassan's weaponized virus. They're monitoring its filtering from our blood.*

As Freund slept, Harrigan rerouted his blood draw tube to Freund's own line behind the nightstand. He replaced his own with a blood-filled segment he saw in the trash, clamped it, and hid the end behind the stand. Then he replaced his serum drip with saline.

Chapter Eighteen

War Room, Baghdad
0551 hours, 23 April 2036

Ismail Mon stood rigid, presenting a poker face to the video camera and large monitor that would momentarily trade his image with that of the U.S. President. NATO forces, including nuclear weapons, had been placed on alert for the two days since the raid.

Sheryl Cox's face flashed on the screen without the courtesy of the diplomatic protocol image of the U.S. Presidential Seal. Mon's staff looked surprised and offended, but he remained stolid.

"Good morning, Premier Mon. I hope it will be that. Please listen carefully. You will order the following three actions without delay. One: stand down all Islamic League forces. Two: release your hostages. And three: permit inspections of Al-Rajda and any other site the inspectors want to see. Do it now. You have no choice."

"Madame President, you have been catastrr-ophically misinformed about our activities. In addition, I cannot control all of the forces currently on alert. The Turks inform me that they will no longer tolerate the abuse of Balkan Muslims. The Syrians have long had trouble in the Bekaa Valley of Lebanon and with Israel. Morocco is worried that it will be attacked by your forces near Gibraltar — which are postured most aggressively, I must say."

"I'm not concerned with your delay tactics, Premier, but *you* had better worry about—"

"I will, however, offer my government's 'good offices' in attempting to quell the situation. Our doctors report that Harrigan and Freund are still suffering from having been poisoned with hormones by that traitor, Hassan. I will return them to Megiddo this very day *if* you return our people. Iraq, as you can easily verify, is at no level of alert. What more can you expect of me—especially after your recent attack into the very heart of our nation?"

"I do not negotiate. Listen closely and watch your screen."

Cox turned from the camera and had it pan toward a large computer screen that depicted the Middle East and the Mediterranean Sea. She turned back to the camera, putting both herself and the screen in Mon's view.

Cox glared at Mon but spoke to Mepps. "Initiate 'Mars Disinfect.'"

Mon watched silently as the President's screen showed lights moving away from naval fleet symbols. His own private monitors began to light up with notices of cruise missile launches.

Cox resumed. "You will be unable to intercept *all* of these *very* powerful conventional warheads, Premier. You have means to verify that they are not nuclear, including watching them destroy hundreds of your installations during the next thirty minutes. I will be able to recall them to their carriers—for later use, if necessary—only within the next three minutes. *You*, therefore, have less than three minutes to issue *valid* compliance orders to each demand."

"I agree. Each demand will be immediately ac-com-modated."

He waited as Cox recalled the missiles, then spoke again.

"You cannot show the world justification for your attack upon our country—your abduction and continuing detainment of our civilian *commercial* researchers. The international community will force you to pay *dearly* in reparations. This transmission is ended."

The guard returned from Harrigan and Freund's room and studied his two monitors. One was a computer read-out of the patients' basic medical status, including a restricted window that he could not access; the other displayed video of the two scientists in their room. The two sick men looked as if they would die soon. However, the data monitor showed that they suffered only from anemia and other effects of aging.

The guard puzzled over this status read-out, concluding that their problems represented just desserts, and wondering what the new serum was that had been substituted last night for their original medication.

The soldier listened with no interest to the pair talking. He sipped his coffee, called for his relief, and waited for it to arrive. He smiled with some satisfaction as he heard boots approaching through adjacent hallways. He perked up, knowing that he might have to render some evidence of his eavesdropping should a superior demand it. He now paid full attention to the data monitor and video screen. He listened closely, hearing Freund address Harrigan.

"Kevin, wake up," Freund said in an insistent tone. "I *know* I should remember more details of what you're so agonized about, but it's not falling into place. Are we prisoners..."

The guard ignored Freund's rambling and Harrigan's reply. "Senile," he sneered. "Completely gone."

He rose to greet his relief, whom he could hear rounding the corner. But his platoon leader arrived instead—along with Colonel Najik. The guard, visibly fearful of Najik, gave his best salute and was dismissed without any report being required of him.

Najik entered his code to view the RESTRICTED DATA window, silently seeking confirmation: *Not a trace of retrovirus, DNA changes, or purging serum. Only the hormonal agent. Now, they are my ticket out — none too soon!*

Najik touched the keyboard's phone button and frowned when he reached his new commander's voice mail.

"Sir, Najik reporting. Only the hormone serum remains. I will escort them to Tel Aviv and return at noon."

Najik turned to the lieutenant.

"Get them dressed to depart now," he ordered the junior officer. "And don't waste time with their personal effects. I'll be presenting them to their families and the authorities this morning when we land at Megiddo. Now, let's have a last look at these two."

The officers briefly visited the scientists, who eyed them suspiciously.

"I know what you are thinking, gentlemen," Najik said grinning. "But I am the one who for days tried to retrieve your friends from the plateau. I did all I could when I dis-covered Bhaszdi's cowardly plot. He received secret orders to kill our friends directly from Hassan. I would have next been killed! As for our altercation in the tunnel, we each did what we believed was duty, yes?" He continued without permitting any reply. "Now, I am happy to report that you will be returned to your families and authorities in Megiddo immediately. You are cured and will feel better soon."

Western imbeciles, he thought with delight.

Najik ordered the lieutenant to have Harrigan and Freund carefully boarded on the jet. Then he waited outside the building, staring nervously from the parked aircraft to the charcoal-filled gash just southwest of it. A fast-rising breeze whisked ash high into the morning sky.

He watched impatiently as two of the lieutenant's soldiers wheeled Harrigan and Freund through the grass toward the jet. One guard handed Harrigan a reddish-pink rose.

"This was in your room, sir," the soldier said.

Najik smirked at tears washing Harrigan's face as a broken cryo-canister marked "zygotes, sapiens" was tossed into a dumpster. A gust carried a loose petal, along with ash from the gouged earth and silvery bubbles from the canister, high into the air. Harrigan nodded, inexplicably watching these soar, then placed the still-vital rose in his shirt pocket.

A shadow rapidly enveloped the area as a huge thunderhead approached from the east.

"Hey... that cloud," Freund called. "Looks like a horse and rider."

A sunbeam from the cloud's reddened edge cut like a sword toward the alluvial plain.

He frowned as Harrigan called out. "I could swear I've seen that before. No, I dreamt…"

"Y-Yes, well," Najik stuttered an English reply, "I'm sure that's all very…i-interesting." Turning to the lieutenant, he said in Arabic, "Let's take off now before turbulence grounds—"

Thunder clapped in the distance and Najik flinched, gaping at the thunderhead.

"One of the preditors!" he cried in Arabic. "I heard—" He halted, glaring incredulously at Freund, who sat smiling at the sunbeam.

"Preditors?" Harrigan said in Arabic. "It sounded more like somebody whispering, but that couldn't possibly…No. It is just thunder, miles away."

"Dr. Harrigan," Najik insisted, "I distinctly—"

The lieutenant's captain approached without saluting Najik and handed the young officer a document. The lieutenant read it and grinned at Najik, who now approached the aircraft's loading ramp. The junior officer blocked Najik's way.

"Excuse me, Colonel Najik. These orders regarding you came directly from the office of the Premier. The captain will escort Harrigan and Freund. You remain here, under arrest."

Najik's stomach wrenched tight, and his breathing quickened. He was handcuffed, hauled inside to his office, and set before his computer monitor. Several officers and men had crowded into the room. One of them reported to Mon's aide on the screen and, in a moment, the face of the Premier appeared to Najik and everyone standing behind him.

"Ah. There you are, Colonel Najik. You compounded the idiocy of Colonel Hassan's order to kill the researchers by sacrificing my soldiers—just to conceal your lies."

"But, sir, I captured Harrigan and Freund for you!"

"You should have at least died fighting alongside your men."

"But—"

"Silence. Your own subordinates have a solution. I concur. Mon out."

Najik looked up at the soldiers' vengeful faces and blanched. They rushed him, dragged him from his desk, and bludgeoned him with their fists until their new commander ordered them to take him to the place on the plateau where he would be officially disciplined.

Najik was unfamiliar with the marshy location and did not know what to expect. As crackling, flashing storm clouds verged upon the forest canopy, he was suspended by his wrists over the marsh from a pulley and left. His feet dangled, barely touching the water. He noticed something triangular surfacing below him in the dirty, amber pond.

———————

Harrigan and Freund sat unguarded but tightly belted into plush seats in the cruising jet.

Looking out the window, Harrigan pondered the last two decades of mystery and discovery. He was glad for the news that they were headed home, although he felt utterly without energy. He took labored, gurgling breaths every few words and spoke in a low, scratchy tone. "I've been thinking, Mannie, what a tough R— c— hm— Ranger I thought I was. Now...I'm helpless and others had to fight a ba— hh— battle...that I caused." He paused, short of breath and aching. "I don't...think I'm gonna make it...Mannie. You?" He was suddenly wracked with coughing and could taste blood.

Freund's voice was slightly stabler than Harrigan's. "No. I believe we're dying...old friend. The serum may have been bogus...or just not effective. Stop berating yourself." Freund paused, frowned, and resumed. "Our work was stolen and perverted to make a weapon to destroy whole peoples. Such a nightmare can't be how God implements the resurrection. But Mon *could* convince survivors that he's the Second Coming, or that he's our savior from a cruel God."

"I'm not sure I underst—!" Harrigan was taken by a shocking thought and more coughing. "Do you think...Mon could trigger...the reincarnation of just about every human back to...Adam and Eve? I couldn't believe my own model!"

"Not reincarnation. Resurrection. A fake one. Maybe M1-RNA's mechanism, left to God, would restore a ruined Eden. But not by human manipulation. A genetic weapon *could* start a cascade, and maybe Mon's evil would unwittingly implement God's resurrection plan. But I cannot believe that. The prophecies say that God purges imperfect souls, reunites them to illuminated bodies and, gives them divine abilities. We must stop Mon."

"It still makes no sense." Harrigan held his breath to avoid more wracking of his lungs. "Why would the same actual soul come back from...what, from some purgatory?"

"Mercy. God was deprived of his creation by sin, and he promised to recreate it. A new Eden, until evil is unchained for a final test. Some form of resurrection is the only prophecy in common among the world's religions." Harrigan raised his eyebrows, but let Freund continue. "One final call prophesied since Elijah and John...even modern visionaries...Kora had visions, spoke of two witnesses. Maybe her purpose is to tell the world we're like Cain. I donno."

The two men fell silent, contemplative.

Harrigan felt his arm grabbed. "Kevin, do you believe what all these years I've tried to..."

Harrigan looked away, his eyes flooding to realize Freund's concern for his soul.

"We can't merit redemption," Freund resumed. "but we can seek forgiveness. We can respond to his call and self-sacrifice by sacrificing our pride and hubris. We can try to emulate the Christ who accepted death to save humankind."

"Yes. Mannie, I get it. Mon played me. I held to my rationalizations and self-importance. I've been blind, and science isn't the tool for all inquiry." He paused for breath, then growled, "The cascade'll happen. It's in the chemistry, the design. But not Mon's way if I can help it! But how? There's just no-huh-ah...not time to develop and distribute a vacci—."

Harrigan let loose a series of coughs and tried to regain his voice. "Maybe I can warn Mon...about the fire he's playing with. Stay his hand. I can't let the human race..."

Harrigan took the phone again and waited for the copilot.

"You may not call out, doctor. We land in Megiddo in twenty-five minutes. But I will check orders just now. I am to read your text to you."

"Text?"

"Yes, yes. I have instruction to obtain your comment: 'ASLI can't help them. MUHAWALA all wrong.'"

Harrigan's eyes popped, but he said nothing. *The firewall hole I set at Hassan's lab! Tykvah must have re-dated folders and backups, the only edit possible. Now, to buy time.*

His mind raced beyond its fog to interpret the text and derive a plan. *If Mon makes FGR a weapon, he triggers the cascade. But if he thinks I accessed and sabotaged his files, distrust of his files could stop or bog down his R & D for years.*

"I must speak...to the Premier."

There was silence on the line as the copilot considered the request, which was technically not forbidden. As Harrigan listened, the connection was made to the Premier's office. A recorded greeting provided instructions, first in Arabic, then in English.

Freund's head tipped back and his eye widened. "Ancient of—!" he mumbled, smiling weakly. His eyes shut and his hand fell from the armrest.

Harrigan listened closely, trying to understand the instructions. "You have reached the offices of the Premier of the Republic of Iraq. Please dial your party's extension. If you don't know the extension, press the keys that correspond to the first three letters of the party's last name."

Harrigan's tears cleared his eyes. He could make out the keypad. He pressed the key for M: 6. Scanning next for O, he realized that it was the same button. He started to dial N but hesitated. His expression tightened in fear. He cleared his throat and forced himself to leave his message:

"M1-RNA can be weaponized and protect your people only if you deactivate my add-on coding for the Y chromosome's SRY gene. Bu-huht...then, it can only affect females and their female offspring.

"You cannot kill your enemy nations' males without making your people su—huh—susceptible. If you deactivate my coding, you can protect selected genetic groups but that leaves males unharmed—intact armies to cru-huh-sh you!" He suppressed another cough. "Give it up! Here's proof I hacked and saved-over your files and backups: My work you stole is in the folder titled 'Asli,' and your failed attempts are in 'Muhawala'." He hung up, coughed heavily, and turned toward Freund.

A locution invaded, "Tetelest," prompting recollection of a lesson from his childhood, *It is paid.* He breathed deeply and easily for a moment, like a man surprised by emancipation.

"Mannie," Harrigan's voice was cracking, tears streaming down his face. His cough returned, now impeding his ability to breathe. "You were right all along. Mon, FGR, and no proof of G—huh-God. Listening to the wh-whisper... trusting, emulating him...offering mys-huh-self...faith, hope."

No response came from Freund. Harrigan tried to turn his head toward him but succumbed to more violent coughs. This time he was unable to pull air back in. Harrigan shuddered with the pain. He knew he could endure it, but the fact no longer made him proud. As he finally managed to turn his head, he saw that a truly appreciated and loyal friend was gone.

Again, Harrigan struggled to inhale, but was unable. He closed his eyes and wondered about his and his staff's families, his hope that the virus he carried might enable immunity research—just in case. And he wondered about the anomalous Kora and humankind's inevitable rebirth. The pain in his lungs increased. Even though he could not draw in air, the scent of the rose in his pocket calmed and comforted him like a mother's embrace.

Iraqi soldiers now feverishly used defibrillator-resuscitators. The plane was under twenty minutes away from landing. Yet Manfred Freund and Kevin Gamaliel Harrigan were home.

END

More Fun & Useful Works by Dan Gallagher

<u>Novels:</u>

The Pleistocene Redemption (TPR, Cypress House hardcover; AncientProphecies paperback). Out of print. Test-readers who read *TPR* as well as the *Ancient of Genes* re-write, praised both!

<u>AOG Anthology-sequel coming soon:</u> *Ancient to Light,* 12 short story pairs, 2nd in the Ancient Beacon series.

<u>Short Stories in anthologies with other authors:</u>
"Dawn of Reason" (DOR in *Planetary Anthology: Earth,* Tuscany Press)

DOR & "From the Reliquary of Job" (*Millhaven's Tales of Adventure* v I)

"Monster in the Sand", "Six Birds & a Cat" (*Fierce Tales: Lost Worlds,* Millhaven)

<u>Nonfiction:</u>

The Secrets of Successful Financial Planning (Skyhorse Publishing, NY) Expert, Zero-bias help for professionals and consumers alike; a fifth of its length is composed of 30 true tales of tragedy & triumph, not boring case studies! Endorsed by readers & experts alike, including Arthur Laffer, Ph.D, Economic Advisor to two presidents.

Essays, business & financial articles, a licensing manual 1992-2017

<u>TV-series Pilot, Proposal & Lookbooks</u> for professional markets:

"Ancient of Genes" Pilot Screenplay. The TV version has a "near-end-first" structure, giving viewers a teasing & limited sneak-peek at action occurring shortly before the story's conclusion.

"$ecret$" version 1 Speculative Fiction / Psychological Thriller:
A war hero, unaware he's located alien tech, rejoins family, fights personal demons… and others' secret agendas. In this psychological / Sci-Fi thriller, war hero, loving father, financial planner Dempsey, seeks peace. But what happens if he can't defeat his trauma-rooted viciousness? What is set in motion when this beloved commander captures an Iraqi archaeological site – with Nephilim medical tech –is tricked by rogue CIA agents, then hounded by psychotic, vengeful characters, each with secret agendas? Imagine "Suits" meets "X-Files".

"$ecret$" version 2 Psychological Thriller: Same as version 1, but without the Nephilim medical technology discovery. Imagine "Suits" meets "Criminal Minds".

For rights inquiries for all of Dan's thrill-rides, please contact The William Pettit Agency

For fun freebies, adventure shorts & humor, become an appreciated "Reader-friend" at AuthorDan.com

Acknowledgments

AuthorDan is indebted to scientists, theologians, and others who assisted this project. The following is a list of those who provided assistance through conversation and/or correspondence.

John J. Collins, Ph.D.: assistance with biblical questions
Margery C. Coombs, Ph.D.: help with *Ancylotherium*
Eugene Gafney, Ph.D.: help with the *Meiolania*
Nick Graham, Ph.D.: fascinating info on theoretical meteorology
Jerry L. Hall, Ph.D.: guidance on genetics: the possible & impossible
John M. Harris, Ph.D.: excellent advice on Pleistocene fauna
William W. Hauswirth, Ph.D.: enlightening help on genetics
Larry G. Marshall, Ph.D.: valuable advice on Pleistocene fauna
Paul S. Martin, Ph.D.: help with geology and fauna
Greg McDonald, Ph.D.: extensive help with fauna
Jim I. Meade, Ph.D.: examples of soft tissue preserved for millennia
Geoffrey Pope, Ph.D.: help with our ancestor-races
Merritt Ruhlen, Ph.D.: linguistics facts & his Nostratic Dictionary
Tom Torgersen, Ph.D.: extremely useful help with geological issues

Several NASA engineers assisted with environmental and aeronautical issues. Friends at Camp Peary, Williamsburg helped with descriptions of intelligence protocols. Many scholars' works were of great help: Francesco Cavalli-Sforza, Ph.D., L. Luca Cavalli-Sforza, Ph.D., Dougal Dixon, Stephen Jay Gould, Ph.D., Svante Pääbo, Ph.D., Steven Pinker, Ph.D.; R. J. G. Savage, Ph.D., Rev. Donald Senior, CP, and Robert Tjian, Ph.D. An especially great resource was the International Society of Cryptozoology, Tucson, AZ. Thanks also to these museums: The Smithsonian Institution (Washington, D.C.), The American Museum (New York); The Natural History Museum of L.A. County.

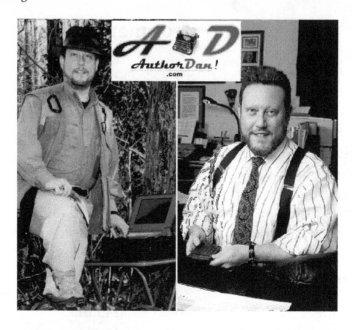

A Writing Style Shaped by Life-experiences

As the youngest of eight in a Catholic working-class family; as a soldier, scholar, family man, advisor, and adventurer, Dan developed a vivid, hard-hitting style:

He has trekked volcanoes, deserts, swamps; trudged Appalachian, Arizonan, and Venezuelan heights & gorges. He has explored exotic locations like Macau, Hong Kong, the Everglades, Bayous, Mexico's Baja… even New Jersey! Attacked by a charging bear, Dan killed it at fourteen feet, evaded a northern Canada wolf-pack and an enraged moose. He's parachuted, been in a knife fight, and numerous other life-threatening tangles. Though he's not seen combat, Dan held command of Mechanized Infantrymen in live-fire assaults, ambushes, and defenses in Germany & the U.S. He has lived in Rhode Island, Alexandria & Williamsburg, VA, and North Carolina.

Other personal experiences inform Dan's writing style. He knows what faith, race, and age discrimination feel like. He helped reform court-marshalled soldiers, consoled the homeless, and took charge in deadly accidents: a C-130 aircraft crash and a 110-mph motorcycle collision. In counseling clients (Dan's pre-retirement financial & business brokerage work), Dan handled hundreds of millions in transactions. He's seen what strengthens and dissolves relationships. Dan has experienced spiritual and miraculous phenomena and investigated those of others. Dan usually pursued simultaneous endeavors (studied Economics, Modern Languages, Finance Math, English, and was a published professional instructor). He's been a lifelong student of Natural Sciences, Comparative Religion, and Cryptozoology. Dan and his wife Laura have been in love for over three decades and treasured raising their four "snit-generating" kids. Several professional and personal tragedies have been profoundly humbling. Yet, through it all, Dan kept sane to help others. He says, "I give psychological counseling to my cat, Watson, who claims to be a saber-tooth tiger. Watson must think I'm gullible: he never tries to convince others of his delusions."

Dan is the author of financial & expository nonfiction and quite a bit of humor, but mostly speculative and adventure fiction, no fantasy. He endeavors to give readers vivid sensory and emotional experiences. His bio is at the AuthorDan website. Reader-friends know his "narrative voice" is never flowery, highbrow, wimpy, politically correct, self-important, pedantic, or whiny. He builds suspense, intrigue, curiosity, fascination, fear, compassion, and other intense emotions, often challenging readers to think deeply or persuading them to act with conviction. His writing always employs plausibility to help readers suspend disbelief. If you read his humor, do not blame him for spontaneous bladder leaks; or, if you read *this* fact-based tale, for nightmares.

Did you enjoy *Ancient of Genes?* Please kindly consider recommending it on social & book websites. Maybe gift a copy to friends/loved ones!